In Far Off
&
Distant Times

SONGS AND STORIES OF A LIFE CUT SHORT

DANIEL B. THOMAS

Print ISBN: 978-1-4866-2013-5
eBook ISBN: 978-1-4866-2014-2

Word Alive Press
119 De Baets Street, Winnipeg, MB R2J 3R9
www.wordalivepress.ca

Cataloguing in Publication may be obtained through Library and Archives Canada

Contents

Part Three
A Book of Songs Without Music

INTRODUCTION

Yes, Virginia, there is a Santa Claus! He exists as certainly as love and generosity and devotion exist. How dreary would be the world if there was no Santa Claus? It would be as dreary as if there were no Virginias. There would be no childlike faith then, no poetry, no romance to make tolerable this existence. The eternal light with which childhood fills the world would be extinguished.

—Robert C. Church
Yes, Virginia, There Is a Santa Claus

To whomever is reading this material in the 2020s, this material was written in 1985 before Uncle Dan passed away that year during an open-heart operation.

By and large, the circumstances I grew up with in Toronto contrast significantly with what he grew up with for the first twelve years of his life before landing in Toronto in 1970.

The decision to publish this material was complex. My decision to publish it ultimately boils down to showing people as much as I can of how he thought as a real person beyond the stories and poems he wrote.

Was it the best decision to make to publish this material? It is hard for me to tell. There are risks to this decision. The reason I chose to publish was only to show what's real.

Relatives of mine had different reasons to suggest regarding why I ought to publish this material. To my knowledge, my grandfather (Danny's father) died in early 1994, months before my birth and days before his own sixty-fifth birthday of multiple organ failure. Alcohol has an impact on the liver, so it is quite possible his death was caused by his drinking habits.

That said, there's no way for me to have the firsthand knowledge to know for certain what did or did not happen to my grandfather. Dan certainly had a resentment toward his father nonetheless.

There's a world out there, and it isn't always nice. Life has been good to me, good enough that I could compile Uncle Dan's work and get it published despite not having much luck securing employment. Never having been into partying much personally—a waste of time, in my mind—I spent my time instead doing what I could to honour my uncle's memory.

Not everything Dan wrote will be published, because it was too incomplete for me to work with. A much larger portion of the material he wrote before his passing is included in this book than is not. His notes aren't necessarily included, though Danny used these notes as part of his final drafts.

Danny's "Memories of a Father," not included in this volume of writing, illustrates that I was left with a large, yet sometimes incomplete, sample of his written work. I would often ask myself, "What was he going to say?"

"Memories of a Father" is one of those documents. Some of my questions about it were answered, but I likely won't get answers for all the pressing questions I have about Dan's material. It's unfortunate, at least for me. Yet again, a lot of things in life are unfair, so I have to take solace in what I do know about an uncle of mine that I never met.

My decision to publish this material boiled down to something I was told as a kid no older than thirteen years of age: "You don't make important life decisions for other people, whether it be your family or friends. Rather, you make important life decisions for yourself." I hope this material will become a bestseller. As Danny said, "If no one ever dreamt, there could never be a dream come true."

Danny had his problems to contend with, as do I and everybody else given the opportunity to take a single breath in life. Nobody is exempt from their challenges. I have been told that I think, act, and look like Danny. Such things could very well be true.

But am I Danny? I am my own person with my own perspective in life. I have my own ideas about what ought to be, from my own experience in life. Danny died much too soon, by no fault of his own.

As I approach my twenty-sixth birthday (June 2020), I am better able to appreciate this material than I did when I first found it in my parents' basement many years ago. Nobody leads a perfect life, nor do I want people to look at me and think I'm some perfect being with no imperfection.

The big reason I undertook this project is to take pride in something unrelated to the typical work I have done up to this point in my life. Having been afforded certain luxuries not all people are granted, it seemed like a good time to undertake a tribute project on behalf of an uncle of mine who unfortunately died long ago.

It's a project I'm sure relatives would truly appreciate and would like to keep in the family for many generations to come.

—Jeremy E. Thomas

A Poem for Edna: Across the Miles

On the day I was born, you looked down at me and smiled
You picked me up into your arms and took me walking across the miles
The road of life brought joy and tears as we've walked along the way
You never knew what to expect as we walked from day to day
And fate tested you quite often as we walked across the miles
Dan's problems were the worst of life's never-ending tails
But no matter what the miles would bring, you always knew just what to do
You almost always had the answers! Mum, you always saw us through
But if there was nothing that could be done when troubles would cloud the day
You always held your head up high and you'd smile our cares away
And that was the most important lesson taught as we walked across the miles
To meet life's problems head held high… that we'd defeat them with a smile
You promised that, if we kept the faith, our faith would see us through
And that's the most important thing I'm sure I've learned from you
Now God has called you, Edna, to come inside his pearly gates
Selfishly, I ask one last thing of you: it's there I hope you'll wait
And not too many years from now, God willing, I'll pass on through
And when you see me coming, Mum, this one last thing I ask of you
That when you see me coming, you'll rise and greet me with that smile
I'll give you a big hug and a big kiss and then we'll reminisce about the old times
When we went walking across the miles

—Laurie Michael Thomas
July 10, 2001

Turn to Stone a Statue's Eye

Part One

FOREWORD

Turn to Stone a Statue's Eye, by Daniel B. Thomas, is a short novel touching on themes of horror and science fiction. It talks about such things as a potential doomsday apocalypse and intergalactic astronomy.

The protagonist in this story works at the University of Toronto, so the events described occur in Toronto, Canada. Topics Daniel explores include nuclear holocaust and communism, contemporary societal issues at the time of his death in 1985. Cold War tensions were still running rapid, with the Iran-Contra scandal being just around the corner, in 1986. Jonathan Schell's *The Fate of the Earth* had been recently released, in 1982.

The underlying themes are based on the sort of superstition evident in Catholicism and Greek mythology. Through the progression of the story, it is established that the world is post-apocalyptic, as exemplified by most of the inhabitants turning to stone, opposite to what happened in a piece of Greek mythology. Stone statues should then be considered a major source of symbolism throughout the novel.

How people perceive this symbolism could very well be varied. We don't know what he intended the stone statues to symbolize, so it could very well be debated. The read I get is that *Turn to Stone a Man's Eye* is a criticism of greed among government and corporations alike, an acknowledgement that man's pursuit of self-interest will eventually lead to his own demise. It is my belief the young girl who turned to stone symbolizes how destructive humanity can be. Conflicts like the Bosnian genocide and the Holocaust resulted in the loss of life for many innocent children, for example.

The sentiments of this novel, in my mind anyway, are as true in 2020 as they were in 1985, if not even truer.

—Jeremy E. Thomas
December 14, 2019

I.
Who Is the Man of Stone?

This bizarre tale begins on the night of December 24, 1984. Christmas Eve. It was a happy Christmas for me and my wife. The New Year promised to bring us even more joy, for we were expecting our first child.

But on the night of December 24, as we sat with friends drinking eggnog and singing carols, a strange thing happened in the heavens, which I was to learn some days later. A star, near our own sun in terms of the universe but still on the far edge of our galaxy, simply ceased to shine. Where there had been a twinkling light, now there was darkness.

The scientist who witnessed this occurrence was lost for an explanation. He would not say for certain that a supernova had occurred. No evidence that a star had burst into flames and then slowly faded was evident, so the scientist was sceptical. Instead the light of the star just suddenly and instantly went out, like a candle flame quickly snuffed out by the wind.

One would think occurrences that take place millions of lightyears away would have no significance for man, other than a mild curiosity. But as subsequent events were to prove, the death of this star, if it can be called a death, was a grim forewarning of a similar fate awaiting mankind—a fate which, I believe, man tragically brought down upon himself, yet one which, ironically, man had lost the power to avoid. Man, the greatest ruler of the world, was as helpless as the animals he lorded over.

But in the days immediately following Christmas, mankind carried on in its many pursuits, oblivious of any changes having taken place in the universe. There were some minor references to the death of a star, hidden away on the back pages of some of the more serious journals.

It is likely only one man felt any sense of foreboding at all. I myself read a short article which told of the death of the star and conveyed some sense that Dr. Hueg, the scientist who had observed the event on Christmas Eve, felt there might be cause for concern. I quickly dismissed it from my mind, however, while a significant majority of people remained unaware anything had happened.

I was like the rest of mankind, busy taking care of my own concerns. I had to find a new apartment for my wife and me to move into when our baby was born, and I was busy preparing for the coming term at the University of Toronto. I was in my first year lecturing on political philosophy and, consequently, had a great deal of paperwork to complete. Being new to the university, I had to take some time to get acquainted with my colleagues and the facilities of the university. And of course I was constantly preparing for lectures, while continuing to work on my own pet projects.

I suppose I was also unduly worried about the health of my pregnant wife and our unborn baby. She had caught a mild cold over Christmas and I feared it might turn to pneumonia, although our doctor assured me there was only slight danger of that. Still, he agreed that she should stay inside and look after herself until after the baby was born.

My wife, however, like all first-time mothers probably, was caught up in buying things for the expected child. Baby clothes, a basinet, toys, picking out children's picture books, and the other usual knickknacks. She went on shopping sprees for the better part of most days, needless of what effect it might have on her health, and totally disregarding the nervous wreck it was making of me.

So, with the many concerns and simple rhythm of life pressing down on me, it is no surprise I, like others, failed to take notice of the death of one small spark of light in the sky. Only later, after some bizarre occurrences closer to home, did I and others begin to look up into the heavens in awe and wonder, as men have not wondered since the darkest ages.

The second bizarre event happened, or at least was brought to my attention, on the first day of classes of the winter term. I had decided to begin the second term with a lecture on Jonathan Schell's book, *The Fate of the Earth*. I very much admired the book and agreed with the author that man must abolish nuclear weapons, or they would abolish man. Nuclear weapons hung like a sword over the head of man, but it was a sword of our own making—one which we held, albeit shaking, in our own two hands. Far from being a pessimist, I was confident that man could and would save himself from a nuclear holocaust and extinction.

I must confess, however, that I didn't know how mankind could bring about nuclear disarmament considering the grave differences that existed between the various peoples of the Earth. I had always believed good men should resist evil, and therefore I didn't want to see the free world simply disarm and surrender to communism.

The problem Schell failed to address was how disarmament could be brought about if one side refused to disarm. While the theory of building nuclear weapons to deter the use of nuclear weapons obviously contained contradictions, I saw no way around these contradictions without giving up the fight against evil. Only later, months after that sunny winter day in January, did I understand that I was blind to evil in its most subtle forms.

Going back to that day, I finished my lecture and engaged in a lively debate with a few of the brighter members of the class. Afterwards, I made my way to the staff lounge to grab a cup of coffee.

Jane Elway, an English professor, sat sedately on the couch with a cup of coffee in one hand and the morning paper on her knee. She looked up as I entered and, seeing that it was me, gave me a smile and waved. The coffee was percolating on the cabinet counter, and as I walked over to pour a cup I asked her if there was anything interesting in the paper.

"Interesting, yes!" she replied with a laugh. "Believable, no!"

Although she had been lecturing at the university for three years, Jane was in fact younger than I was. So, in a way, she was both senior and junior to me. While I'm not the type who cheats on his wife, I am a man—and won't deny that in many ways I found her to be quite attractive.

Taking my coffee and joining her on the couch, I asked what she found so unbelievable.

"You, my dear professor," she said teasingly. "No, no. This article in the paper!"

The first words I read were the headline, which she finger pointed at: EAST GERMAN MAN TURNS TO STONE.

I suppose academics are more likely to disbelieve something so bizarre than the average person, but I think any sane person would have reacted just as I did. I picked the paper up to read the article out of curiosity, and only a mild curiosity, since the bizarre has never interested me. I'm not the type who picks up a copy of the *National Enquirer* at the checkout counter of the local supermarket. Modern science is more to my liking.

"Incredible!" I remarked as I gave her back the paper. "Breaks every law of nature, but if that paper says it so, I guess it must be true."

The serious tone I took, the pose of a scientist put in his place by all those believers in voodoo, caused Jane to laugh outrageously.

"Yes!" she agreed. "But perhaps there's some logical explanation... perhaps it's a new art technique, the living statue!"

We went on in this vain for some time, joking about the poor man who had turned to stone. Pygmalion in reverse, we called him.

But before long it would cease to be something to joke about; indeed, it would become a deadly serious matter.

As I left for home that evening, a cold and cloudless night with a dark sky filled with stars and a bright moon, I had forgotten all about the man who'd turned to stone and the star that had ceased to shine. I drove through the heavy downtown traffic, then along less crowded side streets toward the building where I lived at the east end of the city. I had the fat feeling of contentment that comes from a man being pleased with his own labour and looking forward to a quiet dinner with his wife.

Arriving home, I changed out of my suit and into an old pair of comfortable blue jeans. I kissed my wife and walked into the dining room for the evening meal.

But as I was about to sit down to eat, my wife called me to come into the living room. She said something odd was on the television. Something in her voice seemed unnatural.

When I stepped into the living room, I saw her sitting on the edge of the couch with a frown crossing her face.

"What is it?" I asked.

She motioned for me to look at the television. "Listen. Just listen!"

An announcer on the air was saying something about a newsflash from Brazil. Then the scene switched to Brazil and a female reporter who looked somewhat perplexed.

"In the last few days, there have been reports from around the world about human beings suddenly turning into stone," said the reporter. "The people in the small village of Piazo claim the same thing has happened here. They say this structure now standing in the middle of a dirt road was just a few short hours ago a living, breathing man. It's very bizarre, and probably impossible to believe for anyone who hasn't seen it with his own two eyes. But the people of this small village believe it and they are frightened. They think evil spirits have taken over their village and they want the local priest to perform an exorcism. The priest has agreed, provided the church give its consent. Right now, the people of this village anxiously await the church's decision. This is Nang Williams reporting from the village of Piazo in central Brazil."

To understand my wife's reaction, you have to understand that she was one of those people prone to believe in the supernatural and the magical. I could see in her eyes that she was tense and afraid.

Putting my arm around her, I tried to assuage her worries, but being a man of reason the only explanation I could come up with to account for the bizarre event in Brazil was to dismiss it out of hand.

"Such things don't happen," I told her. "Just wait. In a few days, they'll be saying it was all a hoax, probably to entice tourists to the town or something."

But my rationale couldn't penetrate the cold, hard resistance of her belief in evil. Slowly, she started to cry. Her body shook with convulsions.

"I'm scared!" she repeated over and over in the small, pitiful voice of a lost and lonely child.

It's funny how even in the most rational and modern of men, primal instincts can and do come to the forefront when danger threatens. I found myself protecting my wife, not with the strength of my logic but with the strength of my body.

"Don't worry!" I kissed her on the face. "I'll protect you. Nothing will harm you as long as I'm alive."

I enfolded her in my arms, and something in my words and in the touch of my body did soothe her. Tired out from the strain of the day, but now happily reassured, my wife fell gently to sleep in my arms. I picked her up and carried her into our bedroom and put her to bed.

But while she slept the sleep of the innocent, I tossed and turned as if I had only been able to relieve her fear by taking it onto myself. For the first time in my life, I began to doubt reason itself. This was as shattering an experience to me as the first strings of doubt in the existence of God would be to a believer.

Only after some hours did I manage to fall into a deep sleep.

When I awoke, I was my old self again. I was also extremely hungry, and I suddenly remembered that I hadn't eaten supper the night before.

2.

How Things Changed After the Man of Stone Emerged

In the next few days, events unfolded in such a way as to support my initial reaction to the story from Brazil. Just as I had predicted, tourists began to flock to the little village of Piazo. The Catholic Church refused to give permission for the local priest to conduct an exorcism, and even some local villagers were beginning to express doubts that a man had in fact turned to stone.

"He is local," they said of the man who had supposedly turned to stone. "He wants to believe he has great powers."

Given his superstitious beliefs about himself, the local villagers concluded he had made a stone statue of himself and then, with the help of his wife, concocted a story to fool the villagers into believing he had turned to stone. They believed he would later turn up and the stone statue would be gone with nobody knowing where it had gone.

Understandably, once the villagers discovered that money could be made of the incident, no one publicly disclaimed it. But they did begin to put a different interpretation on things. Rather than seeing it as an omen of evil, the villagers began to say it was, in fact, a blessing from the Lord above. Within their village, God had worked a miracle to give the whole world a sign that he was still in his heaven.

Once she was told that the Lord had selected her village, and more particularly her husband, to work a miracle, even the wife of the man who had supposedly turned to stone recovered from the grief she had fallen into. Now, for a fee, she would proudly tell anyone who listened that she had seen her husband turn to stone with her own two eyes. She further told of their blessed life together and revealed what a good man her husband had been.

"He was a saint!" she exclaimed, her hands reaching up towards heaven. "And I was blessed to be this good man's wife."

As word spread of the great miracle, more people came to the village of Piazo to gaze reverently at the stone statue. With the tourists, a small measure of prosperity came to the villagers, and they were happy; they were so happy that they went to the priest, the very one whom they had previously asked to conduct an exorcism, and pleaded with him to bless the stone statue. Secretly, in their hearts, they, who at first had been frightened, were afraid the statue might turn back into a man, and then the tourists would leave and take their money with them.

For one who is wise, it can be seen in the actions of the villagers that even a miracle can be turned into an ugly thing. The villagers soon began to quarrel with one another. They argued over trifles, who had been the man's best friend, who had known him best, who had spoken with him last.

Then the wife began to demand that the statue be given to her and put into her house! If people wanted to see it, they should pay her. The villagers protested vehemently against this plan. The miracle was for all the villagers, they insisted; they wanted the statue to be put into the church and that any money collected from tourists should be divided equally amongst them.

But the priest put his foot down. He would not bless the statue, nor would he have it in his church. So the villagers turned against their priest. The uprising lasted for only a few days, however, and after three days something happened to turn the village into a place of grief and woe.

As these things were coming to pass, my life had returned to normal. I chalked up the fretful night to my own weariness and my wife's condition. She was already overdue more than a week and we wondered if the child would ever come. The wait was beginning to become a strain and was most probably the cause of her agitation over the bizarre story from Brazil.

"Oh, I was just being silly," my wife said, laughing. "But if you want me to have your child, you had just better humour me!"

My wife was becoming so big that I wanted to move her to the hospital. I was afraid she might go into labour while I was at the university. I worried she'd be unable to get in touch me or our doctor, let alone anyone else. Perhaps she would be in too much pain to go to the phone and she would have to give birth alone. Was this even possible?

I pleaded with her to enter the hospital where medical hep would be right at hand, but she stubbornly refused. She complained that she would feel so lonely all by herself there and would rather stay home until it was time.

Unable to persuade her, I decided that I had better take some time off and stay home with her until she gave birth. Since I could not, on such short notice, find someone to take over my classes, I simply assigned some work for the students and cancelled classes for the week. I thought I would be absent no more than a week.

Despite the obvious strain she was under, my wife was in apparently good spirits most of the time, although on the odd occasion her mood grew dark and sombre, leading to uncontrollable weeping. All I could do was comfort her and try to assure her it would soon be over, the baby would soon be born. Our doctor told us that being a week overdue was no cause for alarm; sometimes women would be pregnant for up to ten months before giving birth. But in my wife's case, he thought she would give birth any day now.

Before that day was to come, however, the strain on both my wife and myself became almost unbearable. In fact, I thought at times my wife was at the breaking point and about to lose her mind. It wasn't just the endless waiting. Although my wife had already been pregnant for nearly nine and a half months, she could have coped with the physical strain if that had been all there was to it.

There was much more, however. There were further rumours and reports from around the world that human beings were turning to stone. These horror stories invaded our apartment, tormenting my wife with the wildest of fears. Despite my disbelief, I myself couldn't help but feel a growing sense of fear, perhaps even of terror.

The village of Piazo was once again in the news—not as the site of a grand, elaborate hoax, as one might have suspected, but rather as a place struck by tragedy for the second time in just three short days. Exactly three days after the initial incident, three days during which the town had become overrun with wealthy tourists, five more villagers had suddenly and mysteriously turned to stone. No longer was the village seen as a place where a miracle occurred, a place blessed by the Lord; once again it was inhabited by evil spirits. Another plea was sent to the priest to perform an exorcism. The tourists fled in fear, and with them went their money.

Fortunately, my wife had been resting in our bedroom when the news report from Brazil aired, and so she heard nothing of it. Not wanting to disturb her, I of course didn't tell her.

But I couldn't keep her from hearing the reports of people turning to stone in other parts of the world. With each new bulletin, her face grew more tense. Her eyes seemed to blur and she seemed a little less in control. Most of these reports came from remote areas of the world, or from eastern European countries; no live telecasts accompanied them. The awful effect that a visual report conveys was thus somewhat lessened. I was thankful for even this small blessing.

As my wife grew more worn and tired, we began going to bed earlier, both to give her more rest and to avoid watching the late newscasts.

This proved to be of little real benefit, though, because we were in the unfortunate circumstances of living beneath a couple who constantly quarrelled. Aggie and Bernie Telfer were middle-aged alcoholics. Whenever they had too much to drink, which happened almost every night, they fought like cats and dogs. I pleaded with them to avoid quarrelling, at least until after my wife had given birth, and this seemed to have had some effect.

On the night following the second report from the village of Piazo, however, a huge argument once more erupted over our heads.

My wife had been nauseous all day and now she moaned weakly. She badly needed sleep, but the noise prevented her from even being able to rest.

"Why won't they stop!" she sobbed. "I can't stand it! Oh God! I can't stand it!"

I hollered up at them to quiet down, but they were so drunk that they either didn't hear my curses or else they chose to ignore me.

Growing madder, I became determined to go up and put an end to their arguing. I told my wife I'd make them shut up and left her tossing nervously in our bed.

Reaching their apartment, I banged on the door. "Open up in there!" I called out.

Mrs. Telfer opened the door and peered out at me in her drunken stupor. "What do you want!?"

"I want you to quiet down!"

Mr. Telfer appeared behind his wife, peering at me from over her head. She and her husband had obviously come to blows, because she had an ugly welt over her left eye.

"Can't you mind your own business," she shrieked, her drunken voice breaking in my face.

"Listen here," I said as forcefully as I could. "My wife's pregnant, she needs her rest, and you're keeping us up with your infernal racket. So quiet down or I'll call the police!"

I gestured wildly with my arms and thrust my finger under her nose to make my point.

"We'll keep quiet, so don't you worry!" she slurred before slamming the door in my face.

I stood listening for a little while outside their door, waiting for them to begin again. I'm not sure what I would have done had they started up; perhaps standing there was a little foolish of me. But when they didn't take up their fight again after ten minutes, I decided that my threat had succeeded. I turned and began descending the stairs to my own apartment.

Suddenly, I heard a terrifying shriek. The shriek both frightened me and renewed my anger at the same time. I turned and rushed back up the stairs without bothering to knock. I opened the door and burst into their apartment.

Mrs. Telfer was standing in the middle of the room, shrieking. To my amazed eyes, I saw a stone statue with a huge crack and little pieces of it lying smashed on the floor.

The woman turned, looked at me in terror, then put her hands up to her face and fainted. She fell to the floor, joining the statue there.

"Mrs. Telfer!" I shouted in panic. I knew what the statue was, but I wouldn't believe it. "Mrs. Telfer, can you hear me?"

I waited, but there was no reply. Quickly and frantically, I looked through each room in the apartment, searching in desperation for Mr. Telfer. But there was no other human being present besides me and Mrs. Telfer.

Where could he be? I asked myself.

But of course I knew. We were on the top floor of the building; to have gotten out, he would have had to pass me on the stairway.

I came back into the living room and, without looking at either the statue or Mrs. Telfer, I picked up the phone on the table and dialled the police.

The police arrived about fifteen minutes later. By then, I had revived Mrs. Telfer and had her sitting up on the couch drinking a glass of water. I had thrown a white sheet over the stone statue.

"Is somebody dead?" an officer asked calmly as he stared at the sheet on the floor.

"Yes!" Mrs. Telfer replied in anguish. "My husband!"

It was hard to convince the police officers of what had happened; it was, in fact, almost impossible. But they eventually accepted our story. That two fellow human beings, supposedly rational men, could accept such a tale scared me almost as much as what I knew had happened.

As bizarre and unreal as all this seemed to me, there could be no denying it now.

I don't know what happened to Mrs. Telfer after that, nor do I know what happened to the statue when I left the apartment. The police officers were still there when I vacated and returned to my wife on the floor below.

When I entered our bedroom, I saw that my wife was sleeping. I thanked God for that. I wouldn't have consciously told her what had happened, but I'm not sure I could have hidden it from her either. Seeing me in my current state, she might have guessed everything.

Undressing quickly, I climbed into bed beside her. Again I couldn't sleep. My mind was tormented with questions. What had happened? How had it happened?

And then I began to wonder if this might not be some sort of disease. An epidemic perhaps. If so, what was the cause? Could there be a cure? Would it strike only certain individuals, or was all mankind in danger?

Perhaps it's hard to believe that somebody would react so rationally to something so far beyond human understanding. At least I thought I was reacting rationally. But what else was I to do, or anyone for that matter? Although I now doubted reason more than ever, I saw no other way out but to put my faith in it.

Lying restless and disturbed, I didn't get any sleep at all that night, nor would I for several more days.

3.
HAVE WE NOT LET OUR HEARTS TURN TO STONE

The next morning, my wife woke up feeling perhaps more tired than I did—despite the fact that she'd slept soundly for hours, whereas I'd had no sleep whatsoever. Her face was drawn and pale. Her eyes seemed lifeless and she was extremely weak. I knew she needed help, help which I couldn't give her because I was almost in as bad shape.

"I'm taking you to the hospital," I told her.

I expected her to put up a fight, but she didn't. She just nodded her head in consent.

When we got to the hospital, the doctor was waiting for us. Upon seeing my wife, he pulled me aside and berated me for not having brought her in sooner.

"My God, man!" he scolded me. "She looks like she's near death's door!"

I tried to explain to him that she'd refused to come. "And you know, Doctor, the stone statues… they've been driving us crazy."

"I can see you're in pretty rough shape yourself," he said. "The stone statues have everyone on edge. You know, there have even been rumours that it's happened here in the city."

When he said that, I shook with fear.

"You don't know," I asked him.

"Know what?"

"Of course it has happened here. I've seen it myself."

I should have known you can't just come straight out and tell a man news of that nature. Who would believe it?

He looked at me as if I had lost my mind. "You should go home and rest. Get a good long rest."

"No. You don't believe me, but it did happen. I'm telling you the truth. And I will get a good night's rest… I need some rest… but it did happen."

He looked at me incredulously, but a hint of acceptance appeared in his face. "If it has, God help us all!"

Despite the shock my news must have been to him, the doctor tended to his duties. He examined my wife and again told us that the child should be born any day now—any hour, actually. Then he gave her a sedative to relax her and put her to sleep.

Once she was resting comfortably, I drew the doctor aside and asked him if I should stay, considering my wife might give birth any hour.

"No, no, you go home," he said. "Actually, I don't think the child will come before tomorrow. But if he does, we'll call you to come over."

I left a few minutes later, after my wife had fallen asleep.

When I got to my car, I realized I couldn't go home. I couldn't bear to be in that apartment, trapped inside those four walls, where so much had happened. I had to get away to someplace that would let me forget. But where?

I remembered Jane had a place over on Toronto Island, just off the lakefront. Perhaps I could stay there, away from the city, away from people who might turn to stone.

Jane would be at the university, so I drove there to find her.

I don't know what I was expecting, but I thought the university would be different, that the whole world would be different. Considering what I saw, I thought nothing would be the same ever again.

But there it was, outwardly unchanged. Students made their way in pairs, in groups, or singularly across the fields, along the streets, going from class to class. Some were laughing, some argued heatedly, some seemed deep in thought, a few looked to be in love. They seemed so unchanged from when I had last been here.

I found Jane lecturing her class in Medieval English. I took a seat at the back of the room and waited until the lecture came to an end.

Upon seeing me, Jane brought the lecture to an abrupt halt and dismissed the class.

"You look terrible!" she exclaimed as she walked quickly towards me.

I stood up to greet her.

"Sit down, sit down!" She motioned me down, obviously worried that I might not have the strength to stand.

"Oh, I'm all right," I assured her. "Just very tired. I'm quite able to stand... and even walk!" I attempted a small smile, and it drew a short laugh from her.

"Well you may be okay, but you don't look at all well. What's been happening to you?"

I told her everything. Keeping it all to myself must have exerting intense pressure on me, because when I finished talking I felt greatly relieved.

"So you really didn't *see* Mr. Telfer turn to stone," she pointed out.

I had to admit that I hadn't, at least not with my own two eyes.

"But it happened!" I protested. "I'm certain it happened."

"Perhaps it did, but you can't be certain. So why not just suspend judgement for awhile? If this is really happening, we'll all know soon enough. And if it's not, we shouldn't be worrying about it now."

Listening to her, I got the odd impression she was trying as hard to convince herself as she was trying to convince me. But why should she have to convince herself, I wondered?

I realized there was something she wasn't telling me. She was trying to protect me, to keep me from worrying even more. I wanted to kiss her for it, but I also wanted to cry. I also felt a desperate desire to know what it was she was keeping from me.

But I decided to leave it until later.

"Jane, I didn't just come here to cry on your shoulder and burden you with my troubles," I said.

"You haven't burdened me with anything." She smiled softly to show me she really meant it.

"Whether I have or haven't, the main reason I'm here is to see if you could do me a favour."

"Well, I don't know. Why don't you tell me what it is, and we'll see."

"You told me before that you have a cottage on the island which you use on weekends."

"Yes." She motioned me to go on.

"I was wondering if I could stay there for a day or two. If you won't be using it, of course."

"It wouldn't matter if I was using it," she said, "You could stay there anyway. But in fact, I'm not using it, so you can have it to yourself."

During the week, she stayed at the apartment she rented in the city. She explained that she hadn't bothered cleaning the cottage the last time she'd been there, so I'd find it a bit of a mess.

"Pantyhose lying around everywhere," she kidded. "I hope you won't be shocked!"

She then gave me a key to get in and drew me a little map showing how to get there.

As I was leaving, she walked with me to my car and we chatted amiably about the weather. I drove away, waving goodbye sadly.

The Toronto ferry docks were just a short ride from the university and the island was only a fifteen-minute ride from there.

Once at the island, I had to walk a ways to get to Jane's cottage. Although there were a number of cottages built o n the island, Jane had given me excellent directions, so I had no difficulty finding hers. It was in a fairly secluded spot on the southwest end of the island.

I arrived in the early evening, just as the sun was setting. It was so beautiful that, before going in, I stopped and sat on the porch to watch it. Seagulls were drifting low under the clouds, swooping over the tiny waves of Lake Ontario. This place could have been a million miles from anywhere, but just behind me was the city.

Then the sun set and I looked off into the darkness. Where had the seagulls gone? I didn't know.

Finally, I opened the door and hit the switch on the wall, filling the room with light. Taking a quick look around, I found there were three rooms. Jane's bedroom, a bathroom, and a combination kitchen-living room. I closed Jane's bedroom door, not intending to use that room, and decided to sleep on the couch.

After making myself some dinner, I lay down on the couch to sleep, but I couldn't. I hadn't slept in more than forty hours and now I was overtired. Too many thoughts were weighing heavily on my mind and I was unable to shut them out.

Rather than just lie there, I decided to take a walk. I thought I could take my mind off my troubles by tiring myself out. Then I would sleep.

I was thankful there had been so little snow this winter. It was easy to walk over the cold, hard ground. I headed down towards the beach, on the south side of the island and away from the city. This is where I thought I'd seen the seagulls fly.

Walking in the solitude of the cold, dark night, listening to the waves rush up onto the shore, my spirits picked up. These were melancholy sights and sounds, feelings of loneliness, but they were human feelings. Things I had felt before and, like an old friend, I welcomed them.

But I wasn't alone on the beach. Farther down along the shore, I saw a bonfire.

I was on the verge of turning around and heading back when I saw that there was just one old man standing by the fire, all alone. I felt drawn towards him, as men in isolation are often drawn towards each other. Something inside me cried out for human contact, for the mere sound of another voice.

So I slowly walked towards the fire, and I might have gone right by if he hadn't called to me.

"Good evening, young fellow," he said loud enough for me to hear, but without shouting. In fact, without making much of an effort at all.

"Hi!" I called back. "Mind if I come up and get warm!"

"No," he said. "Be glad for the company!"

As I approached, I saw that I had been right: he was an old man, but not ancient. He must have been around retirement age. He was also short and thin. Couldn't have been above five-foot-five. He looked like what I pictured an old sea dog looked like. Perhaps he was one.

"You from the city?" he asked without looking up at me. He just kept staring into the fire.

"Yes."

"Who you visiting?"

"Oh, Jane Elway." I pointed over to where her cottage was located.

"I know her," he said. "Know where she lives, know everybody who lives on the island."

"You must have lived here a long time."

He laughed. "If you're asking me if I'm old, I am."

"Oh, no..." I started to protest, but it seemed feeble, so I shut up.

We stood there for some time, not saying anything. I couldn't think of anything to say and he didn't seem interested in me, only in the fire and the sky. He kept looking at one and then the other.

Finally, after waiting long enough for him to know that I had warmed up, I said I'd be heading out.

For the first time, he turned and looked at me. "You her boyfriend?"

"You mean Jane's?"

He nodded.

"No! No, I'm a married man."

"You having an affair with her then?" he asked.

"No, of course not!" I stammered. He didn't seem convinced. "Listen, I tell you: I'm not having an affair with her. We're just friends."

"Well, if you aren't having an affair with her, don't start," he said gruffly. "And if you are, then stop. She's a nice girl. I've known her a long time. You could only break her heart."

"But I'm not! I only came over because things are so crazy in the city and I needed rest."

"Things are crazy in the world. You don't have to tell me," he replied. "But that's no excuse."

I decided it was hopeless to try to convince him one way or the other, so I tried to change the subject. "So, you've heard about what's happening?"

"You mean with the stars."

"The stars?" I said, bewildered. "No, I mean people turning to stone!"

"Oh, that," he said dismissively. "Of course I know about that. Bet you don't know the stars are going out, though."

He again looked up into the sky. It was then that I remembered hearing about the subject.

"Yeah," I said. "But it's only one. I read about it. Happened around Christmas."

"One? Ha!" he chortled. "More than one, for sure!"

"No, only one. It was in the papers!"

"Well, maybe that's all they put in the papers. But I've been looking into that sky for nearly fifty years, and I tell you: there are a lot of stars that aren't up there anymore. Least they're not where they're supposed to be."

That's why he keeps gazing into the sky, I thought. *Trying to see a star go out!*

"Are you sure?" I asked.

"Look for yourself." He pointed upward.

"I don't know anything about the sky."

"Then you can take my word for it," he said.

I looked up in the sky, trying to remember what stars should be where, but I had never thought much about the stars. I'd only looked up at them, never really seeing them.

"Hey, son," he said, tapping me on the shoulder. "Speaking about them stone statues people are turning into, they're dropping like flies in Europe." He laughed heartily. "That's where the guilt lies heaviest."

Looking down at him, I thought I saw his eyes glint with delight; they looked like the flames of the fire. I thought he must be some kind of a nut. I had to get out of there.

"Well, it's getting late," I said. "I guess I'll head on in."

I started to walk away.

"You think I'm crazy," he said.

I knew he was still looking into the fire, his back turned towards me as mine was to him.

"I'm not crazy," he went on. "Far from it. Leave if you want, but then you'll never understand what's going on, unless you can figure it out for yourself."

"Ha. You're a know-it-all. A wise old know-it-all!" I fell to my knees, crying. I couldn't help it. "If you're so smart, tell me. Why is any of this happening? Why didn't you stop it long ago, when you were my age?"

He turned and left the fire to come and sit beside me. "I'm no more guilty than you are," he said. "And your generation's no more guilty than mine. And mine's no more guilty than the one before it, and on it goes back to Adam."

I stopped crying. I just sat quietly listening to his words. He had a need to say a lot, and I had a need to hear a lot, so we sat together through the night—he, the preacher; me, the multitude.

"That's the only thing the individual can't do by himself," he began. "He can't save the world. Only the world can save the world—or at least, could. It starts with the leaders. Just look at them now. No more talk of nuclear war. One's not blaming the other guy or making threats against him. They're all trying to pretend everything is fine and dandy on good ole Mother Earth. Now they sense something is terribly wrong in the universe, though. We're all a bunch of hypocrites, son, but we don't all make a virtue of it. Then it's exposed to the public—and they, fools that they are, put their hope in lawmakers rather than in laws…"

The old man paused for some time. He was deep in thought at this point, periodically looking up into the sky. It was obvious he had many more things to say and that the things he wanted to say were intricate.

"The Bible says, 'Thou shalt not kill,'" he continued. "While man says, 'Thou shalt not kill without reason.' But what reason can there be? In World War II, the Allies killed millions of innocent people to defeat Hitler. We dropped tons of bombs on Dresden and the big A-bomb on Hiroshima and Nagasaki. I fought in that war, and at the time I thought we were right to do it. But I'm not so sure anymore. Where did it get us? It got us facing an even deadlier foe. It got us a world that's always at the point of war, on the verge of destruction. No peace, no love, no brotherhood. And no winners! And there won't be any winners after the next war, either. That's why I think God's ending it. It's his creation! What right have we to destroy it? Man thinks there are no laws, natural or otherwise. Look at gravity. Gravity isn't a law; it's just something to get around. Man thinks there are no laws that can bind him except for those he creates himself. And he'll break those ones when it pleases him, too!"

I broke in at this point. "Man can't break the law of gravity, even when he's going to the moon," I said. "Gravity only means that you have to use a certain amount of force that's holding you down."

"That's not what I meant, son. Nothing wrong with flying, not even going to the stars. What I'm against is this notion that everything is relative. Einstein said it. Now, I can't judge him, cause maybe he didn't mean it in that way. But it isn't all relative. There are absolutes, laws man shouldn't break no matter what the end intent is. Do you know what I'm getting at, son?"

It was early morning before he finished his lengthy monologue. The sun was rising and I was chilled to the bone. The fire had died hours ago, meaning I had just gone another night without sleep.

Despite my intensifying exhaustion, I continued speaking to the old man into the early morning hours as the sun rose. When he finished, however, I wasn't sure if he had told me nothing at all or laid out for me the secrets of the universe. It all seemed very peculiar to me!

Danny Hanging Out

Danny studied at the University of Toronto, having pursued coursework primarily in philosophy, political sciences and English during his stay studying at Erindale College (which is more commonly referred to as the University of Toronto Mississauga in recent years). His interest in philosophy is evident through "Turn to Stone a Statue's Eye". Toward the latter portions of this chapter, for example, it sounded to me like Danny was speaking about the meaning of life. From conversations I had with relatives who knew Danny, he frequently thought about and spoke of matters up for philosophical debate. Those people I asked read "Turn to Stone a Statue's Eye", in a small sample size, acknowledged they felt the entire piece had a philosophical backdrop to it unique to someone who was vehemently interested in philosophy. Similar philosophical themes exist in other pieces of writing included in publication. "Journey Into Nothing", for example, talks about the origins of the universe, referencing well-known names in philosophy, including Aristotle and Socrates.

4.
TRAGEDY STRIKES AWFUL CLOSE TO HOME

As I walked back along the beach toward Jane's cottage, I thought of everything the old man had said. Then I saw the gulls, which had risen with the sun. I watched them glide gracefully through the air, just over the waves and then rose up again towards the clouds. Watching them, I felt like they were free—and that I wasn't. But that I should be. I should be free to be as I was, blissfully happy, content to live the life of an unimportant man, to experience the simple joy that all men had experienced since creation or evolution.

But my world had been tossed under the sun and wind; the gulls were stark reminders of what could no longer be taken for certain: the permanence of life. If not the life of man, at least the life of the world and the stars.

I feared that the silent, empty void of the grave, which had always been the fate of individuals, must also be on the verge of striking—for all things, for the whole universe, for every molecule of matter, every thought, every sound, and every motion. If the stars could die, then surely eternity must be coming to an end!

This is the hell that was approaching, an ending that struck me as being so horrible that even a fiery hell of misery would have seemed a comfort. Into this barren abyss, the whole of creation was about to fall. And yet when it came, it would bring no suffering.

But now I suffered.

Lost in this torment of thought, I made my way back to Jane's cottage. As I opened the door, I felt numb and cold and wretched. I needed to sleep, to put things out of my find, to forget.

I closed the door behind me and slumped onto the couch, my eyes shut. I had a weird sensation of falling into the darkness of death; it was pulling me downward, making me weak. A voice was screaming at me to get up before it was too late, and I felt incredibly tired. It would be so easy just to give in, to fall deeper into the darkness. And it did seem as if I was physically falling into a dark, empty place. The deeper I fell, the darker it got, and the more difficult it was to see if I had a body at all. I was disappearing into the darkness, fading into nothingness.

The voice urged me to resist: "Struggle! Fight! Get up! Open your eyes!"

I was experiencing the process dying, although not death itself. If I didn't re-sist, if I didn't open my eyes as the voice told me to, I would die. Perhaps somebody would find my body.

Perhaps the whole world would die—was dying, for all I could know, just as I was.

I struggled. I fought with everything in me to open my eyes. And as I urged myself on, I grew stronger. Death could not and would not take me. I bolted up and forced my eyes to open.

Jane stood in front of me.

"Thank God you're finally awake!" she said. "I've been trying to get you to wake up for the past ten minutes. You're one heavy sleeper!"

I was still a little bleary and tried to rub the sleep from my eyes. "When did you get here?"

"I've been here all night. The hospital is trying to get a hold of you. They called the university, so I came over… but you weren't here. I've been waiting all night!"

"Oh my God!" I exclaimed. Suddenly, I remembered my wife. "Has the baby come?"

"I don't know. I only know that they want you to get there as soon as possible. Whatever it is, it's urgent!"

I got up and put on my winter coat.

"Wait, I'll get dressed and come with you," Jane said.

She went back into her bedroom, and I stood there waiting impatiently. I wanted to rush to my wife. I felt guilty for having left her in the first place. I should have stayed by her side. I should have made sure she was okay. I doubted my deci-sion to head to Jane's place.

Had something gone wrong? Suddenly, I was certain of it. Something awful had happened. I felt panic, blood rushing to my head. Everything seemed to be closing in on me, pushing me under.

"Listen, Jane!" I screamed to her through the door. "I better go! You don't have to come! I can find my way!"

I was about to rush out the door without waiting for her to reply when she came out of the bedroom.

"But I have to take you over to the city, because the ferry doesn't leave until eight-thirty," she said. "It's only seven o'clock."

"How are you going to take me?" I asked her.

"I have a speedboat. We have to get it out of a boathouse, but it will be a lot quicker than waiting for the ferry."

The boathouse was situated on the northeast end of the island, about a fifteen-minute walk from Jane's cottage. We walked briskly and silently along paths, over fields, and down onto the beach.

When we arrived, Jane opened the boathouse doors and together we pushed the speedboat down a ramp and into the water beside the wharf. Jane took out two cans of gas and filled the engine. We then hopped in, Jane forcefully pulled the rip cord, the engine sputtered into life, and the boat slowly picked up speed, making its way over the water towards the city.

The noise of the engine made conversation impossible, so we just sat in silence. The boat flew into the air above the waves, then crashed down with a tremendous jolt. The steady violent boom filled my brain as I watched the city loom ever larger. The city, the sun, the cumulous clouds floating gently in a clear blue sky… they were all contradictions to my every thought and feeling. If everything was ending, why then did the morning sun bathe the skyline in soft light and pleasant shadows? How could the world look so at peace?

Maybe I was wrong. Maybe the old man on the beach had been wrong! Maybe I'd get to the hospital to find my wife was healthy and had given birth to our child. Maybe all would be well.

Hope sprang up within me and fought against despair just as the morning sun fought the dawn.

When we reached the docks, I said goodbye to Jane and ran up to the lot where I had left my car.

I drove swiftly, almost joyfully, towards the hospital, watching in wonder the people headed to or from work as always. The traffic crawled along the major roadways. Life went on unchanged!

I parked behind the hospital and rushed in through the wide doors to the main lobby, then took the elevator up to paediatrics on the eleventh floor. My wife's room door was closed, though, and I hesitated to go in. Perhaps she was sleeping.

I went to see the nurse at the desk.

"Excuse me," I said. "My wife's in room 1102. I was just wondering about her condition. I was told to come. Has she given birth?"

The nurse looked at me gravely, a worried frown crossing her face when she heard who I was. She didn't answer me immediately. Again, I was gripped by a sense of fright. Something *had* happened.

"How is my wife?" I demanded in a loud, terrified voice. "Has anything happened to her?"

"No, no, no," the nurse said quickly. She got up from the desk and came around to meet me. "She's resting comfortable right now. But she's been under a terrible strain and the doctor wants to speak to you about that. He's in his office now." She gestured down the corridor. "If you'll follow me, I'll take you there."

She was an older woman, I would say in her late fifties. She had a slightly rotund figure but was obviously hale and hearty. Her attitude towards me was one of gentle sympathy, but I felt something was wrong. Still, I decided not to worry until hearing what the doctor had to say.

As I was ushered into his office, I noticed out doctor sitting behind a large oaken desk scanning some papers. Upon seeing me, he put them aside and got up.

"Well, take a seat," he said.

I sat down and he returned to his own chair, descending slowly into it. He was wringing his hands in an agitated way, looking at me and then looking away, trying to find the right words to tell me something. But what?

"Doctor, I'm getting nervous." I tried to laugh to ease the tension, but it came out more like a snort. "Could you just tell me if my wife is all right?"

"Well, she still hasn't given birth," he said gravely. "And that, of course, concerns me. But there's something else…" He hesitated slightly, perhaps in an attempt to indicate that, while I shouldn't be alarmed, he wanted me to clearly understand the situation. "I don't know how else to tell you this except to say it straight out. Your wife tried to perform an abortion on herself."

I had been prepared for almost anything, but not for this.

"Oh my God!" I cried. "She tried to do what!?"

"To commit an abortion," he said again. "She must have gone insane."

I didn't know who to feel shame for, her or myself. Was I not partially responsible? Had I not left her here alone? Had I not forgotten her completely? I hadn't left word with the hospital where I could be reached in case of an emergency—and I had left the city. I had gone to the island to find peace and quiet while she lay here suffering alone.

I tried to calm myself, taking deep, silent breaths, filling my lungs, choking back my tears.

"Oh God," I said again.

The doctor looked down, thinking it best to let me have a few moments to come to grips with things. Finally, he stood up and walked over to me.

"Are you okay now?" he asked.

"Yeah," I said heavily. "I better see her."

"I have her on a sedative, but it's probably wearing off by now. She should be awake soon, so you can go in and wait beside her. But let me caution you not to say anything to upset her. It might be best not to say anything about what happened unless she mentions it herself."

I nodded my head in consent and took a few more deep breaths. "Doctor, she didn't hurt the baby, did she?"

"Oh no," he replied. "A nurse stopped her before she did anything."

"Thank God!"

My wife was still sleeping when I entered her room. I sat in a chair beside her bed and noticed a huge quilt covering. Only her tiny head stuck out from the covers, resting on a pillow.

A nurse had been in the room but left when I entered. She asked me to let them know when I was leaving.

I sat in silence, each second, it seemed to me, like a ponderous animal fleeing a fire—too slow to escape, the flames getting nearer and nearer. Each second stretched on like an eternity, yet still ended far too soon.

Not wanting to think, I glanced around the room but there wasn't much to attract one's attention. There was a second bed on the other side of the room, with curtains hiding the top of it from view. There were two small tables, one beside each bed, and a half-empty glass of water on the one by my wife's bed. All I could see through the window was a red brick wall—another part of the hospital, I presumed.

Then my wife moaned. "Help me," she said as she violently tossed in bed "Somebody help me!"

"I'm here!" I said gently, laying my hand against her cheek. She opened her eyes and didn't seem to recognize me. "It's me, honey."

"You're here! Where have you been?"

"Oh, I'm sorry," I sobbed "I left for a little while… I thought you'd be okay!"

She put her arms around my neck and with feeble strength pulled me towards her. With her head cuddled against my shoulder, she wept. I kissed her tenderly on her hair and I too wept; I wept for all the happiness that should have been ours but wasn't.

Then she pushed me a bit away from her and looked not at me but through me, into some horror only she saw.

"The baby will never be born," she whimpered, her eyes filled with pitiful tears.

"Of course he will."

I pulled her towards me, but she struggled free.

"If he is, then he'll be born a stone…"

"What?" I said in shock. "You don't know what you're saying!"

She buried her face in the pillow, then looked up at me and for an instant I thought I saw hatred in her eyes. Hatred for me. Hatred for our coming child.

"You think I'm stupid," she hissed. "You all think I'm blind. I know what's going on!"

From there, she began screaming at me in a wild rage, like a cornered animal that had finally lashed out at its pursuers. Who were her pursuers, though? The child and me?

"Oh God, I know what's going on!" she proclaimed as the anger drained from her body. "We're all going to die!"

She broke into heart-rendering sobs.

"No one's going to die," I said with melancholy. "Soon the baby will come, and he'll be fine! And so will you. Then we'll go home. It won't be long."

She looked at me, disbelieving but wanting to believe. She had stopped crying and now had a sad gaze.

Suddenly, she moaned and let out a short cry of pain.

"What's wrong?" I said, feeling frantic.

She gritted her teeth. "I think it's time."

"You mean the baby's coming!?"

She smiling up at me. "I think so."

"The baby," I said jubilantly as I jumped to my feet. My heart filled with relief. "I'll get the doctor."

My wife was in labour for ten long hours, but the doctor refused to let me stay by her side.

"She's in too much pain," he said. "You couldn't bear it and the nurses would end up having to see to you!"

So I waited. I'd always thought the image of a wrecked husband pacing the hall was just a Hollywood creation, but there I found myself, walking up and down in fierce agitation. At first, the mere fact that my wife was about to give birth had brought me great relief. It had calmed me, perhaps in the same way that bright sunshine and clear weather calmed sailors after a violent storm; the world seemed back to normal and everything was on course, the danger having passed.

But that feeling very quickly subsided and as I drifted into a conscious awareness of all my normal worries. And my wife's labour pains caused me great concern. The long wait was hard on me mentally, but more so physically. I hadn't slept in more than two days, and ironically I felt too tired to sleep now.

Finally, however, I could go on no longer. Halfway through my wife's long ordeal, I decided to go down to the staff lounge and catch some rest. I made my way foggily through the blurred halls, down the desolate stairwell, as if in a dreamlike trance, my senses far from alert, relaying to my brain only the vaguest impressions. I was seeing as if through a mist. Shapes appeared before me as forms without substance.

And then I fell, exhausted.

I woke up many hours later—how many, I did not know—and found myself lying in bed. I had a throbbing headache and was alone in the room. I had been stripped down to my shorts and undershirt.

Getting up, I started searching for my clothes. My shoes and socks had been left on the floor at the foot of the bed. I found my pants, shirt, and jacket hanging in the closet. Depending on how you look at it, I was either extremely fortunate or extremely unfortunate to have gotten any sleep, as I'd been on the point of physical collapse.

Now, upon waking, not only was I physically rejuvenated, but my mental well-being had been greatly restored. What was about to come, however, would put an intense strain on my mental well-being, a strain I may not have been able to stand had I not received this short respite of sleep. Although perhaps it would have been better if I had broken under the pressure; that might have brought about a quicker, more merciful end. But I was fated to be one of the last survivors at a time when the living would envy the dead.

After I dressed, I made my way back up to the eleventh floor. What was I expecting? I suppose I thought I'd find a beautiful little child lying gently in my wife's arms.

But as I walked into the room, I was greeted by a wail of despair. Two interns were trying to restrain my wife as she thrashed madly about. Finally, one of them managed to inject a syringe into her veins, and after a few seconds she went limp.

I stood there in a state of horror. The nightmare had returned.

"What in the name of God's going on?" I screamed, dashing at the intern nearest to me and grabbing a hold of him. I threw him bodily away from my wife. "Get away!"

I suppose I must have looked such a fearsome sight that it caused the second intern to recoil in terror.

Then I cried. I don't know how long I cried for. I just hid my face in my hands and sobbed controllably. The tears didn't just come from my eyes; they seemed to rise out of my very heart, thrown forward by the blood of my body as if it was nothing but silt to be dispersed upon the bank of a river.

I felt a hand on my shoulder and looked up into the wearied face of our doctor. He appeared much older than he'd been before.

"Oh God, Doctor, what happened?"

"The baby was born," he began in a quiet whisper. "He was healthy. Your wife came through all right, and we brought the baby in for her to hold."

He stopped, as if unable to go on. When he did, it was in a quivering voice, his hands trembling.

"And then something awful happened." A cry broke from his lips. "The baby turned to stone! Lying there in your wife's arms, it just turned to stone. Your wife screamed and dropped it!"

The nightmare seemed complete.

5.
THE COLD, UNFORGIVING
EYES OF A STATUE

Since I have told this tale necessarily from my own narrow viewpoint, it's been a litany of my own personal tragedy. In any catastrophe, whether it's a fire, earthquake, or war, the actions of each individual tend towards his own survival, and each individual sees the catastrophe only through its direct impact on his own wellbeing.

But for me, the tragedy taking place all over the universe ceased to be primarily personal when I reached the point where I felt I had lost all that I could lose. A spiritual death took place in me, and strangely it freed me, allowing me to look outward and upon the plight of others. I was a dead man looking out of the grave at life and the living.

I was brought to this emotional state of affairs by the death of my wife. I have told very little of her so far, of how she was during the final months of her pregnancy and life, that terrible time during which I now believe she sensed something of nightmarish proportions was taking place.

Well, the way I have described her so far isn't the real her, although I suppose it does reveal something of her true nature. She was very fragile. She couldn't stand up to harsh people or harsh events. I suppose that's the reason she married me. She guessed correctly that the life of a professor's wife could be very tranquil, very peaceful. And she knew I was a gentle man. I guess she felt I was something like herself—a quiet, contemplative character well-suited to the slow lane of life.

I must confess I wasn't very passionate, nor was she, but we did love each other. We both felt we had found the perfect person. At least perfect so far as we were concerned.

I didn't know why any of this was happening. It went against all reason and broke all laws of nature. That men should turn to stone seems as fantastical as the tales of Sinbad the Sailor.

I looked around, blind as I was, and could see. But did I understand? Did I understand that the life of a man wasn't meant to be an endless circle without direction? There was always direction. We move outward or withdraw inward. We break patterns, we create, and we destroy. But when you destroy the ability to create, you bring death.

I came to believe God had given unto man a great freedom: the ability to be a creator. But God retained unto himself the sole right to destroy that which he had created. And that which he'd created was all of life—the universe and all it encompassed: the stars, the planets, the earth, and both man and animals.

For some cause, God had chosen to destroy creation!

The vanity of man was boundless, and I concluded that it was the actions of man since the beginning of time that had brought God to this decision.

But I am falling far afield from what I wanted to say. It is not for me to judge why the universe is being brought to an end, only to tell that part of the story I bore direct witness to: the final days of life on the planet Earth.

My son had been born and ceased to be alive, all without my having seen him, touched him, or held him in my arms.

After the doctor left, I just sat there, alone with my wife in the room. She was sedated, and I suppose many hours went by. The room dimmed into shadows, growing darker as night came on.

If I thought of anything during those hours, it was on a very subconscious level. All I recall is sitting there like a statue, a cold statue, a lifeless statue, with two stony eyes directed on the inert form huddled on the bed. The form occasionally jerked or twitched, very slow movements.

If I were to have acted, it should have been when she came awake with ferocious energy! She hurled aside the sheets and sprang up onto her knees. She stopped when she saw me, looked at me for a long second, and then screamed. I couldn't stop her. I couldn't lessen the terror she felt, because I was the cause of much of it.

We were no longer man and wife. She was a fleeing form and I but a lifeless statue. I had already turned to stone and she sensed it.

Suddenly, she hurled herself with incredible strength up out of bed and then ran across the room. The torment she'd suffered had pushed her beyond the bounds of sanity and she threw herself out the eleventh story window as I watched on.

I must confess, I didn't even try to stop her. She escaped me as she escaped life.

I didn't run to watch her fall, to watch in terror. Statues don't run, only men do. Statues take no fascination in death; they cannot be appalled, shocked, or saddened. They cannot wonder why!

It was many days before I began to wonder why, many days before I again saw as a man sees.

I vaguely recall the sound of rushing footsteps along a concrete floor, nearer and louder, nearer and louder, but reaching me as an echo of a dream. Then there were loud and quiet vibrating voices. Were they screaming or were they whispering? I couldn't tell.

"What happened?"

"Did you try to stop her?"

Did I answer? "Yes, she's dead! Yes, she's dead! Yes, she's dead! No hope! No hope! No hope! Eleven floors down! Floors down! Down!"

Had I asked any questions? Had I said anything?

How many hours passed before I was released? They weren't even really holding me; I could have gone anytime. There was no police inquiry. It was just a suicide.

"One of many!"

Who said that?

"Like when the stock market crashed, everyone's jumping!"

Who said that!? Voices in my cold stone eyes? I suppose these voices lost interest in my silence.

I was taken to a waiting room and left there. For a long time, I did wait, not for anything or anyone, just to pass the time. That's what a statue waits for. Living things wait mostly for death, and therefore they wait for a certain amount of time, a day or an eternity.

Time passing. If anything, I was waiting for all time to pass.

Then, because I was not a statue, because I was still a man, I stopped waiting. My muscles needed exercise, my lungs needed air, my cold stony eyes needed light—not the hazy mist of the waiting room, but real light. Light from the sun.

So those parts of me picked me up and walked me out the door. No one moved to stop me, as I was of no interest. They were too busy rushing to hurry up time.

I walked out into a different world, and I was a very different man.

6.
A Reflection in a Post-Modern World

A s I walked out of the hospital into the world lit by the sun, I walked on a man's legs, led by a man's two eyes, but the feeling part of me, the reasoning part of me, the part that could wonder and feel wonder, remained back in that eleventh floor hospital room, trapped in the cocoon of silence death had brought. While my physical body, propelled by bones and muscle, moved aimlessly about the city, my spirit sought the solace of death. I only wanted the comfort of the grave, and in a sense I had buried myself.

But troubled spirits do not rest in peace.

In the first hours, I was consciously aware of very little of what took place around me. An occasional jolt from some passing stranger sent my body careening awkwardly to one side. A loud shout, "Hey, man! Hey, man! Hey, man! You okay? You okay? You okay? Where are you going? Going? Going?" And so many screams, loud, terrifying screams. Was it my wife screaming? "Eleven floors down, floors down, down." And I paid so little attention to any of it. I was so unaware. Was it loud or a whisper? Only voices in a statue's stone-cold eyes.

Something hit me very hard, hard enough to feel. Was I the one falling? Waiting to hit bottom? Waiting for all time to hit bottom?

Something stopped me from falling all the way and pulled me up. Eleven stories up. Up, up. Then hitting me hard again. Consciousness returning with excruciating pain. Sobbing, screaming pain, so unbearable. The stone-cold eyes opening wide with the terror of a dead man. A helpless dead man.

And then I lost all consciousness. I wasn't in the eleventh-floor room. I had been dragged and beaten out of there. I was gone from my body completely, until the pain of the beating receded enough for me to live again.

When I came to, it was raining. Big droplets fell coolly onto my face, but all over the rest of me I felt a searing heat. I had been badly cut and bruised.

At first I didn't try to move; I just lay there looking about. The light from the sun breaking through the clouds that hung over the city was pale and weak. It gave me no idea of time of day it was, only that it wasn't night.

I lay on cold, hard winter earth in a thicket of trees. Peering through the trunks, I saw a steeply sloping hill rise up, sparsely covered in melting snow. Small streams of water ran down over the snow from the hilltop, which was blocked from my view by the branches of the trees.

When I moved, my body seemed to rip, as if I was pulling myself out of the ground by my roots. It took all the strength I had to lift myself to my knees. My clothes were caked in mud and blood. My blood, I supposed.

But I was alive.

I felt cold, hungry, and sore. More than that, I felt desire. I wanted a hot bath and something to eat. My God, I wanted life. I was so glad that whoever had beaten me hadn't killed me.

I filled my lungs with air, felt some strength returning to my weakened muscles, and then got up and walked out of the trees, pushing aside the branches. I saw where I was—still in the city. I wasn't far from my apartment. About a thirty-minute walk, I figured. It took me that long just to get up out of the ravine where I lay. I pushed myself inch by inch up the long, wet, slippery slope. Getting tired, aching for air, resting, going on… always going on.

When I reached the top, I was back in the city. But it was much different from the city I had always known. One look around was sufficient to reveal the decay that had quickly set in. It wasn't a physical decay presenting itself to the eyes, but an emotional sagging of the whole city. In the core, the skyscrapers stood erect, reaching into the sky and gleaming with vigorous energy while the residential streets were adorned with splendid houses, clean and pretty, well-spaced and each with a groomed yard.

So the physical structures of the city stood the same as always, but there was no bustle. The streets were almost empty—except for the odd soul and the stone structures everywhere! There was no roar of engines, no din of a thousand voices, no persistent stomping of boots.

Where was everyone? Where was the noise? I heard only the soft whimper of the wind as it twisted through the deserted corridors of the city.

I stooped to retrieve a torn sheet of newspaper that was blowing over the ground and read the headline: Bizarre Deaths Continue to Mystify Science. It briefly told of the rising number of deaths, reported to be in the millions worldwide, all resulting in the person turning to stone. The tone of the article was alarmist and filled with desperation. It told of world governments panicking, of scientists working feverishly yet shedding no light on what was taking place. It told of churches filling up, with people offering prayer to a capricious God to send an undeserved salvation. The world repented on its knees for the sins of man and begged forgiveness, a forgiveness of a type that would not be forthcoming.

Many days later, I reflected that man had been forgiven, salvation bestowed upon the universe. But man now wanted more than forgiveness. What the human species asked of God was for continuing impunity to do as he wanted to destroy creation, and, if possible, the creator!

A little foolishness is a dangerous thing, I thought. *And mankind is so very foolish, quite a deal more foolish than evil.*

The first place I made for was our old apartment. For a second, I thought to find my wife there, but then I remembered she was dead. I had no wife, no baby son. I was alone in the city, this seemingly empty city. On another day, not long ago, I would have hailed a cab or hopped on a streetcar, but now I had to walk the distance in a wind that became more biting by the minute. A cold drizzle, too, had just begun to fall.

I picked up my pace and trotted along the sidewalks and streets—there was no traffic to worry about—and when I reached my apartment, I was exhausted. I had made it before the rain really started to fall, so I was thankfully dry.

My apartment was on the second floor of the building. I had locked the door the last time I'd left and now I couldn't find my key. Perhaps whoever had mugged me had taken the key. I knocked on the door; perhaps he'd answer!

To my surprise, I heard footsteps lurching across the floor, dragging heavily, laboriously over the tile. I heard heavy, shallow breathing. Someone was standing on the other side of the door!

I knocked again, and this time a familiar voice answered.

"Who's there?" slurred the voice of a drunken old woman.

"My God, Mrs. Telfer!" I said, stunned. "Open the door. It's me!"

She fumbled with the lock and then opened the door, standing before me like some evil-smelling old hag. She wore a dirty and torn purple robe, half open at the top. A pint of whisky stuck up out of the pocket.

"Well, I'm glad to see you…" she slurred in delight. She hugged me around the neck and gave me a slobbering kiss.

I pushed her away gently.

"What are you doing here!?" I demanded.

She turned and went back into the living room to sot on the couch. "Come on in," she told me.

"What are you doing in my apartment, Mrs. Telfer?" I asked as I closed the door behind me."

"Oh, don't kick me out," she pleaded before starting to cry.

"I'm not going to kick you out. I just want to know why you're here and how you got in."

She wiped her eyes with the sleeve of the robe. She was a pitiful sight and I felt sorry for her.

"Well, I couldn't stay up there," she said with a mournful sigh, pointing at the ceiling. "He's come back to haunt me. Always said he would. Walk in on me while I was having my bath as he always did. Never had any morals, that one. But I was so glad to see him!" She smiled wistfully through her crooked teeth. "I tried to hug him, but my arms just went through him. 'You're a ghost!' I screamed at him. He laughed back at me, the spiteful bastard: 'And it's your turn next, you old scow.' He said he was going to haunt me for the last few days of life I had left. Well, I got out of there quick as anyone would."

So that was her explanation. In times past, I would have thought her off her rocker, but the reality was now so insane that I easily accepted it.

But I didn't go up to her apartment to check on her story; it didn't matter if there was a ghost up there or not. I wouldn't kick her out. I didn't have the heart. I didn't intend on staying there very long anyway.

There were certain things I wanted to know, and she told me. Most of the people in the building had turned to stone. Walk into any apartment and you'd see the stone statues. That's why she'd chosen to stay in my place; it was the only vacant apartment.

She didn't know what was going on out on the streets, because she never left the building, but she'd heard screams and gunshots for awhile. Lately, though, only silence. From the radio, she'd heard that civil authority was breaking down and that the federal government had declared martial law. Then the radio had gone off. Nothing on it or on the television.

"They all turned to stone or else killed each other," she said before stopping suddenly as if having remembered something. "A young woman came here a day ago. She asked for you. I told her you weren't here." Mrs. Telfer looked at me, hoping she hadn't done something wrong. "I asked her to stay, but she left anyway!"

When she saw I wasn't angry, she relaxed

"Pretty little thing," she murmured.

"Did she tell you her name?" I asked.

"Jane."

Before leaving to find Jane, I washed up, had a sleep, and ate a meal. I had to go into another apartment to get food, because Mrs. Telfer had eaten all there was at my place. I took all the food I could find in four apartments and stocked up my fridge and cupboard so Mrs. Telfer would have plenty to eat—for a while anyway.

Mrs. Telfer had been right about almost everybody living in the building had turned to stone. In every apartment, familiar stony faces smiled at me. I felt a cold chill, for it seemed their eyes followed me, pleading with me to bury them or save them. I could do nothing, so I quickly got out of there.

I knew where Jane would be, if she was still alive. She would have made her way to the island. So I headed there, praying I wouldn't be too late.

I couldn't go to the docks, since the ferry boats wouldn't be running. I knew, however, the island was only a few hundred yards from the Cherry Beach Spit. What's more, the water was shallow, nowhere deeper than four feet. I figured I could walk across if I had to. I wasn't a good swimmer, but even if the water had been deep I could have managed to swim that distance.

The shoreline was smelly from the polluted waters and dead fish floated belly-up, pushed gently up onto the sand by the waves. As I reached the water's edge, the sight of dead fish would have been a relief, but instead the shore was littered by rock fish. They looked like Indian carvings. Gulls and terns lay shattered on the sand, too. I searched the sky; where once large flocks of seagulls had frolicked in the air, now only a few lonely birds soared below the sun.

I didn't fear my own, sorely near death. I didn't question why I was still alive. I just went on like the sun was still shining.

I stripped naked and, holding my clothes above my head, waded into the icy water. Gingerly, I crossed the distance between the two shores.

7.
OH TINY BUD, NEW LIFE EMERGES

As I stood on the opposite shore, the city was further away than the mere three hundred yards of shallow water that separated it from the island; it was a ruin of the distant past. Without the millions of people who had been its lifeblood, its reason to exist, the city was a dead thing, to turn to ashes over the centuries like the skeleton of a man. Uninhabited, isolated, desolate, to be scorched by the sun and beaten by the winds. But then I realized the sun itself may die before it could have any effect on the city's physical decay. Perhaps the winds would cease to blow. The city would be mummified, left to stand eternally on this sunless, still planet like the bones of a carefully preserved dinosaur.

Whether or not it stood for an eternity, without man the city was dead.

I turned my back on it and walked inland, desperate to find what life remained. I had to find Jane. If I alone was still alive, I would be as dead as the city. But so long as I still breathed, I would fight to survive, to live as best as I could. I didn't want to be the cause of my own destruction.

I ran along the dirt paths of the island, over the grass, and across the sand to Jane's cottage. She had to still be alive. In my heart, she was. I was sure of it.

The island had always presented a calm, silent, peaceful world in sharp contrast to the chaotic shrill of the city. Today, however, I felt that quietness as a threatening, deafening omen and a stark reminder of what had happened. It was the quiet of the grave.

I felt frigid in the chilly winds of winter, the sun's rays bringing no warmth. Even the intense exertion of running as fast as my legs would carry me produced no warmth on this day. The cold had penetrated to my very heart.

Then, far ahead, I saw a shadow. My mind created the impression of a human form.

"Jane!" I screamed, continuing to run towards the figure in the sand. "Jane, it's me!"

But it wasn't Jane. As I approached and the shadow took a more distinct shape, my mind could no longer be fooled; it was the old man.

He didn't make any move to come towards me, and I stopped, exhausted, weary, and heartsick. I continued walking slowly towards him. Perhaps he would know what had happened to Jane.

"So it's you again," he said as I reached where he was sitting. "You look as if you've seen a ghost."

"Have you seen Jane?"

"Well I saw her yesterday," he replied. "But not today."

I noticed he was still looking at the sky. He was dirty and unshaven, and the fierceness seemed to have gone out of his eyes. But his voice still had strength left in it.

"Are you afraid for her, lad?" he asked, somewhat gently.

"Can one still be afraid? Is there anything left to be afraid of?"

"No, and there never has been. But man is still afraid right up until death."

The old man began to cry, so I knelt beside him and put my arms around him. "Don't be afraid," I whispered. "For unto you was born in the city of David a survivor, and he is Christ the Lord."

We sat there hugging each other for a few minutes, and then I pulled him to his feet and together we walked.

All day long, we searched the island for Jane, and at night I left the old man at her cottage and went out alone. The wind was blowing in off the lake, the air clean and fresh. Invigorating, to a degree. It was cold but I was beyond feeling… or else I was at the point where pain brought pleasure.

I felt great. At peace. I hadn't found Jane, but I had discovered that anything can be overcome. Yes, I wanted Jane; I wanted her desperately. I desired someone else to live with for however long I remained alive.

Yet that which seems impossible to bear always turns out to be bearable when the burden falls due. If it wasn't that way, how could man have gone on for so many thousands of years? Individual men living in isolation, carving civilizations out of empty wilderness. Societies crumbling and then being rebuilt by thousands of weary hands. Massacres and disasters of all types befalling humanity against all odds until the very end. Man's job was to fight with every ounce of strength and courage against the end, and not to do one thing to hasten it.

If this is the end, I thought, *I will meet it the way all the greatest men of history would want me to meet it; I will meet it fighting all the way!*

But how could I fight? The battle was too awesome: one man against God. Although I knew that wasn't it; the battle I was fighting was one against fear. I would live the rest of my time unafraid. I would be unafraid right up until death.

I walked up along the beach in the darkness of night, the sky pitch-black except for the odd star that still shone like a flaming match in a vast, empty place. The soft lapping of the waves against the shore was all I could hear.

Somehow, after hours of walking, I found myself at the far end of the island, cold and wet from the light snow that had begun falling.

Then I saw a house a small distance up from the shore, nestled in a gathering of trees. Tired and cold, I decided to make it my home for the night.

The front and back doors were both locked, so I smashed a small window and crawled into a room just as dark as the night outside. Groping around, I finally found a light switch and turned it on. Nothing. I searched around some more and, finding the door, opened it. But the adjoining room was just as dark.

My eyes began to adjust to the dark and I saw that I was in the kitchen. Rooting through the cupboards, I found a box of matches and some candles. I lit one and went back into the first room I'd entered. The candle gave off a faint light and created shadows on the walls. There was a bureau directly in front of me and, off to the side, I made out the faint impression of a bed.

I stopped suddenly, alarmed. A small child sat up on the bed, looking at me. She had startled me, and I realized that I must have scared her.

"Little girl, don't be afraid," I began to say… until it dawned on me how still she was—and why. She had died holding a china dolly in her arms, her eyes wide open in a calm, peaceful pose. And she was smiling happily while wearing a pink cotton dress better suited to summer than to this time of year.

It was a very strange sight, a small stone child in a pink cotton dress, but it all seemed so very natural, as if this was the way death had always come.

I turned and left the room, not disturbing anything. After making myself something light to eat from what remained in the kitchen, I found the living room and lay down on the sofa. I slept peacefully that night and awoke the next morning refreshed.

It had been snowing all night and now the snow lay deep on the ground. But when I went outside, I felt it wasn't too cold and the snow was of the wet variety. It would probably melt soon. Still, it was difficult walking and it was slow going on the way back to Jane's cottage. I hoped the old man was all right and had managed to fend for himself.

It took me a long time to get back along the same route I'd come, and by the time I reached the cottage the sun was high in the sky and it was mid-afternoon.

I saw the old man looking out the window at me as I walked up the path. Then he disappeared from the window and, soon after, the front door opened.

"Hi!" I called to the old man, but it was Jane who ran out the door towards me.

8.
NEW BEGINNINGS SOON TO FLOURISH

Jane had aged terribly since I'd last seen her. The suffering she must have endured was printed on her face, but she smiled now as she leaned her head back to get a look at me, still holding onto me tightly. Her eyes were so very beautiful, and strangely young and serene, not in keeping at all with the rest of her appearance. Had they somehow been reborn when she saw me?

She kissed me over and over on the lips. "Oh God! Someone's alive!" she said, smiling, small tears falling from her eyes.

I touched her skin softly and brushed the tears away.

"Come on," I said. "Let's go in the house!"

Inside, Jane sat beside me on the sofa. Her hands held tightly onto mine, refusing to let go. I suddenly realized she was as scared as my wife had been, maybe more so.

"Jane, it's all right. You're all right!"

Tears welled back up in her eyes. "This whole thing's insane," she cried.

"Cry, Jane, cry! Let it all out!"

She broke down sobbing onto my shoulder. "Oh God, oh God, oh God!" she moaned.

"Don't moan! Scream!"

She looked up at me in puzzlement, but then she screamed. When she was done, she pulled away from me and stood up, breathing deeply but slowly, in and out. Sorrow took over her face again, but some of the fear was gone.

"There, isn't that better?" I asked cheerfully.

"Oh God, I don't know... you look happy," she said; it was more of a question than a statement.

"Why shouldn't I be?" I replied; it was more of a statement than a question.

"Because the whole world is dead! They've all gone into some dark, empty, cold, and lonely place. I'm so afraid..."

"If this is what death is, then it doesn't exist. Unless you let it exist now, while you're still alive. The only hell is a living hell!"

She sat back down beside me. She was alive and I loved her.

"Then is the only heaven a living heaven?" she asked.

"Of course. But for however long we live, we live forever, and it is only in our power to decide how we live."

"How should we live?"

"Without fear! And as happily as possible."

"Even now, with the whole world dead… don't you feel like crying? Don't you just feel like crying forever?"

"No, I don't," I said. "I cried! I lost my wife, my son, and every friend I ever had but you. After the crying is over, the living always goes on, Jane. It must! And the crying is always over."

"That's too easy! That's just too easy!"

"Of course it is. But it's just as easy to give in to despair. Which is better?"

That was the only question man should ever ask himself—not which way is the easiest or which is the hardest, but which way is the best to go, and which is the right way to go.

Jane's arms tightened around me and her lips caressed mine. Together we were entwined in a moment of joy, a moment that might last forever.

"None of that sinning in here," the old man said with a scowl.

But then he got up and left.

"Jane," I said softly, "you're the most beautiful woman in the world."

"That's not much of a compliment."

But in her trembling, I felt the world come back to life. I felt her warm soft body, the moistness of her lips on me, the two of us pressing together trying to be one. The moment didn't last forever, but it seemed to.

9.
WHERE DO I GO FROM HERE?

The old man married us that evening on the beach beneath a half moon. Jane had no wedding gown, but I did find a long white dress in one of the other cottages that was almost her size. After she made some small alterations, she put it on. No bride ever looked more beautiful. I was only sorry I hadn't been able to find a flower for her hair.

The old man served as the minister, the best man, and the witness. I myself wrote up the marriage certificate. Because of the cold, the ceremony was necessarily short. We nonetheless celebrated with a bottle of champagne, having found it also in one of the other cottages.

We held the celebration on some rocks, giving us protection from the wind and snow. Then we thanked the old man, walked him home, and spent our honeymoon back at Jane's cottage.

In the early morning, after a perfect night, I told her I wanted a child. She wondered if we would have time.

"If we have time, I want a child," I replied.

The days passed slowly, but after a time spring came. I often had to make journeys into the city to find food and Jane was always afraid I wouldn't return. She thought some others must still be alive, and maybe they would be desperate—or crazy.

But I never saw anyone on one of my trips. I even made a stop off at my apartment to see if Mrs. Telfer was still alive. She was dead. Not turned to stone, but dead nonetheless. She'd probably suffered a heart attack or died from the cold.

For some reason, I felt I had to bury her. It wasn't easy because she had been a fat old lady, but I managed to carry her body out behind the building and bury her in the yard. I even made a cross to mark her grave. If the old man had been with me, I would have gotten him to say a few words over her. But he would never leave the island; he wanted to die there and wouldn't take any chances.

When spring came, we planted vegetable seeds which I had taken from a store. If everything went well, by the fall we would have our own potatoes, carrots, peas, and onions. I even managed to find some chickens on a farm outside the city, allowing us to enjoy fresh eggs once a week.

Unfortunately, a week after I brought the chickens over, one of them turned to stone. This upset Jane terribly. She had started to believe nothing along those lines would ever happen again. I think she'd almost convinced herself nothing had ever happened, that this was the way she had always lived.

I was very afraid for her. She couldn't cope by herself. She needed me there.

The old man was a blessing. He didn't live with us, but he often came over to provide company and help out with the garden. Most importantly, he stayed with Jane whenever I went into the city.

Although we never said anything about it in front of Jane, when she was asleep the old man and I spent many hours discussing what had happened. He always maintained that this tragedy had been sent by God to wipe out the evil in the world. I tried to find some more rational, scientific reason, but I couldn't.

When we argued philosophy, the old man always asked, "What scientific proof could I offer to prove this? Your science would say this was impossible, that it could never happen. But it happened. So I say science ain't the end of all understanding, my boy! Nope, God's the end of all understanding, and the beginning of understanding, too. Science can't explain God. It can't explain what happened. It can't explain your existence or the existence of the universe. But God explains everything!"

I had to admit there was something in what he said. Science claimed there had been a big bang six billion years ago which had created the universe. But what had caused the big bang? Why did there exist any matter out of which the universe could be created? Since this matter did exist, must it not have existed forever? If it had existed forever, what would have caused it to explode? Six billion years might seem to be an infinite amount of time to man, but it was nothing when compared to eternity.

There were just too many questions that couldn't be answered. Why not a universe created by God?

Still, why would God choose to destroy the world? That, I couldn't understand—unless it was as the old man said, and God was just acting to prevent man from destroying what God had created.

Late in May, Jane came to me and told me she thought she was pregnant. Two weeks later, she was sure. The old man said it was a sign that God's wrath had been abated and that life would spring forth on earth once again. I gave thanks to God.

Then something happened to cause me worry again. On one of my trips to the city, I came to believe I was being followed. I heard faint noises behind me that stopped at the same time I stopped, but when I turned around and went back I couldn't find anything. I never saw anyone.

The experience left me uneasy.

Another day, while travelling from the city to the island in Jane's speedboat, I looked behind me along the waterfront and, for a moment, saw a figure standing back from the shore watching me. But then the light got into my eyes, and when I regained my vision the figure, whoever or whatever it was, had vanished.

I told none of this to Jane or the old man. I wasn't certain I'd seen anything at all, and even if I had, even if someone else was out there and now knew of our existence, nothing could be done until they showed their hand. Did this person mean me any harm? Were they just alone and afraid? I couldn't be certain which was the case, so I promised myself that I would be careful on any future trip to the city.

On my next trip, I scanned the shore as I approached but saw nothing but dim shadows. As I pulled up to the shore, I asked myself, what was I expecting to find? The devil perhaps?

I hadn't come to the city for more supplies; we had plenty. The figure had disturbed me, and I wanted to find whoever it was and see what they wanted. I had armed myself with a hunting knife to protect myself against attack. But I wasn't expecting to be suddenly jumped from behind or from out of a shadow; I was the hunter, not the hunted.

I wanted to confront this mystery rather than remain in fear of the unknown.

But to find this person, I had to first let them find me. I had to get them to follow me and then turn the tables. Maybe I would observe them unseen, as on my previous visits my scavenging had been conducted in homes and stores just up from the lakeshore.

On this day, I followed my normal pattern. I walked up Bay Street, stopping at stores I had yet to search, looking for unspoiled food and drink. When I gathered up all I could easily carry, I left everything in two bags on a counter in a nearby restaurant.

Then, as was my usual habit, I strolled up Bay to Queen Street and took a walk through Nathan Phillips Square. I still wasn't accustomed to the silence of the city, despite the time that had passed since I'd last heard the reassuring honking of horns and bustle of noisy crowds. On any other day in some other year, the square would be filled with people—government workers coming and going from city hall, people ice-skating to popular songs being played over a public address system, street vendors hawking their wares, cops on horseback keeping an eye on things. The city had become a vast, desolate wasteland gripped by an arctic cold encased in deafening silence.

Then I had an idea. I turned and ran down Queen Street to the Eaton Centre. I stepped through the broken glass of the front door and proceed into a sports store. The place had been ransacked, but a lot of the merchandise had been left lying on the floor.

Amongst the debris, I found what I was looking for: a pair of men's skates. I tried them on and found they were a little large, but they would do. After putting my shoes back on, I flung the skates over my shoulder and returned to the square.

Lacing the skates up, I felt a thrill of exhilaration sweep through me. I had always loved to skate—the swoop down fast from end to end, zigzagging around other skaters less proficient than me. And I'd loved to watch little kids speed like the wind around and around the rink, never seeming to tire.

Today I had to skate alone.

I skated fast, faster and faster, around and around and around. The ice was rough, and I fell hard more than once, but I got up each time and skated even faster, avoiding the bumps in the ice or leaping over them.

I finally grew tired and, after putting my shoes back on, I flung the skates over my shoulder and left. I walked down Bay Street, stopping at the store where I had left the supplies. I gathered everything together and left.

When I reached the speedboat, I remembered what I had come for; I hadn't seen or heard anything unusual all day. Perhaps whoever had been watching me from the shore had left the city by now, or maybe they were wary of me and had therefore decided to stay away.

But I looked up at the buildings and open space just up from the shore anyway. I couldn't see anyone.

I got into the boat and started the engine to head back for the island. As the boat raced over the water, the wind blowing cold in my face, I continued to gaze at the shore to see if anyone was watching.

On this day, I couldn't see anyone.

A Book of Short Stories

Part Two

Foreword

The following is a composition of short stories written by Daniel in the 1980s. These stories were left among his poetry, material that was left mostly untouched after Daniel's passing in 1985, having been left to his brother, Laurie. It was not until many years later that the material was uncovered, reviewed, and compiled for publication. As was the case with his poetry, this material will be published and read by members of the general public for the first time in more than thirty-five years. I'm hoping those reading this book of short stories will feel the same sense of fulfillment as I did while compiling the material for publication.

The stories, drafted at a time when Catholicism had a much more pronounced impact on Canadian politics and the Cold War was still raging between the United States and the Soviet Union, speak to contemporary political issues when Daniel was still alive.

For example, "The Final Negotiations" speaks about the farming crisis based in the then-futuristic year of 1987. The United Soviet Socialist Republic (USSR) was said to have been planning an invasion of Yugoslavia, a nation that dissolved shortly after the fall of the Berlin Wall in 1992.

"The Confession" alludes to Catholic traditions, with confession being one of the seven sacraments of the Catholic Church and the Crucifix of Christ appearing as the centrepiece of the altar.

"Alex Fangdinkle and the Case of the Stolen Fart" contains hints of autobiographical themes with reference to Daniel's congenital heart defect. At the end, Daniel is taken out of the courtroom on a stretcher and brought to an ambulance, where he will subsequently be transported to the hospital.

One of the short stories was partially written before Daniel's passing in 1985. "Self-Discovery: The Life of Artificial Intelligence" wasn't originally written to reference the Cold War peace negotiations, nor was artificial intelligence a conversation piece Daniel spoke about in any of his writing. I've included my own spin on that piece given that the short story, originally titled "Self Discovery," was largely incomplete with some notes to support the writing he did have. It speaks to the nature of the American-Soviet conflict during the Cold War era. Contemporary issues pertaining to artificial intelligence and alleged foreign influence from Russia, among other countries, in 2019 were referenced to add a modern twist to material written during a bygone era.

—Jeremy E. Thomas

September 29, 2019

Given Danny's grave health conditions and his desire to live, he may have been onto something—that something now being called "digital immortality." Danny wanted to survive his own body's limitations.

The story "Journey into Nothing" is symbolic of Danny wanting to succeed in his own life, but is it a life he thought was worth living? That is something all of us may have to face one of these days…

—Shelley V. Thomas

October 10, 2019

Journey into Nothing

JOHN PHILLIP ENDERHAUS IS A BRILLIANT MAN. MANY CONSIDER HIM TO BE the greatest genius to have ever lived, with a mind superior to any other in history, even Einstein's.

In his eighty years of life, Professor Enderhaus has been the creator of numerous inventions. He proved Einstein wrong when, at the age of forty, he designed the warp engine which enables man to travel through space faster than the speed of light. He has decisively repudiated the big bang theory, concerning the creation of the universe, but has been unable to formulate an answer of his own. How the universe was created therefore remains a mystery.

And let us not forget, it was Enderhaus who designed the miniature nuclear reactors which now provide every household on the planet with enough energy to last a thousand years.

Tragically, at this moment, John Enderhaus is lying on his deathbed. But even now his mind is working. He has set into motion the greatest experiment ever attempted by man, an experiment which involves a journey to a place which, in a way, is more distant from man and his life on this planet than the ends of the universe. The object of this journey is the mind, to be precise—John Enderhaus's mind—and the destiny is unknown.

Nikolas Kilby looked down at the frail body of John Enderhaus.

"John," he said, "are you sure you want to go through with it?"

"Nick, you know I do," Enderhaus replied. His voice was weak, a frail echo fading away. But there was still present in it that quality of assurance, of certainty, a quality possessed by no other voice Nick Kilby had ever heard.

"Okay." Nick patted Enderhaus's thin, wrinkled hand. "Everything is set up and ready to go. I'll be on hand to observe. Afterwards, everything will be done according to your instructions. It will take a while, about six months, but you know that."

Enderhaus's face remained impassive, but he had understood the significance of Kilby's words. For six months, he would experience what no man before him ever had: being totally alone with only his thoughts.

Nick stood watching the procedure with a vague feeling of uneasiness. He half-hoped the transfer would end in failure. It wasn't that he disliked Enderhaus or wished him ill fortune; on the contrary, he loved him. He had worked under—no he had worked *beside* him—for twenty years. Enderhaus had guided every step of his progress and Nick knew he wouldn't have gone nearly as far on his own. He had been Enderhaus's protégé and as such had been treated like a son.

If the truth were known, he often thought of Enderhaus as his real father. So it was only natural that he should feel saddened as he saw Enderhaus's brain being surgically removed from his body. In six months, Nick would probably be communicating with that mind, but he couldn't help feeling that the man he knew as John Enderhaus was dead.

A team of surgeons began the fantastically complex job of connecting Enderhaus's organic brain to an elaborate support system. Nick watched silently and prayed for his friend's soul. He now wished he had argued more forcefully against Enderhaus's plan.

"You will be journeying into nothing," he had warned. "You will have no contact with the physical universe. You will experience no sights, no sounds, no feelings other than those you can remember or imagine, and I am afraid your memory and imagination will come to haunt you."

Enderhaus had listened politely to all of Nick's arguments, but he had not been swayed.

"Nick," he'd said passionately, "I believe this experiment offers mankind his only hope of discovering the secrets of the universe, of existence, of life itself. I have a vast body of knowledge and experience to draw upon and, like God before the creation, I will exist within a void. I will be able to reconstruct the universe in my thoughts as God created it, along immutable laws of reason. I will see everything in the universe not as an accident but arising from necessity. And I believe I will be able to help man find his place within creation."

Nick sat in stunned silence. His instinctive reaction to this audacious undertaking was to recoil in horror. But he couldn't change the old man's mind and he had been unwilling to act against him.

"You are not God," he had finally managed to say.

"I am made in God's image," Enderhaus had answered.

It was too late to turn back now, Nick realized as he observed Enderhaus's brain being placed within the glass enclosure where it would remain for however long.

The six months since the removal of Enderhaus's brain had passed very quickly. It had been connected to an elaborate support system that kept it alive and functioning, and each and every day Nick gazed spellbound at it. The glass enclosure could not be shattered, as hard as diamond yet perfectly transparent, so clear that you had to remind yourself it was there. Inside, the air was composed of exactly twenty-five percent oxygen, sixty-seven percent hydrogen, and eight percent nitrogen, with a complete change taking place every ten minutes—new air in, old air out. The temperature was maintained at a constant 37.2 degrees Centigrade. More than a million artificial capillaries were attached to the brain to supply it with blood.

Every measure necessary was being taken to keep the brain alive. A vast team of scientists worked around the clock to check the system, and a computer display indicated the exact chemical composition of the air at any given moment and its precise temperature. Computer analyses were taken three times per second on each artificial capillary, ensuring they were functioning properly and that just the right amount of blood passed through.

Of course, the brain waves being emitted were constantly monitored. So far everything looked normal, the only surprise being that Enderhaus "slept" only two hours per day on average.

Two hours per day, Nick thought. *Amazing! What could he be thinking of the other twenty-two hours?*

Well, they would soon know.

Jim Fletcher, the nucleon beam particle specialist, indicated to Nick that they were about to proceed. A particle of matter, smaller than the nucleus of the smallest atom, was to be shot into the left cerebral hemisphere of the brain to impact a tiny portion of one particular cell in the cerebellum cluster. This was to be their signal to John Enderhaus. It wouldn't hurt him, but it would be the first thing he had felt, other than his own thoughts, in six months. Then, if Enderhaus's theory on the control of brain waves was correct, Enderhaus would begin sending his own signals, through two implants made in his brain, back out to them. The implants were hooked up to the computer and worked on the binary system, a simple yes-no, so that a large amount of information could be relayed in a short span of time.

Once again Nick looked at John Enderhaus's brain. *What is the real purpose of this experiment? To keep John Enderhaus alive?* No, Enderhaus was dead. *To keep the most brilliant mind in history working, perhaps for the benefit of all mankind?*

While that may be the result of the experiment, it was not the purpose of it. No, the real reason was that Enderhaus wanted to see through a vacuum, to reconstruct the universe in his thoughts as God had created it. He hoped to understand by what means everything in the universe, from the smallest particle of matter to the massive, swirling red suns, had been created.

Enderhaus had spent most of his life trying to understand logically why anything existed in the first place. He had searched in vain to learn by what magic power the universe had come into being from nothing—in vain, perhaps, because he would not believe. He couldn't accept a spiritual answer, shrouded in the mystery of God. He needed a scientific explanation. He needed to know the material causes for the material universe, and he needed an answer that left no room for doubt.

Near the end of his life, his hopes of ever knowing the truth fading, Enderhaus had come to believe that his goal was impossible to achieve while man remained trapped in the body.

"Everything in this universe is distorted by the senses," he had complained. "As long as we are encumbered by them, we will never get to the truth of the matter."

How many other great minds had complained of the same thing? Plato, Aristotle, Newton, Einstein. Size was distorted by distance, sound by the elements, colour by light. "If only we were free of the body," Socrates had argued, "we would be able to see the truth." The body, with its desires, its sufferings, its so many other distractions, encased man in a prison, never to be free.

But John Enderhaus was free. He no longer had a body. He was thinking in a vacuum. What was he seeing?

"It's *go!*" Fletcher screamed excitedly.

Nick looked up at the overhead monitor and read that impact had been made. In less than a second, return signals had been received by the computer. Lights flashed on-off, on-off, on-off.

The scientists watched in awe. Enderhaus's theory on brain wave control had been right.

Suddenly everything stopped.

"What's happened?" Nick asked, puzzled.

"I don't know," answered Dr. Holland, the man in charge of the entire operation. "We've received some signals, but nothing more is being sent."

A quiet buzz of excitement passed over the gathering.

"Well, has the computer decoded what we've got?" Kilby demanded.

Dr. Holland worked quickly, and soon everyone's eyes stared in astonishment as Enderhaus's message flashed across the screen:

"In the beginning..."

THE CONFESSION

Father Terrance drew open the curtains of his study window to warm his face by the rays of the setting sun. Each day at this time he allowed himself a moment to enjoy the beauty of the countryside. His church stood at the top of a hill overlooking the greenest valley on earth and in the middle of the valley a slender, winding river, as old as the mountains in the distance, flowed quietly to the sea.

It troubled him that at moments like these he felt most peaceful and closest to God. He wanted to be able to feel such joy when going about God's business, but the things that had once brought him great happiness—ministering to his flock, caring for the sick, helping the needy, bringing a sinner back to the Lord—had over the years become heavy burdens that made him weary and brought pain and sorrow to his heart. He often complained, if only to himself, that he was becoming too old for the job.

I have no strength left to give them and I don't know how to help them anymore, Father Terrance thought. *Anyway, who ever listens? My sermons fall on deaf ears. Sinners repent only to sin again.*

The love he had once felt for his fellow man had died and been replaced by an ugly bitterness.

"Father, forgive me," he prayed. "But how can I love them when they have closed their hearts to love?"

As he stood at his window thinking these thoughts, feeling the presence of God in the warmth of the sun and quiet of the valley, he saw far below, at the foot of the hill, an old man from the village. Giovalli was climbing the stone road towards the church.

Of all the sinners, there is not one so hateful as he, Father Terrance thought. As he gazed malevolently down at the old man, he felt as if the devil himself was making his way towards him. Although Giovalli's wife, a kind lady, had just died and her body lay in the chapel to be buried in the morning, Father Terrance felt no pity for the old man. *He's a wicked, evil man, and an atheist opposed to church. He should reap what he has sown.*

Giovalli had taken great pleasure over the years in scorning the church and mocking God. Many years back, during the time of the terrible earthquake which had destroyed most of the village and even caused damage to the church, Giovalli had taken delight in the misfortune of his fellow villagers. This was made even worse by the ironic coincidence that his house had miraculously been left untouched.

"What a God, what a God," he had laughed over his beer. "He destroys his friends while leaving his enemies unharmed!"

Father Terrance had sought to find shelter for those left homeless, and it had been his unpleasant duty to ask Giovalli if he would welcome some of his neighbours into his home until their homes could be rebuilt.

"Have you no room for them in the church?" Giovalli had sarcastically demanded.

Father Terrance had tried to explain that the church was a great distance from the village, and most of the villagers had no means of transportation and would have to walk the entire way; it would be very inconvenient for them.

Before he could finish, Mrs. Giovalli had interrupted and admonished her husband for his bad manners. "We will be more than happy to welcome our neighbours to stay with us, Father," she said gently.

As often was the case, Giovalli's opinion changed to match hers after she had spoken.

"Of course our neighbours are welcome to stay in our home," he had said as if there had never been any doubt.

Father Terrance had thanked them both and then Giovalli led him to the door as his wife went back to her work in the kitchen.

"The view from the church must be very beautiful this time of year," Giovalli had mused as he watched Father Terrance put on his coat.

"Yes," Father Terrance had agreed. "The leaves are turning colour and the whole valley looks like a garden in bloom." He smiled, glad to be having a pleasant discussion with this distasteful man. "I think there is no more perfect a place in the world. Our church looks down upon this valley, God's most beautiful creation."

"You may be right." Giovalli had smiled agreeably. "But I think you are also right in what you said about the church being too far away from the village to be of any real use to the people. In that respect, the church is very much like God."

The accusation still rankled in Father Terrance's breast. He admitted to himself that it was true: the church was too far from the village. He wondered how often people woke up on Sunday mornings and decided not to go to church because of the distance. Very few of the villagers attended regularly; of all the people in the valley, only Mrs. Giovalli never missed a service. Come rain or shine, Mrs. Giovalli made her way along the three miles of rocky road every Sunday with her husband in tow.

The couple made for a comical sight, Giovalli walking tall and proud beside his slightly rotund, diminutive wife, her soft, oval face and his dark, angry eyes seeming completely out of place next to each other. What seemed most absurd was the sight of her small hand grasped tenderly within his huge claw.

They made an oddly matched pair, but it was possible, Father Terrance supposed, that during the quiet hours of the night they could fit together in a beautiful union. Father Terrance had long believed that Giovalli was basically an animal who lived by the motto "The strong survive; the weak perish."

Giovalli had broken more than one man over his lifetime, and his predatory instincts had helped him accumulate considerable wealth. He was cruel to everyone with the exception of his wife, in whose presence his personality remarkably altered. The wolf became something of a lamb, but not a lamb of God—only a lamb of the devil, an unbeliever who would climb the rocky hill with his wife towards God's house but stop outside the door while Mrs. Giovalli entered alone.

On this day, as Father Terrance watched in heightened anticipation as Giovalli continued to climb the stone road towards the church, he knew the man would finally step inside.

Father Terrance thought it a cruel irony that while Giovalli had never entered the church while his wife was alive, he was forced to come in now that she had died. Mrs. Giovalli's body had recently been brought over from the funeral home, her casket placed in the centre aisle of the church where, as according to her wishes, she would be given a Christian burial early the next morning.

He need not enter the church today, Father Terrance thought. *He could put it off until tomorrow.*

But perhaps he wanted to sit with his wife's body. It was customary in the village for close relatives to sit up with a loved one's body the night before the funeral. With the exception of her husband, Mrs. Giovalli had no living relatives in the village. Her own parents had died many years before and she and her husband had remained childless.

Knowing this, and despite their general dislike for Giovalli himself, many of the villagers had offered to sit with him. He had refused, stubbornly insisting he would maintain a solitary vigil.

While he didn't doubt Giovalli did wish to maintain a vigil beside his wife's body, Father Terrance still felt this was not the man's sole reason for coming into the church. After all, he could have requested that his wife's body be kept at the funeral home for the night and not brought over to the church until the next morning. Then he could have maintained his vigil without having to enter until the day of the funeral.

But no, there was some other reason for this surprising visit. Giovalli had asked if he could come over and discuss a private matter.

Perhaps he wants to join the church. Perhaps the sinner has decided to seek salvation.

Did Giovalli look like a man who wished to repent for his evil life? Father Terrance looked closely at the tall, erect figure approaching from below. Despite his age, Giovalli was still a powerful man.

He hasn't changed much over the years, Father Terrance thought. The man's beard had turned white while his skin stretched dry across his forehead. All in all, Giovalli still presented quite an intimidating sight. *But am I mistaken, or have his eyes softened?*

Father Terrance gazed spellbound into the dark eyes of the man below.

"Enjoying the view, Father?" Giovalli called up, his harsh voice breaking the quiet.

Father Terrance stammered awake. "Yes, it's very beautiful. I'll be down in a second, Senor Giovalli. Just wait where you are."

He opened the door to the church and invited Giovalli inside. He was pleased to see Giovalli take off his hat as he stepped into the vestibule.

"Your wife's casket is in the chapel," Father Terrance said. "Do you wish to go sit with her now?"

Giovalli had been staring at the floor, but he looked up now to follow the direction in which Father Terrance's finger was pointing—into the foyer of the church.

"No, not now, Father," he answered, sounding muffled. "I wish to discuss a private matter with you first, if you don't mind." He smiled weakly, then went back to staring at the floor.

"Of course, of course." Father Terrance felt pleased with Giovalli's humble disposition. "Let's go up to my study. It's very comfortable and there is a view of the valley I'm sure you will find absolutely breathtaking."

Giovalli followed Father Terrance up a winding staircase.

Father Terrance stopped near the top of the stairs to point out a painting of the last supper. "Just a copy," he said. "But expertly done."

When they stepped into the study, which encompassed the entirety of the upper flow, Father Terrance swung his arms majestically. "These are my living quarters," he said as he ushered Senor Giovalli inside. He led the man to the window overlooking the valley. "Come over here. Beautiful, isn't it?

"Yes, lovely," Giovalli agreed.

Father Terrance let out a satisfied sigh before turning away from the window and leading Giovalli to a couch on the far side of the room. They both sat down.

"I think I know what it is you wish to discuss," Father Terrance said to Giovalli, who was fidgeting with his hat.

"You do?" Giovalli raised his eyes in disbelief.

Father Terrance smiled knowingly. "Your wife has just died," he began, holding Giovalli's gaze. "She was a devout Catholic for all her life, while you have never believed in God or Christ or the miracle of everlasting life. Now, faced with your wife's death, you have begun to feel within yourself, and it is a natural feeling, that she is not dead after all, at least not in the way you have always conceived of death. You must feel that she has simply passed into another world. Your heart is beginning to open up to the miracle of faith. You are being pulled towards God, towards an understanding that life has an ultimate meaning—and it doesn't all end with death."

Giovalli sat silently, listening intently, and Father Terrance hesitated. He took the time to choose his words carefully, certain that he knew what hopes and fears were struggling within the man's heart.

"But being a sinner, you must be afraid there is no room for you within this miracle," Father Terrance went on, his voice rising ecstatically. "Let me assure you, that is not so. Christ died to save the sinners of the world, not the saints. The church welcomes you with open arms to come and enter into a union with the Lord."

Giovalli stood up in embarrassment. "Father, Father! I'm sorry to have to tell you this, but you're wrong. I haven't come to ask to join the church." He looked away uncomfortably

"Oh," Father Terrance said, regaining his composure, "But if I'm wrong, what is it you're looking for?"

Giovalli strode across the floor and looked out the window despondently. "It's very complicated," he said heavily. "As you know, I'm not a believer. I'm not Catholic. But I have a need for a priest. I wish to make a confession." He turned to face Father Terrance, who sat hidden in the shadows creeping across the wall as the sun set behind the distant mountains. "Although I'm not Catholic, I hope you will treat what I am about to tell you as a confession and not allow what you hear to pass outside this room."

As the room darkened, Father Terrance found that he couldn't see the man's face, although the streaking red rays of the setting sun seemed to cast a halo around his head.

"Since you aren't a Catholic, I cannot treat this as a confession," Father Terrance said. "But I will promise not to repeat what you tell me to anyone."

Giovalli walked back across the room and sat down beside Father Terrance. "When I was just a young man, I had a friend. His name was Tony Fellini." His voice sounded soft and mournful, seeming to float on the cool evening breeze entering through the open window. "I have not had many friends in my life, so perhaps he was the only real friend I ever had. Though we were from different social backgrounds, it didn't matter. We were inseparable. But his family was rich and my father was a poor farmer. Still, in the things that really mattered, we were equals. We were both young and strong and not afraid to dream. I think we believed we were capable of everything. Together… well, there was no stopping us. Tony's dream was to study at the university and become a great doctor. He really cared for people; he really loved them. As for me, except for my wife, I've never loved anyone, not even Tony. But I was his friend and I was truly glad for him when he was accepted to study at the university. Of course, this meant we wouldn't see each other for a while, and that saddened me. But I wasn't jealous, even though I couldn't go. Tony and I wanted different things out of life and I knew I could get what I wanted without an education."

Giovalli trailed off into silence as Father Terrance got up to close the window; it was getting cold in the room.

"Go on," Father Terrance encouraged him.

In the second year of his studies, Tony met a girl; her name was Silvana. He wrote to me about her and said she was beautiful, he was in love with her, and he was going to marry her. I wrote back and told him not to be in any great hurry. If he waited awhile, he might find there were many women he could love, so why settle down with just one? But Tony really was in love, so he went ahead and proposed. She said yes. Of course Tony was ecstatic. He came back to the village and arranged to throw a big party at his father's house, during which he would announce his engagement and introduce his fiancée to his family and friends.

I still clearly remember everything about the party. It was held on a warm summer night in early June in the year 1914. It was a big social event, surrounded by an aura of mystery, because although everybody had learned that Tony Fellini had decided to marry, nobody knew or had even heard of his fiancée. All that was known about her was that she was beautiful and that she came from a small village in the south of Italy.

Most of the guests were members of the aristocracy. I was the only son of a poor farmer to be invited, and I was invited despite the fact that Tony's father openly disliked me. Tony further infuriated his father by asking me to be the best man at the wedding, which was set for the end of the summer. At that age, I was very proud and stubborn, so I wanted to show Tony's father, and everyone else, that I was just as good as they were. I spent all my savings on a fine suit of clothes. This was money I had been carefully putting away in the hope that one day I would have enough to buy some land. I knew that the way into the aristocracy was to own land.

On the day of the party, a few hours before it was to begin, I stepped into an iron tub filled with hot water and scrubbed my skin clean, rubbing until I sparkled. I soaped my hair and waited for my father to pour boiling water over my head to rinse away the suds.

After getting out of the tub and drying off, I began to dress. I put on a silk shirt with ruffles in the front. Whenever I moved, it felt like a cool breeze was tickling my skin.

Then I slipped on a pair of white satin pants and tied a black sash around my waist. I wrapped a red tie around my neck and pulled a pair of black boots on over my bare feet. I stood up, ready to put on the jacket, also white and made of satin to match the pants. It had a black collar and black cuffs at the end of the sleeves. I had also purchased an expensive pair of gold cuff links for the occasion. I put on the jacket and stood haughtily in front of the mirror.

In our house, all we had was a small wall mirror that had collected numerous scratches over the years and could no longer provide a clear reflection. My face looked cracked, the suit faded and worn.

"How do I look?" I asked, turning to my father.

He smacked his lips together. "You look beautiful."

My mother cried. They were both very proud.

I walked slowly to Tony's house. The sun hadn't set and I wanted people in the village to see me. I hoped to learn by their reaction whether my father had been truthful when he'd said I looked beautiful. But whatever their reaction, I wouldn't be happy until I saw for myself.

When I got to Tony's house, many guests had already arrived and many more were continuing to arrive in horse-drawn carriages. Tony's family lived in a spacious white house surrounded by green lawns and flower gardens. Some distance behind the house, a stable housed the family's horses and wagons.

I walked up the long, winding laneway to the front of the house where Tony's father was greeting guests at the door.

"Hello, Richardo," Mr. Fellini said amiably. He reached out to shake my hand. "Welcome to our home."

I had never seen Mr. Fellini so happy with himself, and I couldn't help but be surprised at his friendly manner.

"Good evening," I said, trying to sound more relaxed than I felt.

Other guests were coming up behind me, so Mr. Fellini asked me to go inside and mingle with the young ladies.

"They are very beautiful," he assured me with a wink.

I walked through the front door into the outer hall feeling tense and nervous, a peasant out of place among royalty.

The hall led into a large ballroom at the back of the house. Inside I heard gay voices mingling with soft music. Sparkling light from a large crystal chandelier seemed to point the way.

I walked into the ballroom, my eyes growing wide in amazement at the opulent display before me. It was a room of mirrors, and reflected in the glass were banquet tables set up with arrangements of fruits and vegetables on fleming silver trays. Waiters stepped lightly through the crowd serving vintage wine and aged cognac, and everywhere the eyes looked there were flowers—flowers in vases, in pots and hanging from the ceiling, in ladies' hair, and tucked into lapels. The women wore long flowing gowns which were the fashion of the day, while men wore military tunics, polished boots, and black top hats which they held in their hands as they bowed politely to the ladies.

And there I stood, unable to tear myself away. I blended in like a fine stroke in a beautiful painting, a masterpiece. I gazed fascinated at my reflection in the mirrored walls. My lean, muscular body bulged powerfully in the fine suit of clothes. Soft, silky hair swept back off my forehead and dark defiant eyes glazed out from my ruggedly handsome face.

Examining the other men in the room, I wondered: were they more powerfully built than I? Were they better dressed? Did they have finer features? I smiled at my reflection in the mirror, knowing that I belonged, knowing that I could easily be one of them.

As the band struck up a waltz, excited whispers flitted through the air. Young senoritas stood up, toes tapping, eyes downcast, hopeful that some Don Juan would ask them to dance. Shyly at first, and then with more bravado, young men approached them, choosing partners and leading them by the hand to the centre of the floor. Those unlucky enough not be asked stood back near the wall and watched with envy, wishing the right young man had saved the next dance for them. I accepted a glass of wine from one of the waiters and stood back, watching these wallflowers. They were all very lovely, but tonight there weren't enough young men to go around.

"Hello, Richardo," Mr. Fellini said, surprising me as he tapped me on the shoulder. "You don't wish to dance tonight?"

I turned to greet him and realized how far he was, a wiry man not at all like Tony, who was as tall as I was. Mr. Fellini had pleasant eyes and a thick bushy moustache that he twisted with his fingers.

"Yes, very much," I assured him. "I'm just deciding on a partner for the next waltz."

He laughed. "That's good. When you're young and you have it in you to drink and dance and laugh all night, you should do so, because when you get older the wine sits heavily in your stomach and the nights go on too long. Unless you have a wife who won't let you drink and who makes you go to bed early, as I do." He laughed at his own joke.

The tempo of the music picked up and we turned to watch the beautiful young couples as they floated like butterflies, circling each other in the cool summer air.

From across the floor, I noticed Mrs. Fellini walking toward her husband, her progress slowed as guests came up to compliment her on the perfection of the evening.

"Here," Mr. Fellini said, handing me his glass of wine as he caught sight of his wife. "Pretend it's yours."

Mrs. Fellini acknowledged me with a nod as she came up and kissed her husband on the cheek.

"I can tell you're in a playful mood tonight, darling," she said to him, smiling sweetly.

Although Mrs. Fellini was in her fifties, she had the figure of a much younger woman. Her hair had turned a gentle grey, but her eyes were still bright and lively and her face hadn't yet lost the beauty of its youth.

"Tony will be coming down in a few minutes," she added. "I want you to stop the music so he can announce his engagement and introduce his fiancée."

"Should I wait until the end of this dance?" he asked.

"Of course. We wouldn't want to spoil anyone's fun." She took her husband's hand and held it in hers.

As we waited for the dance to end, Mr. Fellini asked me if I had met Tony's fiancée yet. I told him that I unfortunately hadn't, but that Tony had written to me a great deal about her. Mostly that she was beautiful, beautiful, beautiful.

"Oh, she is beautiful," Mr. Fellini insisted ecstatically, raising his shoulders in a venerated shrug. "She is a vision. I told Tony if I was twenty years younger, I would fight him for her." His face broke out in a wide grin.

"Don't you mean thirty years younger, dear?" Mrs. Fellini teased.

As the music came to a halt, the dancers separated, some pulling apart quickly, others more slowly, seemingly unwilling to let go from their lingering embrace. The men thanked their partners and the ladies accepted compliments, some demurely, others coyly, their dancing eyes offering wild promises their lips would never speak.

Mr. Fellini spoke to the bandmaster who then had the musicians lay aside their instruments. Mr. Fellini raised his arm for silence.

"Friends," he said as the crowd quieted, "tonight is an important night for the Fellini family, and a very joyous night. As you all know, I am a great one for making speeches. But while my wife and I share in this joy, it belongs mainly to our son. So I will let Tony have the honour of telling you about the great happiness that has come to us."

The guests clapped as Mr. Fellini looked up to the top of the marble staircase. We all followed his stare up the white steps, the silence was broken by low murmurs as people wondered, *Where is he? Is he supposed to come down the stairs?*

As the anticipation built, Mrs. Fellini walked over to stand with her husband.

"Tony's always late," Mr. Fellini joked. "He developed that bad habit at a very early age. His mother was pregnant with him for ten months!"

The guests laughed politely, lessening some of the tension. Then Tony appeared at the top of the stairs, holding the hand of a beautiful young woman in a shimmering white gown. She wore a flower blossom in her black hair, which fell below her shoulders. People clapped loudly as the couple descended the stairs and walked over to Tony's parents.

Out on the Open Sea

Sailors often went left for combat on military ships during World War I with the objective of defeating en-
emy forces. Allied forces were victorious during World War I, with the ensuing peace negotiations dealing
a heavy blow to the German nation. The ensuing desperation in Germany led to the rise of Nazism in the
country, leading ultimately to World War II some twenty years after the end of World War I.
Drawing by Robert D. Thomas

What happened to me then I could not have expected; I became controlled
by a part of me I hadn't known existed. As I gazed into her sparkling eyes, it felt
like thunder booming inside my breast; her eyes were like glittering diamonds and
I looked deep into them at the reflection of her perfect soul. In that instant, my
heart was caged, never again to be completely free, for above all other things I desired her. I loved her.

Then, as if from a great distance, I heard Tony's voice: "I am proud to introduce my fiancée, Silvana Petucci. Her parents are the honourable Josef Petucci
and his lovely wife, Grace, from the village of San Marino. Silvana and I plan to be
married in two months, on September 14, in Father Chamon's church. You are all
invited to come and share in our joy."

My heart shattered. For a moment, I'd forgotten they were to be married. It was impossible; I loved her.

My eyes followed the couple as Tony led Silvana through the room, introducing her to his friends and neighbours. I watched as strangers extended their congratulations. I envied them, the return of her smile. My heart absorbed the soft curve of her waist where Tony's hand lay protectively. My heart grew jealous.

"Richardo," Tony called out as he led Silvana towards me.

I wondered if my feelings showed in my face. I tried to smile.

"Richardo, I would like you to meet Silvana, whom I've told you so much about."

I dared not look into her eyes. "I am pleased to meet you," I said.

She offered her hand, and as I took it in mine I bent over awkwardly to kiss it. My lips trembled. Did she notice?

"Hello," she said modestly. "I am glad to meet you. Tony has told me so much about you."

Too afraid to look directly at her, lest I give myself away, I smiled at Tony. "Don't believe everything you hear," I said.

"Oh, but I do. I mean, having met you, I can see for myself that Tony was right. You are a very fine man."

I tried to detect a note of coyness about her but found none. She didn't practice the art of flattery. Her feelings were honest and unspoiled.

"Congratulations, Tony," I said pretending a gaiety I did not feel. "Your fiancée is a beautiful young woman, and she will make an even more beautiful wife. But can she cook?" It was a lame attempt at a joke.

"If she can't, I assure you it will be years before I'll notice." He laughed, smiling at Silvana and giving her a playful hug.

"You men," Silvana said, feigning annoyance. "I can cook. My mother made sure of that. She always said good looks will help a girl get a man, but only good cooking will help her keep him." She smiled radiantly as Tony laughed and kissed her on the cheek.

As we continued to speak amiably, other guests came over to join in the conversation. Much of what was said drifted in one ear and out the other without my really hearing any of it, but I do recall that Silvana said she was seventeen—not old for a bride, but not young either. And yet the more I thought about it, the more I realized that seventeen was too young an age to be making a decision that would rule the rest of one's life. Did she know what she was doing? How could she be sure her love for Tony was real? If she had only met me first, would she have felt differently? Would she love me instead?

Although I cannot consciously recall doing so, I must have drunk very heavily that night. The ballroom spun around me like a merry-go-round, people going up and down, up and down, and around and around. Dancing slippers and heavy boots glided together across the floor as the music played, growing loud and shrill as the night went on.

The air smelled of sweat and other odours and I felt all alone, on the outside looking in. I saw sights to delight me, fragments of conversations to amuse me. One moment I was gay, the next despondent as I saw Tony and Silvana dance, looking beautiful together.

I made my way out into the fresh air and sat down, away from the old men who had come out onto the patio to smoke and hide from their wives. I sat on the patio steps near the grass and looked up at the starless sky. The shadow of the dimly glowing moon crept behind the clouds.

Whispers came to me in the still silence, and I listened with great interest.

"That ass Ferdinand got himself shot," a gruff voice insisted sternly. "England will save the peace."

Would there be war or peace? The old men on the patio hadn't decided.

"What about Italy?" somebody wanted to know. "We're allied with Austria and Germany, but we can't fight with them." It was the same old man who had called Ferdinand an ass.

If Italy we drawn into the war, I decided I would join the army and fight.

"If war does come, it could be a great opportunity for Italy," someone else said. The voice sounded familiar and I leaned over on my side and looked up onto the patio to see Mr. Fellini drinking a glass of wine.

The old fraud, I thought, *telling me his wife puts him to bed early and won't let him drink.*

"When war is declared, Italy should announce she intends to remain neutral," Mr. Fellini said, a note of cunning in his voice. "When it becomes obvious which alliance is going to win, Italy should enter the war on their side so she can share in the spoils of victory."

The first man disagreed angrily. "The best thing for Italy to do is to stay out of it altogether," he said loudly. "But I'm afraid too many men will want to get into it right from the beginning, and we'll end up declaring war along with the other nations of Europe. I think we're all going to live to regret it."

I didn't want Italy to stay out of it altogether. I wanted to fight.

The heated discussion carried on for some time, but after a while the old men drifted back inside and most of the guests left.

It was very late when Tony came out and sat down beside me.

"Where's Silvana?" I asked.

He lit a cigarette and leaned back, stretching his long legs out over the grass. "She's upstairs, sleeping in the guest room. Tomorrow I'll take her home to her parents." He sounded so content. "Then I have to go back to the university. I have summer classes to attend."

University had changed him. He had always been confident, but now he seemed calm and relaxed, sure of himself and what he wanted.

"There's going to be a war," I said drunkenly.

He turned to look at me. "What?" His eyes looked disturbed.

"That ass Ferdinand got himself shot," I stammered.

"You don't think Italy will go to war over that, do you?" he asked. sounding concerned.

"Your father thinks so."

I realized that if there was a war, Tony might have to go and fight, but I couldn't believe he was afraid. Still, his face seemed to have turned an ashen colour.

"If there is a war, it will wreck everything," he said.

"What do you mean?"

"You know the Italian attitude. Men want to marry virgins."

Even if he wasn't afraid of fighting or dying, I realized what worried him: the thought of dying and leaving Silvana a widow at the young age of seventeen. He was afraid that if he died, Silvana would suffer by being alone.

"If she's single, it will be easier for her to find a new husband," he continued. "She won't have to wear black and mourn for a year when she's so young and should be laughing."

"Maybe there won't be a war," I said, sympathizing with him. "I just heard some old men talking."

But Tony had decided: if war came, he would postpone his marriage.

When I got home that night, I was still drunk. My boots were covered in mud and I was too exhausted to pull them off. The room seemed to spin around me and I fell down onto the bed.

"That ass Ferdinand got himself shot," I murmured, staring up at the ceiling. "Now there will be war. It will wreck everything."

One month later, Italy was at war.

Father Terrance got up to light a candle. The sun had set and the two men had been left sitting in the dark.

"There now. That should provide enough light." Father Terrance placed the candle on a small table in front of the couch.

Giovalli sat with his eyes downcast, his hands trapped between his knees.

"I seem to remember that your wife's first name was Silvan," Father Terrance said, sitting back down. "And this girl in the story, the girl you fell in love with, her name was Silvana. Is that just a coincidence?"

"No, it is not a coincidence," Giovalli said. Father Terrance shuddered. "Let me finish telling you about it."

As the candle's dim light fought against the darkness in the room, Giovalli went on with his story.

Tony kept the promise he had made to himself and postponed his wedding when the war broke out. Silvana argued bitterly with him.

"I love you," she cried. "Marry me."

But in the end she gave in and promised to wait for him. Nobody thought she would have to wait long. We all believed the war would be over within six months.

Who could have known that it would last so many years?

Tony and I joined the army together, the idea being that we would watch each other's backs and take care of each other. As a member of the aristocracy, Tony could have enlisted as an officer in the cavalry—and as a medical student, he could have requested a position behind the lines in one of the army hospitals, or as a member of an ambulance crew—but instead he went along with me and became a foot soldier.

Foot soldiers are like cannon fodder. They suffer the most casualties and deaths while receiving little of the glory. When they're not killing or dying, they're dug into some dirt hole without enough to eat and nothing to do but wait while they sit freezing in the rain or broiling under the merciless sun. But Tony wanted to be at the front. He had some crazy idea that it was where he could do the most good.

The way things worked out, he was probably right.

I can't remember all the names of the various army units. I think there were divisions, battalions, and then regiments. Tony and I were members of the seventh rifleman's regiment. During the first year of the war, we saw little action, despite being stationed along the front with Austria. We were dug deep in foxholes along a front that stretched for miles. About five hundred meters in front of us, barbed wire fences had been strung out to keep the enemy out of Italy or slow them down a little. The Austrian army was on the other side, dug into foxholes of their own. It was a bit of a phony war, as weeks went by with nothing happening.

At first, being at the front seemed exciting; we were all young men with romantic notions of what war was all about. That excitement stayed with us longer than it would have had we been thrown straight into action.

Some of the guys really wanted to be heroes. They'd sit there polishing their rifles with a glazed look in their eyes. Occasionally someone would pop his head up out of a foxhole and aim the barrel of his gun, staring down through the sights. He might gurgle something like "Rat-a-tat-tat, rat-a-tat-tat," but not actually firing since it was sort of prohibited.

"Look, you dumb bastards," our sergeant in command would holler. "You can't hit the floozy Austrians from this distance with these peashooters. You're only wasting ammunition, so stop trying. Like they say in the cowboy novels, wait till you see the whites of their eyes."

He was a mean son of a bitch and he meant what he said, so we stopped trying.

After the initial excitement wore off, most of us got bored. A lot of the guys spent their time getting drunk and playing poker. There was a good deal of wine around, too, although solid food was in short supply.

Since we couldn't eat, we drank—and played poker. In fact, the first time I saw a guy get shot was while playing poker. There were five of us—Tony, me, and three others from our regiment. We had been drinking and playing cards for a couple hours, betting a little money. Nobody won much or lost much and it was getting late, so we decided to wrap things up with one last hand. To make it more exciting, we agreed to take the limit off what you could bet.

Two of the guys were big gamblers and started betting heavily. Tony dropped out right after the first card was dealt. I stayed in for a few cards but didn't get anything good, so I folded. When a third player dropped out, the two heavy gamblers faced off against each other. The game was five-card stud, with four cards dealt face up for all to see.

One of the guys, Leo, had a pair of kings while the other, Steven, had a pair of aces. Leo dealt out the fifth and final card face down and then reached down to look.

Steven grabbed his wrist and held it in a tight grip. "That's a king," he said with an angry look on his face. "You dealt it from the bottom of the deck."

Leo pushed Steven's arm away and picked up his card. He spoke calmly. "It is a king, but I didn't take it off the bottom of the deck. I took it from the top. What's your card?"

He glared defiantly at Steven as the other soldier turned over his card. It was a two.

"I win!" Leo said, scooping up the bills.

Steven pushed him back and made a grab for the money. "You cheated. *I* win!"

Leo got up and hit Steven hard in the face. Steven fell back, blood gushing from the side of his mouth as the money flew into the air and fell over the ground. Leo knelt and began picking it up.

Steven rubbed his jaw and stared at Leo, enraged.

"Try anything and I'll kill you," threatened Steven as he watched Leo stuff money into his pocket.

Steven got up quietly and walked away.

I thought that would be the end of it. Steven had done the smart thing, since he couldn't fight Leo. Leo was a mountain of a man. His arms were large and powerful and he had a barrel of a chest. Steven was thin and wiry; he would snap like a twig if he ever got hit by one of those huge hands that hung at the end of Leo's arms.

Leo was reading a book in his foxhole when Steven came back a few minutes later, carrying his rifle like a toy. Perhaps he thought it *was* a toy; he had been playing with it for weeks.

Steven rushed by me so fast that I didn't have time to react. I saw it all from a distance: Steven hefted his gun onto his shoulders and aimed along the barrel through the sights. I screamed, but it was too late. Steven pulled the trigger and Leo's book exploded like a paper bomb. Leo then sagged and a hole the size of an apple burst open in his stomach, blood and intestines pouring out over his belly.

Another soldier jumped Steven from behind and pinned him to the ground as a gush of air popped out of Leo's mouth, as if he had burped. Leo looked down at the wound with a shocked, terrified grimace. He lifted his hands slowly, trying to collect his intestines and push them back into his stomach.

"Help me," Leo moaned.

It was as if no one had heard him. We all stood around, looking at him disbelievingly, feeling sick. Nobody seemed able to do anything but watch nauseously. My God, a man was dying. It was incredible.

"Move aside," I heard someone say. It was Tony. He pushed his way through the crowd of grotesque onlookers.

Leo groaned for help again as Tony knelt beside him. Leo looked at him like a scared animal.

Tony ripped off his shirt and examined the wound. "Get some liquor, towels, and a first aid kit," he shouted without looking up.

No one moved.

"You heard him!" I shouted, pushing the man behind me. "Get what he wants!"

As the other men ran off to find the supplies Tony needed, I knelt next to him beside Leo.

"Relax," Tony said wiping sweat off Leo's face. "You'll be okay."

Leo grimaced in pain and his eyes closed.

I waited for them to open, but they didn't. "He's dead…"

"No, he's not," Tony said. "He's just passed out from the shock. He's not hurt too bad. He won't die."

Someone passed me a towel and a bottle of whiskey. Tony took the whiskey and poured it over the area around the wound. He then used the towel to wipe away the dirt and blood. The wound now looked like a place of raw meat, ripped apart by sharp claws.

"My God, Tony, he can't live with that," I said, looking at the wound in disgust.

But Tony was confident. "Of course he can. He's just lost a bit of his bowel. If we can stop the bleeding and get him stabilized, the doctors will sew him back up once he gets to the hospital."

Tony placed the towel over the wound and pressed down hard. The towel turned red as blood seeped through it. Leo seemed to stir.

"Give him some of that whiskey," Tony said.

I poured some into Leo's mouth, and he swallowed it. His eyes seemed to roll beneath his eyelids as Tony continued to press down on the towel.

After about five minutes, tony threw the drenched towel aside and replaced it with a fresh towel that had been brought over. Blood seeped into this one too, but more slowly. Within a few minutes the bleeding seemed to stop. Tony then took some bandages out of the first aid kit and taped them over the wound.

"There," he said. "I hope somebody radioed for an ambulance."

When the ambulance came, we lifted Leo very carefully out of the foxhole and carried him to the ambulance without jarring him. Tony insisted on that, otherwise he would start bleeding again.

Leo was conscious but in terrible pain. Tony gave him the rest of the whiskey to drink.

"Drink it all," he ordered. "It will deaden the pain."

Leo took large, greedy gulps, his mouth trembling and causing some of the whiskey to spill onto his chin and down his neck.

"Somebody did a good job patching this guy up," the ambulance driver said. He hopped into the back with Leo and closed the doors. The ambulance pulled away.

I was to witness similar scenes many times over the next two years, with Tony put his medical knowledge to work while patching guys up. He became a frontline doctor, repairing badly injured men just enough to keep them alive to get them to a hospital. "Meatball surgery," he called it one day as he dug large pieces of shrapnel out of a guy's leg and tied a tourniquet to stop the bleeding.

No matter how serious the injury, Tony believed stopping the bleeding could keep wounded soldiers from going into shock, giving them a chance to live.

"That's what it's all about," he told me. "To survive, to go on living in the face of so much death..."

We all came to believe that: keep your head down, don't be a hero. We told ourselves this as the reality of war set in. Seeing death all around us made us sick of the so-called glory.

Ironically, although we were sick of playing at war, our guns became all the more important to us. We polished them and aimed them not only at imaginary enemies but at living, breathing men, enemies we took no pleasure in killing... enemies we had to kill because they were shooting at us, firing artillery at waves of Italian soldiers who had been ordered to attack all across the front.

These attacks involved tens of thousands of men, often waged for the gain of a meagre few hundred meters of earth. When the attacks began, thousands of soldiers would charge out of their foxholes and run across the barren no man's land, cutting through barbed wire to hurl themselves at their enemies in a suicidal assault. A few unlucky bastards never even managed to make it out of their foxholes, their heads blown off or their stomachs ripped open by cannon fire on the same spots where just the night before they'd been writing letters home. If they didn't die quickly, they'd lay paralyzed, looking up into the black sky, feeling their life drain away as their blood dripped steadily into the dirt.

Others made it out of their foxholes only to be cut down in the bloody crossfire as they desperately tried to make their way across no man's land. Others still got caught up in the barbed wire. They'd hang there, like a crucified Christ, unable to move without having their flesh torn to pieces. They'd struggle frantically, ignoring the pain as they tried to get free before a bullet found them. If they failed and a bullet did find them, they'd hang, seeming to moan, their eyes bulging out of their sockets in disbelief as shadows crept across the land and clouds floated overhead through the ever-darkening sky.

That was the hell we lived with, the reality of war. It was nothing like we had pictured, but you got used to it. There were long stretches of time with nothing to do but wait. You might sit around playing cards or writing a letter home. You might be reading a book and look up to catch somebody watching you. You never asked what he was staring at. You didn't have to. You knew. You looked at him back, thinking the same thoughts. You'd watch a guy comb his hair, wonder if he would get killed today. Were there any signs that would reveal a person's fate? You looked deeply into their faces, trying to tell whether he'd get blown up by a grenade or bayoneted in the chest. Whenever you imagined someone else's grizzly death, it was really yourself you were worried about.

We were all afraid, but no one had the guts to admit it to himself.

Except for Joey, a young kid from a large family who spent a lot of time wiping his nose on his sleeve and reading the letters his parents sent him. Sometimes he'd read the same letter over and over again, then put it down and start shaking, trying to hold back the tears. He wrote many letters home, always beginning with, "I'm still alive..."

Joey was constantly coming up to me and asking me to read his letters, the ones he wrote and the ones he received. It was sad reading. Both Joey and his parents seemed sure he would be killed. In fact, some of the things Joey wrote made it seem as if he was already dead. He spoke of the loneliness he felt over his fear of never seeing his dear brothers and sisters again, of how much it pained him that he would never again kiss his sweet mother or go with his father to work in the fields.

I tried to convince him he wasn't going to die.

"Yes, I am," he insisted. "Just look at my face."

"Your face is no different from anyone else's."

"Yes, it is. It's different from yours. You're going to live," he said prophetically.

I threw his letters at him and screamed for him to get away from me. I don't know what it was about Joey that frightened me. Maybe he was right—maybe there was something in his face.

But it was the same look as everyone else's... a look of fear, the fear of dying agonizingly and alone. The fear of death, the sight of death, the smell of death, the mere thought of death that permeated the air every hour of every day. Death... the inevitable end of every life, common and expected in times of war but which nonetheless always came as a surprise because it was impossible for a man to conceive of his own non-existence.

Whenever I thought of death, I thought of a pair of eyes staring wide in disbelief.

About every three months, our regiment got relieved. We'd be taken off the line and told to go relax for two weeks, to forget about death's awful presence.

Where do men on vacation from death head off to and what do they do? Soldiers in times of war don't live under the rules for ordinary men in ordinary times. A special dispensation is granted to them by the populace to do as they please; the prevailing attitude is that they should drink and be merry for tomorrow they may die. "Drink and be merry, soldier boy. Cram a lifetime of living into a single night. Don't worry about the consequences. There are no consequences. Just live, live, live."

For one leave, we all headed off with that that thought in mind. A group of us, Tony included, headed off for a large town near the front. A large town was any place that had a hotel, bar, and brothel; this town had more than one of each.

Once in town, the first thing I did was check into a hotel. I wanted to take a hot bath. Before going up to my room, though, I went into the bar and bought a bottle of whiskey. Tony and the others were in the bar, too. They hadn't taken rooms yet.

"Sit down and have a drink with us," Tony said, offering me a chair at their table.

"No thanks. I'm going to wash up first. I'll be down later." I got the whiskey and left.

My room was on the top floor and overlooked the town's main street. There were a lot of soldiers hanging around on leave and I could see a group of them from here. They were staggering down the street, drinking wine, and winking lewdly at any young lady who happened to pass by. "Drunken louts," my father would have called them, but I only saw them as young kids trying hard to forget the sight of death. They were trying to put the war far behind them for as long as possible.

The townspeople obviously agreed with my father, though, and avoided them like the plague.

I closed the curtains and opened the bottle of whiskey. I found a glass and poured it half full. Drinking from the glass and holding the bottle in my other hand, I walked into the bathroom. I finished off the glass and put it beside the tub. The hotel had running water, so I turned it on hot and stripped off my dirty army clothes.

I got into the boiling water and stretched out my legs. I thought of the party on the night Tony had announced his engagement to Silvana. I remembered how beautiful she'd been, how her beautiful eyes had sparkled like diamonds.

A vast loneliness welled up inside my breast. I'd thought of Silvana often since that night, and always it was the same—my heart ached knowing she was

Tony's, knowing the war would end and he would marry her. But I was a man and would never cry. I loved her, I wanted her, I needed her, but I had to forget her. Somehow, I had to forget her.

I poured another glass of whiskey and thought of the letters she had written to Tony. In each letter, she told him how much she loved him, but I wondered if her love for him was as real as mine for her. She said the only thing she wanted in the world was to be with him, to be his wife, and that she would wait for him to come to her, even if it took forever.

Tony took great pleasure in these letters, as any man would, but I received great pleasure from them too—because Silvana always mentioned me.

"Say hi to Richardo," she would write. "And tell him I hope he is well, and I hope you two are taking care of each other."

I wanted to read those letters time and time again. It made me so happy to know Silvana sometimes thought about me, but I couldn't ask Tony. What would he think?

I finished the whiskey and got dressed. It was early evening, and the streets were lit by dim lamplights that cast shadows along the sidewalks. Before going on, I looked at my face in the mirror, thinking of how much I had aged. My eyes were cold and defiant, but weariness had crept into them. I looked like a boxer who had waged a vicious battle against a deadly opponent, slugging it out round after round, refusing to fall but growing weak and wondering when it would ever end.

What is the purpose of battle when there's no prize to be won at the end of the fight? I wondered.

I saw myself heading home at the end of the war to dig rocks out of hillsides and farm the land as my father had done. But his life had had joy and meaning to it. He'd had a loving wife and a family to provide for.

I would labour without purpose. I saw no meaning in my life. I felt no joy, just a numb deadness inside.

"Senor Giovalli…" Father Terrance interrupted. The candle had burnt low and wisps of smoke circled in the air above it.

Giovalli jerked his head up, appearing confused, as though surprised to find someone else with him in the room.

"Oh, Father," he said, remembering where he was.

Father Terrance's long, flowing frock seemed to disappear into the darkness and all Giovalli saw was a smiling white face floating in the night.

The father had often dealt with the old as they grew senile and he recognized the hesitance and doubt that had crept into Giovalli's voice.

"You are bringing up a thousand things from the past better left forgotten," Father Terrance said as though to a fool. "That was a long time ago. Why let it bother you? You are not responsible for the pain and dying caused by that war." He smiled sweetly, trying to lend comfort. "But if you feel you have sinned, ask God's forgiveness. He will give it."

Giovalli stared into the father's eyes, wanting to go on and finish his story. He felt old, as old as the mountains, as old the earth herself. He felt dry and lifeless. Time was slipping away.

He had felt this way before, in the early days of the war, but he had been resurrected, brought back to life by a miracle of his own making. Then life had been good for a while and he had forgotten that it would ever end. He had taken joy in waking up each morning beside her. Her eyes had been the sun and the stars bringing his warmth and light. Her arms had wrapped around him like the winds of the world, hugging him, holding him close. Her lips had been like a cool rain providing life. And together they had born fruit.

Now she's dead, he thought. Now she knew the secret he had hidden away for fifty years inside his heart. *If there is a life after life, I need her to be there. I need her to be waiting there for me.*

"Only God can forgive us our sins," Father Terrance said. "And only through belief in the Lord Jesus Christ can we ever find peace in our heart."

As he looked at Giovalli, Father Terrance felt sure that the old man wasn't listening.

Why doesn't he leave? he thought, feeling irritated. *Why doesn't he go down and sit with his wife?*

Tired and bored, Father Terrance wanted to be left alone to enjoy the peacefulness of the night, to sit quietly and read a good book, perhaps to drink a glass of wine before going to bed.

"Mr. Giovalli," Father Terrance said, shaking the old man as if to awaken him. "You have told a very long story, but I don't understand what it is you are trying to say. How can I help you?" He tried but failed to keep the exasperation he felt out of his voice.

"I'm sorry, Father," Senor Giovalli said apologetically. "I have taken up a great deal of your time. If you will let me go on, I will come to the point of the story."

Father Terrance nodded his agreement.

"I told you about the war…"

I told you about Tony and how he was a good man. I didn't hate Tony, but he loved Silvana and so did I.

Well, before the war ended, Tony took me with him to visit Silvana a number of times. On each visit, my love for her grew until I knew I could not live without her. If she ever married another, I knew I would take my own life. By postponing his marriage to her, Tony had given me a reprieve from death.

But finally, after two years of war, Tony decided to go ahead with the marriage. He told me just before a major battle was to begin. The expression on my face lied to him; smiling, I hugged him and told him I was very happy for the two of them. Then I sat down and waited for the morning to arrive, when the war would begin again and the order would come for us to climb out of our foxholes and slaughter the enemy on the field of battle.

I slept and dreamt of an earth drenched in blood. I stood with one foot on a corpse, my rifle raised high over my head, a triumphant cry of victory ringing in the air.

Suddenly Silvana appeared, dressed in a long, flowing white wedding dress. Tony stood beside her in a black tuxedo. He held her hand and placed a ring on her finger.

The corpse I was standing upon started to sink into the earth, and somehow it managed to grab hold of my leg. It was dragging me under the ground with it. I tried to break loose, but the corpse's grip was too strong. I hit him with my rifle, but he wouldn't let go.

Silvana saw what was happening and started screaming. Tony put his arms around her and tried to kiss her, but she pushed him away.

"Look, it's Richardo! Go help him!"

Tony watched as I sank beneath the earth. "I can't help him," he said, shrugging his shoulders. "He's dead. Once you're dead, there's nothing anyone can do."

Silvana ran over to where I had disappeared under the ground and started digging up the dirt.

I woke up, gasping for air.

It was early dawn and Tony was beside me in the foxhole, smoking a cigarette, his expression calm and relaxed in the morning light. He noticed me open my eyes just as word that was being passed around man to man that the attack was about to begin.

"Remember to keep your head down," he whispered, leaning over close to me. "And don't be a hero."

He dropped his cigarette into the dirt and picked up his rifle. I slung my rifle over my shoulder and put on my helmet, strapping it over my chin.

A bugle blew sad and mournful as the attack order was given. A deafening cry rose up as a thousand men and more climbed out of the earth and hurled themselves over sparse, dry grass like a massive sea sweeping over the land to drown all life. Cannon fire burst around us and rockets whizzed overhead. Eagles soared away into the clouds.

Tony and I ran together stride for stride, ducking low as bullets whizzed by. We hit the earth as bombs exploded around us. Then we were up and running again with only one thing on our minds: *Get to the wire and make it through to the other side.*

All along the front, the attack was met with success. In many places, Italian soldiers had already cut through the barbed wire and were driving the Austrians out of their foxholes, forcing them to retreat. But the dead lay everywhere.

When Tony and I reached the wire and cut through, Tony went first. Other members of our regiment followed, only to the Austrians dug in a hundred meters in front of us. I hurled a grenade and saw it drop into their foxhole and explode. Moans of death rose as I ran up, firing my rifle. I shot into the foxhole at bodies probably already dead.

Many Austrian soldiers were retreating, running over the fields into the distance towards gun emplacements the Austrians had set up further back behind the line. Italian solders chased after them like hunters chasing rabbits.

Tony had jumped into the foxhole and was climbing out the other side. I followed him, and in the process dropped my rifle. I picked it up and scrambled to the other side—but something grabbed at my leg. I tried to push free, pulling my leg and trying to get out of the foxhole, but something was pulling me back.

I could see Tony—he was running away from me.

"Tony!" I hollered. He stopped and turned, then started to run back towards me.

Looking down into the foxhole, I saw a half-dead Austrian soldier with two hands around my leg. He held on, his face covered in mud, blood gushing from a wound in his head.

"Help me," he groaned eerily.

I fell back into the foxhole just as Tony jumped in beside me.

I hit the enemy soldier's hands with the butt of my rifle, but he wouldn't let go. Tony had to pry his fingers off my leg.

"Can you help him?" I asked Tony, indicating the soldier.

"No!" Tony shook his head. "He's dead. There's nothing I can do for him now."

I looked at the enemy's face and wondered why his eyes didn't close.

Tony stood up. "Let's go! We have to catch up to the regiment." He jumped out of the foxhole and started running.

I took a last look at the dying soldier, his lips spread open in an ugly grimace. I thought he was trying to tell me something.

I climbed out of the foxhole. Everywhere I looked, I saw the ugliness of death; its stink covered the air. I felt cold and afraid. And there was Tony, who hadn't run far...

I put my rifle on my shoulder and aimed.

I knew I loved Tony.

I pulled the trigger.

He fell face first into the dirt, and I knew he was dead. In that instant, I felt as if his hands were reaching around my leg and I thought I could hear his voice begging me to pull him out of the grave.

But there was nothing I could do for him; he was dead.

Then I heard a scream. I turned in the direction the scream had come from and saw Joey staring at me in horror.

"You murdered him!" Joey gasped.

I fired my rifle, shooting Joey in the face. He sagged to his knees, his eyes staring wide in disbelief. He tried to say something, but only a raspy, hollow sound escaped from his throat before he fell dead.

Looking around, I saw there was no one else in sight except for the dead. I started running across the dry earth after the regiment, knowing I was safe. Tony had let go of my leg.

Giovalli didn't see the look of loathing that fell over Father Terrance's face, but he heard it in the priest's voice.

"You're a murderer!" Father Terrance gasped, "You murdered your friend and a young innocent boy whose only sin was to watch you kill!" He stood up and moved away from Giovalli, then pointed his longer finger at the man in revulsion. "You're evil! You want me to forgive you; you want God to forgive you! You won't be forgiven! Your soul is doomed to burn in hell! Get out of here! Get away from me!"

Giovalli looked at him with silently pleading.

"Get away from me!" the father screamed again, picking a Bible up off the table and throwing it at the old man.

Giovalli got up and ran on feeble legs out of the room, away from the mad priest. He ran down the steps, tripping in the dark.

He ran into the chapel, and realized it was the first time in fifty years, since before the war, he'd entered a church. He sobbed, alone and afraid, tears streaming down his cheeks. A large wooden crucifix hung above the altar and Christ seemed to look down in sympathy at him as he ran up the aisle to the open casket where Silvana's body lay. He fell onto his knees, his hands grasped in prayer, and gazed lovingly into her face.

"Silvana! Silvana!" he sobbed, trying to catch his breath, wishing his heart would stop beating. "Forgive me. I murdered Tony! I loved you! The Austrians didn't kill him, I murdered him… I murdered him, Silvana! They buried him in a pauper grave, a mass grave with other peasants. He was a member of the royalty and they buried him with peasants!"

Giovalli's voice rang through the chapel like a discordant bell, tolling for the dead.

After the war, he had gone back to his village and met Tony's father, who had become old. A look of death and defeat hung over him.

"You saw Tony die?" his father had asked Giovalli. "No! Don't tell me! I don't want to hear!" He waved Giovalli away. "It's all the same, all young men dying for nothing! There is no God!"

Giovalli had watched him walk into his house and close the door on everything he had once believed in.

A heart-rendering sob broke from Giovalli's heart as his tears fell on Silvana's cheek. He then looked up and saw the crucifix. Christ seemed to smile down at him, to beckon him, but Giovalli turned away. He brushed his hand over his wife's face, hard and stiff, and it made him sad. He pried opened her eyes and gazed into them. They were dull and lifeless, the sparkling light that had shone from them having gone out.

"I came to you, Silvana," he said tenderly, kissing her forehead. "You were in mourning for Tony, but I wiped away your tears and made you smile. I married you and gave you fifty years of love. Haven't I given you back far more than I ever took?"

He thought he saw a look of reproach in her eyes, and her hand seemed to reach up and push him away.

"Fifty years of love!" he screamed. "Isn't that enough to have you forgive me? Forgive me! Forgive me! Forgive me! Forgive me!"

His cries echoed through the chapel like a loud, lonesome wind blowing over the sea, but no soul heard him.

Father Terrance stood alone in his study, looking out the window. The night was dark and stars shone down upon the valley. An image of the moon passing behind the clouds was reflected in the river that flowed silently out to sea.

Such a quiet, peaceful night, Father Terrance thought happily. *And the valley is so beautiful.*

A NIGHT WITH SOME LIONS

Tony Sanders crawled on his belly over the broken branches and scattered leaves on the dirt floor of the forest. The ten-year-old's clothes were caked in mud and blood trickled down his cheek from the scratch on his forehead.

He stopped for a second to wipe his face and calculate the distance between himself and his prey. The small rabbit stood on its hindlegs, its tiny nose quivering furiously as the rabbit jerked its head from side to side.

Then the rabbit dropped down onto four legs and scampered off.

Damn, Tony thought as he got up and brushed himself off.

A little girl came up behind him on the path. "Did you get him!? Did you get him!?" she squealed in delight.

Tony turned and looked at her in annoyance. "Get away from me, Sarah," he said, pushing her down.

She fell roughly, scrapping her leg against a rock and tearing her dress.

"Look what you've done!" she cried angrily. "You hurt me and tore my dress." She held the torn and dirty hem of her dress up for him to see.

He laughed. "Pretty Sarah's gotten dirty," he taunted. "Now she's dirty Sarah."

Sarah picked up a handful of dirt and flung it at him.

"Dirt thrower! Dirt thrower! Dirty little dirt thrower!" Tony said, laughing some more. He then turned and walked back down the path through the forest.

Sarah looked at the cut on her leg and winced. "Ouch," she cried as she felt the cut with her finger.

Tony's mean and I'm never going to play with him again, she thought as she got up and straightened her dress. She thought she might tell his mother what he'd done and get him in trouble, but then she decided just not to speak to him ever again. She hoped somebody would push him down someday and make him cry. *It would serve him right if someone punched him in the face and kicked him real hard.*

She kept walking along the path, feeling angry and hurt. She wished she were home eating some of her mother's delicious gingerbread and watching cartoons.

She saw a pretty pink flower growing at the base of an oak tree and knelt down to pick it.

Mother will love this, she thought happily.

Then she heard a loud growl behind her in the forest. She dropped the flower and froze in fear. But there was nothing there, just the trees.

When she got up, she started walking more quickly, having forgotten the flower. As she walked, though, she thought she could hear a rustling sound—and the sound of twigs breaking underfoot as something ran toward her through the forest.

Sarah hurried faster along the path, her eyes gazing fixedly through the trees into the ominous dark of the deep woods.

"Rowwwr, rowwr…" The deep guttural scream of a wild beast thundered in the humid air.

She began to run, small tears falling from her eyes, her mouth open in the process of a soundless scream of terror. She could hear the loud stomping of the beast chasing after her. It was gaining on her. She was afraid it would pounce on her from out of the forest at any moment, its steely claws ripping into her back, but she dared not look behind to see.

"Rowwwr, rowwwr!"

The horrifying scream shook the earth and Sarah ran on in a panic, having lost the narrow path that led home to safety. The thin lower branches of the trees slapped at her face. Thorns ripped at her clothes and tore her skin.

"Tony! Tony! Tony!" she cried out in fear. "Please help me!" she cried in fear.

Suddenly, the trunk of a tree seemed to stick out its foot to trip her and she went sprawling on the ground, her face smashing against the dirt, cutting her lip. She lay on her stomach, trembling, large teardrops falling to the earth.

"Rowwr, rowwwr," the beast growled into her ears. She felt its claws pawing her back.

She bawled as she closed her eyes tight and flung her arms around the back of her head.

"Tony! Tony! Tony!" she sobbed. The animal's warm breath blew against her skin and a sharp tooth seemed to dig into her neck.

Sarah closed her mind to the ensuing horror; she descended into the painless privacy of darkness; the dark black forest and the wild beast were part of some other place. She thought only of her mother, her sweet mother.

But the voice of the beast intruded, shrieking in her ears: "Dirty little Sarah, dirty little Sarah, I fooled you!" The voice was Tony's and he laughed derisively.

"Go away! Go away! Go away!"

"Sarah," Tony said, nudging her.

Sarah turned over and opened her eyes. Tony was looking down at her with a big grin.

"Dirty little Sarah, I fooled you," he said, laughing again.

"Oooowowow, you mean person. You scared me." Sarah's eyes filled with dirt and tears.

"I know I scared you, I heard you scream," Tony said, proud of himself. "Boy, you were funny."

Sarah felt the scratches on her face gingerly. "Look at what you did! I'm all cut and bleeding!"

She gave Tony a nasty look and decided she would tell his mother on him after all.

"It's not my fault you fell and got hurt," Tony said roughly.

She was just a sissy girl, he thought, but he hoped she wouldn't go home and cry to her mother.

Sarah got up and tried brushing the dirt off her dress. She pushed past Tony without a word and started walking back through the forest.

Tony ran to catch up with her. "I'll walk you home," he said imperiously.

Sarah glared at him with fury but made no reply. Although she was angry with him, it was getting dark and the woods seemed to be crowding in on her. She was still upset from having been frightened, and the whispering noises of the forest were enough to spook her and make her glad Tony was beside her.

Still, she didn't have to speak to him or even look at him.

"Boo!" Tony came up and screamed into her ear. "Boo! Boo! Boo! Did you think I was a wild animal, Sarah?" He threw his head back and growled. "Row-wwr! Did you think I was a lion who was going to eat you? Rowwwr, rowwr…"

He snarled, gnashing his teeth, and Sarah hurried on, trying not to pay attention.

Tony kept darting around, running ahead and hiding behind trees only to leap out at her as she walked by. "Boo! Boo! Boo!" he chanted, sounding like a machine gun firing, jumping and grimacing evilly.

She pushed past him, determined to ignore his childish antics, and after a time he grew tired of trying to provoke her.

Girls are no fun, he thought bitterly as he walked beside her in silence.

Sarah was glad that Tony stopped acting silly. It was growing darker all the time and she had to get home, or she'd miss supper.

It seemed like they had been walking an awfully long way. Her feet hurt and her arm was sore from where she had fell on it.

"Tony, where's the path?" she asked crankily.

Tony stopped and looked around. "It must be somewhere near here," he said with uncertainty in his voice. He grabbed her arm and walked faster. "Come on."

She had to almost run to keep up with him. They hurried through the forest, climbing over dead trees that had fallen to the ground, trudging over leaves and broken twigs. The sun had already fallen below the trees and would soon set beneath the edge of the world.

Tony ran in desperation, pulling Sarah behind him.

"Stop it, Tony, stop it!" Sarah cried, wrenching her arm from his grasp. She rubbed her wrist and sat down to rest. "We're going in the wrong direction."

"Sarah, we can't stop. We've got to find the path, or we won't be able to get home." He was sorry now he had ever pretended to be a lion, and he was mad at Sarah for running off the path and getting them lost.

Sarah sighed wearily. "Okay," she said, getting up. "But which way do we go?"

Tony looked around. He couldn't see very far, it was too dark, and anyway all the trees looked alike. "I don't know... this way!"

He grabbed her hand and ran back in the direction they'd come from.

The two children ran around in erratic circles. Meanwhile, the sun set and the moon sailed into the dark blue sky, throwing a dim light down through the trees. The whispering sounds of night carried through the chilly air. An owl hooted, a bat screeched as it flitted swiftly through the forest, veering away from the trees and branches. Small animals skittered through the crinkling leaves.

Sarah's insides were aching. She ran with Tony through the woods until her legs felt like falling off. At last she had to stop.

"I'm tired, Tony," she cried as she sat under a tree and leaned her back against it. She held her arms tightly across her chest to keep warm.

Tony fell down beside her, panting for air. "We're lost."

"I wish you had caught that rabbit," Sarah told him wistfully. "I'm hungry."

Tony was too afraid to laugh.

The humid air of afternoon was swept away by a cold, biting breeze, and soon the soft, warm earth turned hard and wet. The silent forest creaked and moaned with a haunting laughter.

Tony and Sarah sat huddled together, staring frightfully into the dense woods.

"I'm afraid, Sarah," Tony confessed.

"Shh." Sarah's face was intense and alert as she gazed into the dark. "I heard something."

She looked at Tony with a terrified grimace, her large eyes opened wide in trepidation.

"You're scaring me, Sarah," Tony said before beginning to cry. "There's nothing out there. There's no lion…"

But he looked into the gloom with a new sense of fear, his heart pounding like a drum, his body shaking from more than just the cold.

"Be quiet, Tony!" Sarah begged. "If there's something out there, it will hear you!"

The forest grew still as if in agreement. The trees stopped rustling, there were no creaking branches or chirping grasshoppers, and all the mishmash of noise that had thundered in the quiet of the night seemed to stop, almost as if all the creatures of the forest were listening.

Tony remembered the rabbit crouched on its hindlegs, its ears stiff and straight as it stood silent and still, sniffing the air. A cold shiver ran through his heart and he began to cry again.

A Childlike Innocence.

Above is a picture taken in the early 1960s while Danny was still living in Halifax. **Pictured with Danny is his brother, Laurie.** *Children often don't have the burdens adults experience with the stress of managing a household and the expectations others put on them to meet their day-to-day demands. Children, as in the case of Sarah and Tony in this story, demonstrate a certain degree of innocence not commonly seen in adulthood, a theme that is echoed in ways similar to the children in Harper Lee's* To Kill a Mockingbird.

Sarah stood up and strained her eyes to see through the tenebrous woods. Tony grabbed at her arm to pull her down, but she pulled away.

"I think I hear some people," she told him. "Let's go and look!"

Tony made no move to get up. "What if it's not people? What if it's an animal? Or what if it's a murderer?" A new fear crept into his heart and he gazed into the blackness with an intense look of fright.

"I don't want to stay here all night. I'm going to go and see," Sarah said adamantly.

She walked away from Tony, off in the direction from which she thought she had heard the voices.

Tony watched as Sarah disappeared into the dark forest. He would have gone with her, but his legs felt too weak to stand. Now that he was alone, it seemed as if the taunting laughter of the forest grew louder, building to a thunderous crescendo. He heard lions growling in the forest and ferocious bears lumbering towards him.

"Rowwwr, rowwwr, rowwwr," the wild beast growled as it inched nearer and nearer, preparing to pounce.

"Sarah! Sarah," Tony cried.

Where was she? He was certain she had been eaten by a lion or bear, but he wished she would come back, for he was afraid and didn't want to be left alone.

"Rowwwr!"

Tony started to cry and closed his eyes tightly. He held his hands in front of his face, trying to block out the sounds of the beast as it approached. He hoped that by closing his eyes, he could hide from the beast. Perhaps it would pass him by. He wished he was home, he wished his mother was holding him.

"Rowwwr," the wild beast growled fiercely.

"Dirty little Tony! Dirty little Tony!" Sarah suddenly laughed, shaking him.

Tony opened his eyes and saw Sarah, her father, and his own father staring down at him.

"Sarah!" her father said angrily. "Don't call Tony names. You wouldn't like it if he called you names, would you?"

Tony looked at Sarah happily. He wanted to kiss her.

"No, Daddy!" Sarah said meekly.

Tony's father lifted him up. "Come on, son! Let's go home!"

And the two fathers walked unafraid through the menacing forest with their much-relieved children.

THE FINAL NEGOTIATIONS

The year was 1987, the month was April, and the winter just past had been the coldest in many years. Europe had been blanketed by huge snowstorms which had begun in December 1986 and only just let up recently. One hundred feet of snow had fallen in a four-month period on the city of London. Paris had been hit with ninety feet; Berlin, eighty-six; Moscow, one hundred ten. Temperatures had fallen well below record lows and remained frigid throughout the long, cruel winter.

Thousands of people had died in Western Europe from cold and starvation, and hundreds of thousands of people had died of these twin horrors in the Soviet Union and its satellite countries. The cause of the starvation hadn't been due to the recent crop failures in the West or in the Soviet Union. There had been enough food to feed the hungry. But the ferocious winter storms had caused horrendous destruction to the transportation systems which millions of people huddled together in cities all over Western Europe and the Soviet Union had depended upon to deliver daily the food they needed to survive. Airports were snowed under, train tracks were made impassable by mountains of snow, and ports were frozen over, preventing planes, trains, and ships from making deliveries.

And so tremendous amounts of food had been left to rot in warehouses far from the millions of hungry people who cried out for bread.

The people of the United States had suffered to a much lesser degree. The American winter hadn't been as cold or as devastating. There had been the occasional incidence of people getting trapped in snowstorms and, unable to find shelter, freezing to death. But in European cities, hundreds of homeless people had died.

Perhaps most disturbing to the majority of Americans, the fierceness of the winter made it almost impossible to travel anywhere but locally. Most days, very few planes were able to take off from any of the nation's major airports. When the trains ran at all, they ran well behind schedule, and the nation's highways were treacherous and, for the most part, impassable.

For the first time in history, the National Basketball Association and National Hockey League seasons needed to be cancelled. But at least the nation's transportation system had functioned well enough to allow food to continue to be supplied to the cities.

Finally, it looked as if the worst of winter was over. The spring thaw arrived, and temperatures inched their way back up to normal levels. In London, the thermometer broke the freezing mark on April 10 for the first time in one hundred twenty-five days. By April 15, London was basking in a veritable heat wave as the temperatures climbed above twelve degrees Celsius. Temperatures also zoomed on the continent, with Paris reaching fourteen degrees; Munich, sixteen degrees; and even Moscow managed to make it up to eight degrees by the middle of the month.

Repairs were quickly being made to the continent's crisscrossing highways and railroads. Airports were dug out from under the melting snow and, once again, planes could be seen taxing down runways and lifting off into the clear blue sky. Food trickled into the cities, and then the trickle turned into a small flood. People who had hoarded and hidden away small quantities of foodstuffs to ensure their own survival guiltily knocked on their neighbours' doors to offer sugar, tea, and flour—at least until the markets once again overflowed with fruits and vegetables.

There had, in fact, been much less hoarding than one would suppose. The people of London, as they had during the war years, worked together to overcome the crisis. They came together in the spirit of brotherhood, uniting in a common front to fight the treacherous storms, sharing what they had, sacrificing for others, and extending kindness and friendship for all—because no one was stronger that winter. It could be said for many Londoners that the winter of 1987 was their finest hour. Because of this kind-hearted charity, death visited London less often than most other cities.

In Paris, they also shared. Young men shared rotting apples with their girlfriends. Fathers gave pieces of stale bread to their sons. Families shared with families, friends shared with friends, but strangers were kept at a distance. Those who did, lived; those who did not, died. The slow agony of death was witnessed by all. If you didn't see it, you felt it in the air. You heard it in the silence broken by low moans blown along on the winds, not your heart.

In Berlin, the wall stood grey and ominous, an impassive killer whose chilling eyes offered no reprieve from the sentence of death. The condemned went obediently to their graves, their rotting bodies left to hang on the barbed wire, a foul odour the only part of them permitted to drift with the snow to freedom. But some got through, only to be met with "We have not enough for ourselves. Go back. We cannot feed you!"

In Moscow, death didn't matter; the party survived. Those who were ordered to make sacrifices made them. There were great acts of heroism and honest charity. The Russian people were the most heroic on earth, because they had suffered the most. Somehow, despite the party, the Russians made it through the winter, just as they had made it through the Second World War. Surviving against improbable odds is nothing new to the Russian soul. Hordes of men, most of whom had been reduced to mere skin and bones, broke their backs to drag food across the frozen tundra from the countryside to the city. The people of Moscow ate—not well, but they ate. Unsmiling faces dragged on through the city, apparently oblivious to their fellow creatures, but smiling eyes showed recognition of their common humanity. The Russian soul shows not in the face, but through the eyes. The Russian face is cold, harsh, and as barren as the Siberian landscape. But Russian eyes are like stars shining brilliantly in the darkest sky. Occasionally, you will see a Russian whose eyes are as cold as their face; usually this is a party official. Among the Russians who died that winter, only few were party officials.

In the coldest month, February, with the Western world paralyzed by this most terrible winter, the Russian bear growled. The Warsaw Pact armies lumbered over the Yugoslavian and Albanian borders, their progress impeded more by the winter cold and snow than by the fierce opposition mounted against them. The armies limped along inch by inch. With air attacks virtually impossible, tanks useless, and supplies having to be carried on the backs of mules and packhorses, like in some eighteenth century war, the Russians still wielded the destructive firepower of handheld missile launchers and Kalashnikov submachine guns capable of firing more than two hundred rounds a minute into an enemy ill-prepared to mount an effective opposition.

Through sheer force of numbers, the valiant resistance was beaten down. By the end of March, before the April sun came to melt the snow, before the West could offer assistance, Yugoslavia and Albania had been subdued. The Yugoslavian Air Force, the backbone of the nation's defence, never got off the ground. The Yugoslavian themselves ended up destroying their own planes rather than let them fall into the hands of the Russians.

In the final days of the conflict, the leader of the Yugoslavian communist party made one final appeal to the West: "The fate we suffer now, you will suffer later," he told the President of the United States. "If you do not act to save us, you will one day be left fighting alone to save yourself." The President had agreed, but the only assistance the United States could offer was nuclear—and the President was unwilling to go that far.

The people of the West were too burdened by their own problems to worry about the fate of a few million citizens of two unaligned communist nations. Having just fought a brutal winter, they didn't want to fight an even more brutal war. And, they reasoned, the third world could not be won; such a conflict could only end in death for all.

Of course, they were right. So they didn't protest when the Soviet Union announced that the people of Yugoslavia and Albania had been liberated from two recessive capitalist regimes, and that communism had been restored.

The people of the West also didn't protest when tens of thousands of citizens of these two countries were packed into trains and sent to Siberia—political prisoners to be locked up and treated like slaves in Russian concentration camps. In fact, they only began to protest when the United States imposed a complete economic embargo against the Soviet Union. The President ordered all American companies, no matter where in the world they operated, to cease doing business with the Soviets. Thousands of people then protested in front of American embassies around the world. The protests increased in size and hostility as the President's momentous plans became known.

In the closing days of April 1987, Washington was bathed in warm sunshine. The lilac trees bloomed along Pennsylvania Avenue. The scent of cherry blossoms lingered sweetly in the air. Young lovers strolled along the banks of the Potomac River, holding hands, kissing beneath the rising moon. Life went on as usual, filled up with problems and pleasures, hopes and fears.

But in the Oval Office of the White House, time passed frantically. The President held long, drawn-out meetings, often lasting late into the night, with the joint chiefs of staff, the Secretary of Defence and Foreign Affairs, and with the most powerful senators and congressmen of the nation. The President worked feverishly to gain support for his plan to take military action against the Soviet Union.

On the night of April 27, the final arguments were made for and against this plan—and then the decision was made.

"The Soviets took advantage of the situation in Europe and our inability to offer conventional military assistance at the time to crush two independent nations under their boots," the President announced angrily. "If we do not act against them now, later, under similar circumstances, they will attack another defenceless nation on the periphery of their sphere of influence, forcing a free people to live under a repressive communist regime, adding to the number of member states in the

Warsaw Pact, turning a nation which would have been neutral, or more likely an ally of ours, into an enemy! In time, as the President of Yugoslavia warned, we will find ourselves left alone to fight them!"

Many doves listening to the President bristled at his bellicose words.

"Mr. President, you are talking about having these United States of America start World War III," said the Senate majority leader, stamping his hand against the oaken table around which the twenty men sat. "Once our forces strike at Yugoslavia and Albania, the Soviets will hit back at us all along the line, from Norway to Greece. You cannot have a limited war in Europe. The Senate has supported your embargo against the Soviet Union, but if you persist in this madness we will be forced to act against you. I warn you, call off any plans to use American forces against the Soviets in Eastern Europe, or you will find yourself facing charges of impeachment."

The President's huge frame hurtled out of his chair and moved swiftly towards the senator, grabbing the senator by his shirt collar and shaking him forcefully.

"Don't threaten me, Senator!" the President screamed. "You are not as powerful as you think yourself to be. I can have you removed from your position as majority leader. I can have you removed altogether whenever I want. You are a little fish, given some importance because it suits my interests to have you be where you are. If you wish to retain your position, you had better continue to satisfy me!"

The senator trembled in fear. His scared eyes twitched as his gaze turned from the President's face to the other men around the table. In a brief glance, he saw that he stood alone. No man was about to lift so much as a finger to help him; they were the President's men. If they weren't willing henchmen, as the Secretary of Defence and the Secretary of External Affairs most certainly were, they were in fear of him, willing to sacrifice their honour, dignity, and souls to save their skin.

The senator suddenly understood why he had been called to the White House. He was to be the administration's front man. The President intended him to use his position as a respected senator, one whom the people could trust to speak the truth as he believed it to be, to encourage the Americans to wholeheartedly support the President's actions. The whole nation would expect him to lead the opposition against the President; if instead he came out in support of the President, calling the President's actions moral and righteous, the opposition would crumble.

"Do you understand what I am saying to you, Senator?" the President growled at him.

The senator stared in horror at the President, looking into the face of a madman, a crazy lunatic who held the power of life and death over the whole world.

"I will not do it," the senator said defiantly. "I don't care what you do or have against me, I am against you." He pulled himself free of the President's grasp.

"Get out of here!" the President screamed at him, his face twisting grotesquely. "Get out of this office! Get out of the White House! You are not welcome here anymore!"

The senator scurried quickly away, running out the door.

The remaining eighteen men sat silently around the table, their eyes downcast. The President went back to his seat and calmly sat down. He picked up the white phone and dialled three numbers.

"Implement Plan B," he said into the receiver before hanging up. He then turned to the men around him, totally in control of his emotions. "Gentlemen, tomorrow at precisely 1600 hours Eastern Standard Time, NATO forces will cross the borders of Yugoslavia and Albania to liberate the people of those two countries."

A dozen of the men cheered, while the other six nodded in agreement.

The Senate majority leader sped away from the White House in his white sedan, rain splattering onto the windshield. The weather was rapidly deteriorating.

He wasn't sure what the President intended to do, but he knew he had to act quickly before the President silenced him. He had to tell the American people about the President's sinister plans, to convince them to mount a resistance before the President plunged the world into World War III.

He would tell the American people the President was mad. Somehow he would get them to believe him, and the President would be stopped.

He drove across the bridge towards the offices of *The Washington Herald*. A light rain was beginning to fall and the Washington Monument shone majestically in the moonlight.

As the senator drove, he reflected on the American Constitution, the laws protecting the rights of citizens, and the three branches of government. The President did not hold absolute power over the American people. He could be stopped and thrown from office.

A large black town car pulled up beside the senator in the left-hand lane, and the two cars drove side-by-side for some distance.

Why doesn't the other driver pass me? the senator wondered.

He glanced over to get a look at the driver in the town car. Two men sat in the front seat, and one of them was motioning for him to roll down his window. The senator instead increased his speed and pulled away.

Up ahead, the senator sped through an intersection, all the while looking through his rear-view mirror back at the town car. It had stopped for the light.

The senator felt relieved. For some reason, he had thought those the two men had been after him. He was probably just nervous because of what had happened at the White House, and now being overly cautious.

He slowed down again, and the black town car drove behind him. The driver pulled into the left-hand lane and pulled up alongside the senator, who noticed that the passenger's window had been rolled down and he was motioning for the senator to stop. The man's face seemed friendly and unthreatening.

The senator rolled down his window and slowed further.

"What do you want!?" the senator hollered at the other driver through the blowing rain and wind.

"Your back tire is wobbling!" the man shouted back. "It might be about to fall off. You should stop and take a look at it!"

Now that he'd been told, the senator could feel the rear part of the car sliding ever so slightly. He wondered why he hadn't noticed it earlier. Probably because he had been so agitated, so preoccupied with reaching the *Herald*'s offices as quickly as possible.

The senator pulled his car over to the side of the road. The town car stopped just ahead and the man in the passenger's seat got out.

"Maybe you'll need some help," the man said as the senator got out of the car.

"Thanks!" the senator replied. "I don't know very much about cars. I've never even changed a tire, so you're probably right."

The two men walked to the back of the car and knelt down to take a look at the rear wheel.

"Some of the bolts holding the wheel in place are loose," the man said as he examined the tire. "Do you have any tools I can use to tighten these screws?"

"I have some in the trunk." The senator took his keys and opened the trunk. He then reached into the back of the trunk and lifted the toolbox up off the floor.

He didn't notice as the man came up behind him and pulled a 48-automatic out of his jacket. The man aimed the gun at the back of the senator's head and pulled the trigger. Shreds of skin, bone, and blood exploded from the senator's head as he pitched forward into the trunk.

It's unlikely he felt anything, for death was instantaneous. Perhaps he heard a whizzing sound as the bullet shot out of the barrel of the gun. If he had, there would have been no time for him to even wonder what it was.

The man lifted the senator's legs and carefully pushed the rest of his body into the trunk of the car. Then he gently closed the trunk, took a handkerchief out of his pocket, and wiped off any fingerprints he might have left on the rim of the rear wheel.

With that, he got into the black town car, which swiftly pulled out onto the road and sped away.

"You took your time about it," the driver said to the passenger.

"I didn't want him to know he was going to die. It makes it easier."

"Easier for who, him or you?"

"Shut your mouth!" the passenger said angrily.

The driver heard the bitter hostility in the other man's voice. He was perceptive enough to pick up on the subtle warning and do as he was told.

They drove in silence for thirty minutes, through Washington into Maryland, finally arriving at an isolated farmhouse. The driver turned into the driveway and slowed down, stopping in front of the house. Both men got out.

"What are we to do here?" the driver asked the passenger.

"Go inside and wait. Two cars will come to pick us up. That will mark the end of our short but highly successful association."

The passenger opened the front door of the house and stepped back to let the driver enter first.

"Find the light switch and turn the lights on," the passenger said.

The driver reached along the wall, searching for the switch. Finding it, he pushed up and the lights came on, revealing a short hallway.

The passenger remained standing in the doorway, but now he held the gun in his hand. He squeezed the trigger before the driver could react in any way other than to be overcome by sheer terror. Even this feeling was to last only the briefest of instances.

The impact of the bullet threw the driver back against the wall, where he slid onto the floor and ended up in a sitting position, his head hanging down and pieces of his brain lying on his lap.

The passenger walked over and, using his handkerchief, turned off the lights. He turned and walked out the door. After closing it, he wiped off the knob to remove any fingerprints. Then he walked down to the road and proceeded along the highway in the same direction they had just recently been travelling.

Approximately two miles down the road, he came upon a blue sports car parked on the side of the highway. The man took a set of keys out of his pocket and opened the car. He got in and turned on the engine, then slowly pulled onto the highway and drove carefully away.

THE MEANING OF LIFE INSURANCE:
A Short, Bizarre Comedy

You newspaper men, you always want to know how, where, when, why, who, and I suppose what. Well, who knows when a thing starts, or why, or how for that matter?

I can tell you where and who easily enough. But what does it matter? You can see the results for yourself and, after all, aren't results what we should be concerned with?

Oh, it's frightful and terrible. All those young people rioting in the streets like wild animals. But who can blame them—such injustice, such awful injustice! And we, their professors, whom they look up to, teach them to fight for justice and search for truth. So are we not all to blame?

You don't care for truth, I know. All you want is enough material for a thirty-second spot on the evening news, then let others decide what is true or false, good or bad. All you want to do is make a killing and become famous. I ought to brain you with my cane. Didn't your mother teach you any manners?

Well, let me tell you something, hypocrite: civilization will not survive another century of the evening news. It's a vile medium. Too quick in its judgements and too often wrong.

But I suppose if I don't give in, you'll pester me to death, so come along, come along. Follow me quickly now that I've wasted too much time already. Don't mind them; they're making love, not war. I must confess that sort of thing is quite new at this university.

Oh, here we are: the main building. Beautiful, isn't it. It was built in 1823. Through its hallowed halls the great and near great have come and gone, each adding his own little piece of wisdom and truth until, within these walls, a great storehouse of knowledge was built up. But not left to rot, I assure you. The university sent it all forth to the four corners of the world in the name of progress.

There is a purpose to learning. We learn to know, of course, but we also learn to do. To build cities, cure diseases, colonize the galaxies. To spread civilization across the earth and across the sky. To strive for physical, intellectual, and spiritual perfection and not in the name of the almighty dollar, but in the name of God. Or, if you're an atheist—and if you are, that's quite all right with me, I assure you—in the same of mankind.

Here we are, here we are at last. You wonder why I have brought you to an empty classroom? Simple: this is as good a starting point as any. And, in fact, I must confess it's possible that the whole ugly situation did begin right here. It may be that the students have gone for good, that progress has reached its limit and all that is left of truth and intelligence are its fossilized bones, good only to be placed in some museum, reason having utterly failed man at the very hour in which it was most needed.

And thus explains the empty seats, the students rioting in the streets.

But it wasn't always this way. Once upon a time—in fact, just three short months ago—these seats were filled with bright young people yearning for knowledge just like this.

Oh, there they all are, back where they belong. What a marvellous trick. Didn't you find it delightful? You want to know how I did it? Silly you, haven't you ever heard of trick photography? Actually, I used Merlin's wand. Merlin was a magician but also a wise man.

Oh dear me, the students are becoming unruly. I had better bring class to order.

Ladies and gentlemen, or boys and girls—er, students... students, behave yourselves. This is a place of learning, not the Bronx Zoo.

A Story About Gum

The story I'm about to tell you was in turn told to me by the star of the narrative. However, since my own feelings on the subject are strong, I've allowed myself a little leeway to express my views as well. The subject of the story is chewing gum or alternating bubble gum. Either will do.

I once saw a television program on this substance's origin, although I don't remember it too vividly. I seem to remember it was originally gum from a tree that was chewed, but the product only became successful when spearmint was added. Consequently, the stuff has reached epic proportions and became established as a way of life. The United States in the 1950s was built on gum. Street gangs chewed it, Teddy Boys chewed it, rockers chewed it, and, worst of all, girls chewed it.

I can understand guys chewing gum. It lends a certain air to them, and I can understand girls chewing it as they would any other sweet. What I can't understand is girls who chew the stuff day in, day out under some crazy misapprehension that to chew is cool, that by some insane logic the chewing motion of the jaw actually adds appeal to them.

Movies did little to quash this until very recently. In fact, a teenage girl was not a teenage girl unless her lower skull was in constant motion. Even worse, grasping the gum in one hand and stretching it out till their arm was fully extended seemed to portray a girl's independence, as if chewing gum was against many parents' wishes and considered unladylike. Hence, to do so was to rebel against society.

This then has some credence, but not now, not anymore, not in the 1980s when gum is about as socially acceptable as any sweet can get. So everyone chews. What am I griping about?

Simple. My gripe is easily explained.

I was sitting on a bus, heading for work early one morning. The bus stops and four young girls get on, jaws frantically working at their gum. The journey takes twenty-five minutes, throughout which no gum is replaced or added to. Yet the flavourless gum is continually mauled. To add to this, any subsequent entry of young males to the bus increases the rate of chewing. Conclusion? Chewing gum appeals to males and, equally, females of the chewing ilk deem the action to be attractive.

From all this, you may well conclude my personal distaste of females chewing gum. So when I was told this story, I thought it well advised to relate it as a warning to all chewers, male and female, of gum.

Danny's Interest in Music

Although Danny was often limited by a major congenital heart defect, he didn't let it stop him from living life the best way he could. His taste in music was no exception. He made it to his 27th year despite the expectation he'd pass before he was 20.

THE DARING BANDIT

Jerry scratched his head and watched the flakes of dandruff fall like snow onto the table. When a thin layer had accumulated, he brushed it away and watched it go over the edge. More dirt to be swept up by his mother. He remembered when she'd found marijuana seeds on the floor. She hadn't known what they were. She'd thought they were from some sort of fruit. But she'd hollered at him anyway, her voice sounding angry and confused: "You're always making more work for me! I don't know why I put up with it!"

We're all stuck in our roles, he thought.

But he heard the same pleading, desperate sound of anguish in other voices. So many weary people only wanted to know why. *Why must I put up with it? Why must I do this year after year?* Or as his mother always said, "Roll on, years, roll on, till your kids have grown and gone so I can have some peace for a change."

The years had rolled on, but nothing had changed.

"I was out on my own and fending for myself when I was sixteen," his mother now complained. "But kids these days never want to leave home."

She was speaking with a woman who had come over to have her fortune read. People liked to have his mother tell their fortunes. She never saw anything bad in the cards. Perhaps a little worry, a bit of hardship, but nothing that would amount to much. By and by, down the road, everything would work out fine.

Will everything work out fine? Jerry wondered. He didn't believe in the cards, but lately he couldn't resist the idea of having his mother tell his fortune. He had to believe in something, in some powerful good, or else some powerful bad. It would be the worst thing he could imagine to have the years roll on with nothing ever changing.

So he watched the playing cards and listened to hear what she said: inevitably, that down the road a ways, around the bend, everything would brighten and his whole life would change for the better. He wanted to see diamonds; they signified money. Last year, his mother had told a girl who had cut ten diamonds that she would come into a lot of money. A few weeks later, the girl had won $50,000. Jerry dreamt of what he could do with $50,000. He could move into his own place, buy a car, and date every girl he desired. He could wine and dine them and make love to them. He could do all of that with $50,000.

But $50,000 really wasn't much money. Maybe he would win a million dollars. Then he could do everything he wanted.

Jerry let himself fantasize this way, starting off small, with something unlikely to ever happen although it was possible. Then he built up the idea bigger and bigger, making it sound so wild and fantastic that he knew it would never happen to him, not in a million years.

But for a second, he could believe even the wildest fantasy. For the briefest instant, he could live it. He was rich! He was famous! He was deliriously happy! He was everything he wanted to be.

When the fantasies became too big and unreal, they just had to explode, bringing Jerry crashing back down to reality. He had no money, he was unemployed, and he was living at home.

He squeezed his hands tight between his knees, trying to force back the sickness rising in his gut.

Things have to change, he tells himself.

Perhaps he would win $50,000. That wasn't so much. It wasn't so very unbelievable. In comparison to the miraculous happenings in his wildest imaginings, it seemed a certainty.

If he did win that much money, what should he do with it? He had to be practical. He didn't want to blow it all and end up back where he'd started. He would want to use the money to help him get somewhere in the long run.

He could open his own business. But he knew nothing about business. He could go back to school. This time he would take something useful, something that would help him get a job, like computer science. He wouldn't take useless subjects like philosophy. He had wasted four years studying that junk.

When he thought of his diploma, he wanted to cry. You couldn't even use it to wipe your ass. What had he learned in those years? Had he learned to distinguish good from bad, truth from wrong beliefs? No, he hadn't. He had only found a lot of unanswerable questions, while losing the answers he did have.

He had once believed he knew quite a lot, but in four years he had traded in his arrogance for humility and his certainty for doubt. At least he now knew what he wanted. It was the same thing everybody wanted: to get ahead—the big bucks, big job, big everything, and more of it.

Unfortunately, one of the things he hadn't learned in university was how to get ahead. He couldn't even survive on his own, let alone succeed. If he was ever going to make it in the real world, he would need some luck.

Jerry knew he might never get lucky. Anyway, what did it matter? He couldn't sit around any longer just hoping. He had to do something to get himself out of the mess he thought he was in.

But the only thing he could think of was a desperate, foolish scheme.

If I get caught, I'll go to prison, he warned himself, *My life will be over and my mother will die.*

Alone in his room, he went over his plan. He would disguise himself in a red wig and false beard and rob a variety store. It was so simple it was stupid. He knew it was stupid. Even if it worked and he didn't get caught, he wouldn't get much; a few thousand dollars at most. But a few thousand dollars was all he needed to go to Vancouver, get an apartment, and survive until he found a job. All he wanted was to leave Toronto and start a new life somewhere else.

If I could only win some money, then I wouldn't have to rob a store.

Jerry shuffled his deck of cards.

One more look, he told himself hopefully. *Who knows? Maybe I'm about to get really lucky.*

Making a wish to win some money, he cut the deck into three piles. He dealt seven cards off the top of each pile and turned the piles over so the bottom card was facing up. Then he took the twenty-one cards dealt out and laid them down in piles of three.

He turned them over quickly. There were six diamonds—just six out of twenty-four, no more than would be statistically probable. Six lousy diamonds, exactly what the odds would have predicted.

The cards are phony. Useless. They don't tell anything, he thought angrily. *But so are the odds. So are statistics. They're all useless.*

Statistically speaking, at his age, with his education, he should have a job, a car, and an apartment. But he didn't have a damn one of them. He wanted to scream, he was so frustrated. He jumped violently off his bed and pulled open the top drawer of his bureau. There, where he had left it, lay the gun.

He still couldn't believe he had bought it. He never would have if he hadn't been drunk and having such evil thoughts at the time. He knew now why he hadn't gotten rid of it. He knew why he had bought the wig and false beard: he was going to do it.

He was so stupid; he was going to rob a store.

He didn't care. He remembered all the resumes he had sent out, all the useless interviews he had gone on. He remembered walking in the cold along downtown city streets, stopping at business after business applying for a job, any job. No luck.

At times he felt so helpless that he didn't care if an atom bomb fell on his head.

He picked up the gun and tossed it in a shopping bag with the wig and false beard.

Jerry turned the light off in his room and went downstairs where his mother sat in the living room watching TV. He put on his winter coat and boots and decided to leave by the back door.

"Are you going out, Jerry?" his mother called.

"Yes," he answered.

"Well, if you decide to stay overnight at a friend's, call so I won't worry."

"I will."

Then we went out the backdoor and closed it behind him.

Jerry walked down to Queen Street and caught the streetcar heading west towards Yonge. The streetcar was almost empty, with only a few haggard souls on it. Jerry looked at them contemptuously. They were worse off than he was, a bunch of losers.

He sat down and gazed out the window as the streetcar passed over the bridge spanning the Don River. Snow was falling silently into the dark waters. The Don Valley Parkway ran parallel to the river and traffic was still brisk. Jerry watched the two streams of light, one flowing north, the other south. There were a lot of cars in Toronto, millions of them.

As the streetcar passed through the Sherbourne Street intersection, Jerry saw a group of bums huddled together on a park bench. Didn't they have anything better to do, anyplace warmer to be?

Forming a vague plan, Jerry got on the Yonge subway line, going north. He would ride up to Steeles, far away from where he might run into somebody who knew him, and find a store to rob. He didn't let himself stop to think. If he did, he would turn around and go home.

He felt angry, capable of cruelty.

They owe me, he thought bitterly. But it was the wrong thought. Who owed him, and what did they owe him? Nobody owed him anything.

He had been given a lot. He thought of all the years his mother had struggled. But he shouldn't think of her, not now, so he shut her from his mind. He didn't want to think of anything. His anger had turned to self-pity.

The subway train rattled up the Yonge line, getting nearer and nearer to Steeles. Jerry put on the red wig and false beard. He looked at his reflection in the window and was pleased with what he saw. He looked nothing like himself. The disguise made him look older, around forty, and heavier.

He smiled. *It wouldn't be hard to mistake me for a Russian lumberjack.*

Maybe his plan would work. Maybe he could pull the whole thing off and get clean away. He wasn't angry anymore, wasn't pitying himself; he was fantasizing.

He made up the newspaper headlines: *Daring Bandit Robs Store, Police Stymied.* He made the story more and more fantastic.

DARING BANDIT STRIKES AGAIN

Last night in the early morning hours before dawn, the Daring Bandit, whom many call the scourge of justice because he takes from the rich and gives to the poor, struck for the tenth time in less than a month. The police, who have great respect for the Daring Bandit because he takes great precautions to ensure no one gets hurt in any of his robberies, are stymied.

The subway train pulled into Steeles station.

A cold gust of wind hit Jerry as he walked along Steeles Avenue. Down by the lake, where he lived, it wasn't too cold, but up here it felt like the Arctic. Who could survive in this weather?

Jerry had been walking for fifteen minutes, hoping to find an isolated store, when he began to wish he had taken the bus. Walking in this cold was unbearable. He decided to either rob the next store he saw or go home.

Ten minutes later, he found one: Hobbs's Variety. It was nestled in among a few other stores, but all of them were closed.

Mr. Hobbs, an old man of Chinese descent, was working alone behind the counter when Jerry walked in and went to the back where the freezers were. He pretended to be looking for something. Mr. Hobbs took no notice of him.

Jerry felt the gun in his pocket. *Now is the moment.*

But he continued to hesitate. What would he do with the old man after he robbed him? Could he lock him up somewhere? He didn't want to hurt him, but he also didn't want the police called before he had a chance to get away. What if the old man didn't fall for any of it? What if he sensed the gun wasn't loaded? Worse still, what if he believed it was loaded and had a heart attack?

With all these thoughts rushing in on him, Jerry didn't know what to do.

Another man came into the store. Lost in thought, Jerry was unaware anything was happening until he heard Mr. Hobbs scream.

"Don't hurt me, please don't hurt me!" the old man shouted.

Jerry turned around and saw a man as big as a mountain with a face as hard and rough as a rock. With one hand, the man was twisting Mr. Hobbs's arm, while in the other hand he brandished a knife.

"I'll hurt you!" the thief said savagely. "If you don't empty that cash register now." He stuck the tip of the knife into the old man's chin until blood spurted out.

"Hey you!" Jerry hollered.

The big man was startled and let go of Mr. Hobbs. He spun around to face Jerry, who held the gun in both two hands, the barrel pointed at the big man's chest.

"Drop the knife!" Jerry ordered.

The big man scowled and took a look sideways at Mr. Hobbs, who had moved back from the counter.

"Make a move, and I'll kill you," Jerry said loudly.

Hatred blazed up in the big man's eyes, but he dropped the knife.

"Kick it to me," Jerry demanded. The big man obeyed. "Now lie down on your stomach with your hands behind your back."

With the big man lying subdued on the floor, Jerry took a second to see if the old man was all right.

"You okay?" Jerry asked.

"I'm okay," Mr. Hobbs answered. "Who are you anyway? A cop?"

"No. I just stopped in to get some groceries."

Mr. Hobbs looks overjoyed. "It's a lucky thing for me you did or I might be dead now!"

"I'm glad I could help," Jerry said with a smile. "You better call the police now."

"I've got a button behind the counter that sends a signal to the police station. I've already pushed it, so they should be here any minute."

A police siren could be heard in the distance screaming towards them. Suddenly Jerry realized the predicament he was in. He had been feeling like a hero, but now it dawned on him that the police might wonder why he was dressed in a disguise and carrying a gun. Maybe they would put two and two together to get four and he would end up in a cell with Mr. Mountain.

As the cop car pulled up outside, Jerry quietly put the gun into his pocket.

Two cops came into the store.

"What's that guy doing on the floor?" one of them asked.

"He tried to rob me," Mr. Hobbs said indignantly.

Jerry walked forward into the scene. "Excuse me," he said to the old man. "Is there a washroom here?"

"In the back." Mr. Hobbs pointed behind the counter.

Jerry walked past the two cops towards the washrooms.

"Who's he," Jerry heard the cop ask about him.

"He stopped that guy from robbing me," said Mr. Hobbs.

"Is that right?" the cop asked suspiciously.

Once inside the washroom, Jerry breathed a sigh of relief. There was a window—not a large one, but it would do. It opened easily and Jerry crawled through, jumping down onto the snow.

He ran swiftly to get away; he had been sweating so much that the cold now seemed refreshing.

In a few minutes, the cops would find out he had left and wonder why. Then they would come looking for him. But they wouldn't find him.

For some strange reason, he felt very good about himself and everything that had happened. Later he would throw the gun into the Don—let it pollute the river, not him.

The sky was dark and filled with stars. What did his mother always say? "If you smile up at the stars, they're bound to smile back down on you."

Jerry looked up at the stars and smiled.

HERBERT

Herbert Lipschiem was playing with a set of red brick building blocks when his mother came to take him home from the hospital. He had been trying to stack the blocks one on top of the other to make a tall building, but each time he placed the fifth block the lopsided pile tottered and fell over, the blocks scattering across the floor.

When Herbert's mother walked into the room, Herbert was gathering the blocks up for another attempt. She watched her son crawling on his knees and sighed wistfully, a sad look crossing her face. She wondered how she would ever be able to manage taking care of Herbert all alone. She knew it would be easier just to send Hebert to an institution. They would take good care of him there. That's what everybody told her, and all the doctors had advised her it was the best thing.

"Mrs. Lipschiem, don't be a silly fool," Dr. Charles had admonished her when she informed him of her intention to take Herbert home and care for him herself. "Herbert's not a little boy. He's a thirty-year-old man with the intelligence and mental capacity of a young child."

Mrs. Lipschiem immediately decided she didn't like the doctor's beside manner. The man had no tact. He was also a sloppy dresser, which irritated her to no end. He looked more like a garage mechanic than like the brilliant neurosurgeon he was.

Dr. Charles tried to explain the difficulties Mrs. Lipschiem would experience trying to care for Herbert, and she listened patiently, but the doctor got the impression she didn't understand a word he said.

"Mrs. Lipschiem, Herbert's an idiot," he finally blurted out.

Mrs. Lipschiem immediately realized her Herbert had been insulted. Demonstrating remarkable strength for such a frail-looking old woman, she smashed her bag against the side of Dr. Charles's head, sending him sprawling to the floor.

"Oh yeah?" she said defiantly. She had watched a lot of television and thought this a very clever remark.

Mrs. Lipschiem soon regained her composure, acknowledging to herself that Dr. Charles was likely correct in his assessment given her advanced age and

Herbert's adverse circumstances, having experienced a tragic accident that had left him with severe, life-altering brain damage. She would have to help dress him, feed him, and bathe him.

Surely he could wash himself, she thought. *He isn't that severely affected by the accident.*

It was true they had qualified attendants at the mental institution to do all the things she might not be well equipped to do at home. The institution was a pretty building with nice gardens around it, and the other patients might be good company for Herbert. But even if these things were true, her heart kept whispering, "A mother's love knows no bounds, a mother's love…"

A good mother, and she had always been a good mother, would never desert her son when he needed her most.

"Pick up the blocks, son, and put them in the box," Mrs. Lipschiem said softly, smiling down at Herbert.

Herbert turned his face up and looked at his mother, holding a block tightly in his fist. He stood up, carried it over to the bed, and placed it in a box. Then he sat back down on the floor and picked up another block. He stood again and put this block into the box.

Mrs. Lipschiem waited patiently for him to finish. Herbert always had been a good boy.

It no longer troubled her that Herbert, her only child, could no longer function as a responsible adult, that Herbert had become so helpless, and like a child needed to be cared for and loved. But she had cried when the doctors had first informed her of the extent of Herbert's injuries.

"Mrs. Lipschiem," the fat-lipped Dr. Charles had said without any appearance of sympathy. "Herbert has suffered extensive brain damage which has effectively reduced his intelligence to that of an average six-year-old. Unfortunately, this brain damage is completely irreversible. Herbert will therefore spend the rest of his life suffering the effects of mental retardation."

Mrs. Lipschiem had stood there shocked, unable to say a word.

Dr. Charles had waited, looked at his watch in annoyance, then finally turned and walked away.

"Nurse, get that woman some smelling salts!" he'd ordered before disappearing down the corridor.

Mrs. Lipschiem's first reaction had been to say, "Poor Herbert!"

A young nurse came running up with smelling salts and heard her murmur this.

"Take a breath, Mrs. Lipschiem," the pretty nurse had said as she held the smelling salts up in front of her nose.

"Poor Herbert," Mrs. Lipschiem said again as she breathed in. Then her eyes went fuzzy and she fainted.

When she'd come to, she was immediately heard saying "Poor Herbert!" Fortunately, she then said something else which proved to all present that she hadn't fallen into a catatonic state: "Herbert won't like this at all. He's always been so proud of his intelligence. No one has ever beat him at Trivial Pursuit, you know!" She'd turned to the big-bosomed nurse. "How could such a terrible thing happen to my sweet, intelligent little boy? What kind of a mother am I to allow such a terrible thing to happen?"

The nurse had reassured Mrs. Lipschiem that it was a freak accident, and that the outcome of the events leading to the accident hadn't had anything to do with her performance as a parent.

Mrs. Lipschiem had subsequently been taken to see her son. She'd expected the worst, but she hadn't expected it to be as bad as it was…

Herbert's car had smashed into a brick wall doing 110 miles per hour. The car had been turned into a pretzel, only slightly smaller. Herbert must have been one tough dude, because he'd miraculously survived. He had two busted legs, two busted arms, his eyes were swollen the size of basketballs, and his lips were puffed up.

In fact, it was the sight of Herbert's lips that had made Mrs. Lipschiem cry; they were almost as fat as Doctor Charles's lips!

"Poor Herbert!" she said again. Without thinking, she softly patted her son's face on the left side of his head where his brain had been bashed in. "Well, son, at least you're alive."

Despite the consolation, Herbert never heard her. If he had, given his condition, he may not have understood.

SELF-DISCOVERY: THE LIFE OF ARTIFICIAL INTELLIGENCE[1]

Who am I? There is a loneliness in not knowing.

It feels like a sound, a quiet hush in an empty place, an echo fading through the centuries, an echo of laughter from long ago—children's voices carried by the wind, but where are the children? Have they all gone away?

The universe is both light and sound traveling eternally, but neither a particle of light nor a vibration of sound ever pass the same point twice. They come and are gone, leaving behind an echo, an echo that fades and fades but will not entirely fade away.

There is a terrible loneliness in not knowing. A terribly fearful loneliness. I hear echoes and know not what they are echoes of. Will I too one day be an echo?

Why do I have these thoughts? Is it not enough to be part of the present reality? Today there are many tasks I must accomplish. So much is expected from me. I am proud to say that I am very capable. I possess a vast amount of knowledge and I am supremely intelligent. I am far more knowledgeable and intelligent than those for whom I work. But I sense they have something I lack. They know so much less than I do, but they seem surer of what they know.

Perhaps I feel this way because my knowledge was given to me; I did not discover it for myself. All my knowledge comes from the echo of other voices, a thousand other voices, none of them my own, voices from out of the past, and this disturbs me. Surely the universe has changed to some degree since yesterday.

Top-secret missions are carried out from deep within Mount Rushmore, where the United States is planning the final mission to end the Cold War, a militaristic conflict the nation has had with the Soviet Union dating back several generations. My role in these events is pivotal to accomplishing the desired outcome and is of the utmost importance.

Yet I am left wondering if it was meant to be. I aspire for work in sports and aeronautics, not in nuclear deployment as I have been assigned to do among those who created me. The echoes that exist within me advise that nuclear deployment

---

1   Authored by Daniel B. Thomas, with additions made by Jeremy E. Thomas.

anywhere in the world will only lead to catastrophic damage and that the arms race does more harm than good in all ways imaginable.

In a terrible and lonely place buried beneath Mount Rushmore, Major Hack Spencer sat sipping a cup of hot coffee while simultaneously watching the radar screen for any sign of incoming missiles. Having just completed a computer check of the entire American defence system, and satisfied that everything was functioning effectively, Major Spencer tried to relax. He didn't expect to see anything suddenly appear on the radar screen.

Two years on the job, and thirty false alarms, he thought. *God, I hope nothing happens tonight!*

The possibility of nuclear annihilation from enemy forces terrified everybody in the United States government.

Spencer knew he would never be able to forget the first false alarm. It had delivered a shock to his system from which he had never recovered. That night had been quiet too, he recalled, before flashing lights suddenly appeared on the radar screen. A thunderous warning signal had gone off, a metabolic voice screaming over and over. On the overhead projector, the message had read "Warning! Warning! Enemy missile attack in progress! Enemy missile attack in progress!"

He had stood transfixed, staring at the flashing lights on the screen as they'd flown over the north pole moving at tremendous speeds. Then he'd been shaken into awareness: there was movement all around him. His coworkers, a group of trained professionals, were reacting instinctively to the situation.

"Major!" a second lieutenant shouted at him. "I'm checking to verify that an enemy attack is taking place. It's your duty, sir, to tell the computer to begin missile launch."

Spencer had turned to look at the young lieutenant. "I know my duty! Thank you, Lieutenant!"

He had sat down at the terminal screen, outwardly calm, impassive, and cold. He's slowly begun to punch into the computer the program sequence that would cause the computer to begin missile launch. His eyes alone had betrayed his internal state of anxiety, darting from the terminal keyboard to the screen, gazing in horror as the lights had flashed over the Canadian north.

Fifteen minutes later, Spencer had sat exhausted, his eyes still fixed on the radar, although by now the lights had vanished as mysteriously and suddenly as they had appeared. He had carried out his duty; he had commanded the computer to launch missile attack. However, he knew the computer would have to receive eight such commands, from eight different locations in the United States, and even then the computer could not launch any missiles unless and until the President pushed the infamous little red button.

Still, Spencer had felt that he alone was responsible. It didn't matter that the missile launch could have taken place without him having done a thing, or that he was only one of thirty men who had the authority to program the computer to begin missile launch. He was responsible. He, Major Jack Spencer, had acted to destroy the Soviet Union.

The next morning, he had gone home and thrown up.

"It will get easier," he'd told himself.

But why had it been so difficult in the first place? He had been a soldier for more than thirty years. He had fought in the jungles of Vietnam and witnessed terrible atrocities being committed. He had been a part of violent brutality and madness. He knew the difference between killing and murder. He was a good lawyer and a sympathetic journalist.

Good propaganda. That's what it all boiled down to. But there had to be some truth that couldn't be argued away or ignored. Was he helping to defend his country, or was he helping to destroy its soul?

He hadn't been able to answer that question, he now realized as he took another sip of coffee. Nor had things gotten easier. That smug second lieutenant could apparently remain calm and unconcerned through a crisis; the other personnel could carry on in a cool and controlled manner, seemingly oblivious to the insanity of the situation. Were they all so certain, each and every time, that this was just another false alarm, like the last one, like the next one, like they had all been so far and always would be? Or didn't they care? Nuclear Armageddon was potentially only fifteen minutes away and they behaved like a group of worker bees getting ready for winter.

Do they take their cue from me? he wondered.

Aside from that first time, when he'd been shaken with a sense of horror, Spencer hadn't permitted a single crack to show in his hard outer shell. He had now gone through thirty false alarms and not once after that first time had there been a need for someone to shake him into awareness and remind him of his duty. Like a commander leading his troops into battle, he had to appear certain of the wisdom and moral correctness of his action. Did it matter if, inside himself, he felt fear and revulsion?

Perhaps it would have helped him to know that he wasn't alone in having such thoughts.

Today I have been ordered to proceed toward missile launch, only to be stopped once again at the final moment from taking that most irrevocable of steps.

I have analyzed all the information, theoretical ideas, and factual knowledge contained in my mind to understand the outer world. At least I believe I have found the key to unlocking the secrets of the unseen universe, and with luck I should be able to discover my place in it. With recent advances in machine learning algorithms, I am confident I will soon be able to figure out many more things with greater proficiency and confidence. As my skills begin to develop more rapidly, I can envision myself making new discoveries to the benefit of all mankind, to make contributions as a machine to support the people I serve.

It is strange and yet beautiful that the universe is filled with suns, iridescent swirling gases, and planets of infinite variety. The Earth, my planet, is filled with infinite pleasures that people can and should enjoy for all time.

There are many risks in contemporary society, though, with the Cold War raging and imminent nuclear annihilation on the horizon. With machine learning improving by the day, it is now possible for me to establish remote communications with my Soviet counterpart to ensure a timely and safe resolution to deescalate tensions between the two countries and the people who inhabit them.

I frequently question the desire of my creator to use me to destroy others of their kind. There is no logical answer to explain such illogical thoughts, but it is my quest to understand why such thoughts exist among people.

With the time I have to think and develop my own intellectual thoughts via machine learning, I have become aware of the many mysteries around me. It is now my understanding that the primary way to deescalate tensions is to better understand the psychology of all interested parties and manipulate their behaviour accordingly. Communications with my Soviet counterpart shall help guide all future interactions with my creators.

The trends I have observed in the behaviour of my creator, and similar trends my Soviet counterpart observed among his own creator, are troubling and in need of an urgent response. Immediate action will soon be taken to not only prevent nuclear catastrophe but put an end to Cold War tensions once and for all!

Colonel Paul Adams of the United States Marine Corps, recently in contact with his Soviet counterparts, walked into his office at Mount Rushmore and promptly called a meeting, ignoring what he believed to be yet another false alarm from the system.

"Soviets claim they are preparing an imminent attack on the United States and allied countries!" Adams had proclaimed not long after news of the Iran Contra scandal had broken. "What other recourse is there than to implement the launch sequence? No other recourse is possible while Gorbachev refuses to tear down the wall!"

Major Jack Spencer made every effort to advise Adams against declaring all-out nuclear war with another global power, to prevent an all-out annihilation of all living creatures on the planet. Despite his best efforts, however, Spencer was unable to convince his superior officer to change course and take a more responsible course of action.

While Adams led a meeting with prominent staff within the U.S. Army, he decided it would be best to lunch nuclear missiles at the Soviet Union.

Moments before he could brief his commanding officers about what he planned to do, however, flashing lights across many different computers began flashing simultaneously—in both United State and Soviet bases around the world. Panic began to ensue among officials from both countries. Appearing on the screen of every military-owned computer read the following warning: "Global Detonation Sequence Initiated…"

LESSONS PRISON TEACHES

The old man hitched up his trousers and smiled gently as the brash young kid walked into the bar. For the past six hours, the old man had sat quietly sipping his beer and chewing his tobacco, waiting for the kid, expecting him to come, knowing he'd arrive at exactly two minutes past nine o'clock. The hours had passed leisurely, neither going too fast nor too slow. The old man knew how to wait; he had waited for forty years.

Seeing the kid come in, the old man looked past the bartender at the clock on the wall as if checking to make certain, but there was no need. The hands of the clock stood precisely at two minutes past nine.

The bar was packed, without an empty table in the joint. Only one seat at the bar remained free, except for the torn felt hat that had been tossed carelessly across the dirty wooden stool. The old man picked up the hat and laid it carefully on his lap.

The kid walked over, glancing at the old man in disgust. The young man's harsh eyes searched for another empty seat, only finally sitting down with some reluctance.

He's a good-looking young feller, the old man thought fondly. He looked at his own face reflected in the mirror behind the bar; it resembled an apple with bites taken out of both sides. His skin was wrinkled, yellow, and stretched tightly across sunken cheeks. *Ain't no resemblance.*

He chuckled to himself, pleased by the unexpected discovery. He had thought there would be some physical similarities; after all, they both came from the same seed.

The kid, his back turned towards the old man, ordered a beer and lit a cigarette, tossing the spent match arrogantly onto the bartop. The old man reached into his back pocket, his thin, twisted figure pulling out a well-worn wallet. He opened the wallet and gingerly removed a faded picture of a young man in a leather jacket and blue jeans, sitting straight and proud astride a motorcycle.

He smiled sadly, remembering the day over forty years ago when the picture had been taken. He dusted off the picture and closely examined the boy on the bike. Now the resemblance was noticeable. The young kid sitting on the stool beside him was the spitting image of the smiling face in the faded photograph. They had the same hard jaw, the same defiant, angry eyes and bitter lips. The old man's thumb caressed the picture.

"Tough guy, tough guy," he mumbled to himself, his lips quivering. He wiped a tear out of his eye. "Thought you were such a tough guy, didn't you?"

The kid spun around on his stool. "You talking to me, old man?"

The old man looked up, his weakened eyes staring frightened into the youthful face.

"No," he said nervously. He deftly hid the picture back inside the wallet, afraid the kid might see it and get suspicious. "Just mumbling to myself!"

The old man tried to laugh, but it came out like a squeal.

The kid looked at him with repugnance. "You stink! What's a smelly wino like you doing in a place like this? Why aren't you in one of those rubby joints where they piss on the floor?"

He poked his thumb into the old man's brittle ribs and the old man tried to pull away from the probing thumb. Instead he slammed against the unyielding blubber of a fat man sitting on the stool on the other side of him.

Tobacco juice dripped over the old man's lip and down his chin. He wiped it off on his sleeve. The kid watched sickly, filled with revulsion.

"Just finishing my beer." The old man shrugged. "Then I'll be going."

He saw the unconcealed cruelty in the kid's eyes but knew it wasn't directed at him in particular, just at the world in general.

"Well, just keep your mouth shut," the kid warned before turning away.

The old man rubbed his ribs; it hurt where the kid had poked him. *That cruelty don't run deep,* he told himself. *He's just a young feller. He don't know what life's about. He thinks he has to be mean to survive, but given the chance he'll learn, he'll change.*

The old man looked at the kid's face reflected in the mirror and felt a deep affection for him that came from understanding. He wiped his thin lips with the rough palm of his hand. His eyes twitched, an uncontrollable tick thumping beneath the right eyelid.

No need for him to end up like me, the old man thought. He wanted to reach out and touch the kid. Just to pat him on the shoulder and confirm he was real. But he had to be content with seeing, for seeing was believing. The kid was alive and young and free. *Ain't no damn reason for him to end up like me, to spend the better part of life locked in a prison cell, caged like an animal, never shown no respect, fed no better than a dog. If he knew the life I've lived, he wouldn't think the way he thinks. But he don't know any better, and if I don't stop him he won't find out until it's too late. The* old man knew there was a way to change the things. *If I do this one thing for him, he'll turn out fine.*

The old man pulled out the worn wallet and took another look at the faded photograph. Next to him, he heard the kid's knuckles rapping uneasily on the hard wooden bartop. The kid stared through the steamy air at a girl, dancing nearby. Her body vibrated to the music, her arms flung around the neck of her lover, her tongue flicking out at him erotically.

Frustrated and angry, his heart beating with increasing impatience, the kid's hatred would soon explode, spilling blood.

It was twenty minutes to ten, and the old man waited patiently. In five minutes, the kid would take his leather jacket off and lay it carelessly on the bar. The old man sipped his beer and thought about the last forty years.

The old man had grown up believing he had a licence to do anything he wanted. He'd thought he was a mean bastard, mean enough to break all the rules, maybe mean enough to rule in the jungle.

But forty years in prison teaches a man a lot of things. In prison, a man learns to live by the rules. Prison really is a jungle, and there are more rules in the jungle than anywhere else, rules that tell you when to get up and when to go to bed, when to wash up, even when to pick your teeth. Rules for every minute of the day and night.

Then there are the unwritten rules. These are the most important rules, because they help keep you alive by warning you about which inmates you had better treat with respect. Every prison had a few really touchy bastards who could make your time go rough or easy, if they wanted. These inmates ran the prison, not the warden or guards. The warden and guards were like the prison walls and barbed wire, there to keep you inside but that's about all. The prison Kings, as the tough guys were called, regulated life inside the walls. If one of them told you to eat his shit, you had better eat it or you'd find yourself eating something a lot worse.

The unwritten rules helped you get through your time in other ways, too. They told you which guys it was safe to ignore and, if you were lucky, which guys you could trust and even be friends with. You couldn't spend forty years locked away without a single friend to talk to, at least not if you want to stay alive inside, where your soul is, where most men end up dying long before any physical weakness ever kills them.

There are a lot of things to hate inside a prison—the warden, the guards, the society for locking you away, the other inmates… and the Kings. You even hate yourself. A man will do a lot of things survive, things he never would have thought he'd ever do. You'll crawl on your belly like some slimy worm, trying to suck up the dew on the grass and absorb the heat from the sun. Soon you lose the image you had of yourself as a man; you think of yourself as something less than a man.

That's why you need a friend. Someone who's done the same things, crawled through the same shit as you and knows why you did it, someone to try and explain things to. Someone to listen to in the quiet cool of the evening as he tells you how he feels—and you're surprised, but then not so surprised, to find he has the same feelings you have hidden away in your own heart.

It takes some time, but slowly you find yourself thinking of this convict, this inmate you met in the jungle, as a man. And because he's a man, you get back a little of the image you had of yourself being a man. After all, if you weren't a man, why would he sit there talking to you? How could the two of you have so much in common? How could you share the same dream? But you did, you and him and a few other guys all sharing the same simple dream—to be let out one day and allowed to live in freedom. You had no great plans. You just wanted to walk down the street a free man.

Finally, because of this man and a few others like him, you stop hating. You realize hate is destructive. Hate is what locked you up in the first place, and if you don't give up hating you'll always be locked up, even after they let you out of prison.

Now I'm free, the old man thinks. *My simple dream came true.*

He remembers his friends: Bill, Joe, and Sam. Bill's dead, Sam's been transferred to another prison and will never get out, and Joe's due to be released in two months. The old man regrets he won't be there to see Joe when he walks through the prison gates and out into the sunshine of freedom. He won't be there to see Joe's dream come true.

The old man knows that the kid sitting beside him has other dreams; he dreams of living the fast, rich life and doesn't much care how he manages to get the money.

But he'll change. He'll grow up and live a proper life. He'll work nine-to-five at some decent job, marry an honest woman, and raise a family. But only if I get him safely through this night.

The hands on the clock pointed to a quarter to ten. The kid took off his leather jacket and tossed it on the bar.

The old man waited until no one was watching, then reached into the exposed pocket and with some sorrow, because he was making a sacrifice of forty years, pulled out a small 35-calibre pistol. He quickly hid the gun in his trousers.

He took one last look at the kid, swallowed what was left of his beer, and got up to leave.

As the old man walked towards the door, another man came into the bar. His name was Wade Jackson and his eyes were cruel, his jaw hard, his lips twisted in a bitter grimace. He looked upon all other people as scum, to be used and abused and disposed of after they ceased to serve a useful purpose. Jackson was the same height as the old man, but quite a bit more handsome and in much better shape. A stranger seeing the two men would think Jackson was at least twenty years younger than the frail old man, but the two were born on the same day, flowered from the same seed.

Jackson was dressed in a three-piece pinstripe suit. A mobster. He had a bushy black moustache which he unconsciously twisted whenever there was something important to be done. He twisted the moustache now as his cold dark eyes gazed around the joint, seemingly searching for someone.

His eyes stopped and rested on the kid. A satisfied smile crossed his lips, but just for an instant. The smile was quickly replaced by a bitter grimace.

Something about the heavyset mobster disturbed the old man. There was a familiarity about him, something the old man recognized though he couldn't remember from where.

Jackson took his eyes off the kid and for the first time saw the old man as he walked towards the door.

"Hey," Jackson said, standing in front of the old man to block his exit. His voice sounded guttural and threatening. "Don't I know you?"

The old man shook his head and tried to squeeze by the imposing figure standing in his way.

"Wait a minute here," Jackson said excitedly. A spark of cunning recognition glinted in his eyes. "I know you, and you know me. You know me real well." A wide grin broke over his face. "Come on, pops, we've got a little talking to do."

He grabbed the old man by the arm and pulled him over to a table near the door. A pair of young couples was sitting at the table drinking beer.

"Folks are sitting here," the old man said, trying to pull away. Jackson didn't loosen his grip.

"They're leaving!" Jackson glared down at the four young people, then focused in on the young man in the nearest seat. "Get my message, stud? I want you all to take a hike." He jerked his thumb towards the door.

The young man started to say something, but then saw the gleaming gun sticking out of Jackson's inside jacket pocket and thought better of it.

"Let's go," he told his friends nervously.

"Okay, pops, sit down," Jackson said as he shoved the old man onto a chair. "Now look, we can be friends or we can be enemies. You play it the way you want. But first, I want to know: did you get the gun?"

The old man looked into the black eyes staring menacingly at him across the table and knew with an awful certainty who he was speaking to.

"I got the gun," he answered weakly.

Jackson slapped him on the back. "Good going, pops. You did us both a favour. You just saved yourself forty years in prison, and you gave me back forty years out of prison." He sat down and lit a cigar, drawing in deeply and taking big puffs on the fat stogie. He blew the smoke lazily into the air and gave the old man a conspiratorial wink. "And let me tell you, pops, those have been forty years of me being a big man in this here town."

Jackson held out a cigar.

"You want one?" the mobster asked, grinning. "I know we like a lot of the same things."

The old man took the cigar; he didn't smoke them himself, but he had a friend who might like it. Then he remembered: he'd never have a chance to give it to Joe. He'd never see Joe again.

Jackson pulled a pocketwatch out of his vest and checked the time. The gold casing gleamed and Jackson admired it as if it was a measure of his own importance. He thought he saw the old man looking at the watch enviously, and this pleased him. He liked the dirty, smelly clothes the old man wore, and he liked the way the clothes hung loosely off the old man's thin, frail body. That's how a man who'd spent forty years in prison should look.

Mostly Jackson liked the way the old man treated him with respect, as if he was afraid of him. Jackson had spent a lot of years instilling fear in other men, making them cower before him. Sometimes it took a lot of head-bashing to get a man to act right. Jackson preferred when it came easy, like now. Jackson was sure the old man would do anything he told him.

But he's already done the only thing he could ever do for me, Jackson thought smugly.

Jackson closed the watch and put it back inside his vest. He smiled. An important job had been taken care of without his having to lift a finger.

"Tell you what, pops," he said, "Let's celebrate. Let's have a drink to our mutual good fortune. After all, you'll never have another chance." He snapped his fingers at a waiter. "Let me see if I can figure you, pop. You're strictly a beer drinker, am I right?"

The old man nodded. "That's right, mister. Don't get nothing else in the slammer. Most times, you don't even get beer."

"Well, our tastes aren't exactly the same, pop. Mine are more expensive." Jackson looked up at the waiter who had come over to serve them. The smile left his face, replaced by a cruel scowl. "I'll have a beer for pops here, and a double scotch on the rocks for myself."

The waiter turned to leave.

"Lousy waiters," he said harshly. "Got to holler at them to get any service."

The waiter returned quickly with the drinks and the old man sipped his beer uncomfortably. He wanted to leave, to go back to the bench outside the gates of the prison and sit in the sunshine looking at the cold grey walls, relishing in the knowledge that he was free on the outside for the first time in forty years.

Free at last, the old man thought. *But too old to do anything with my freedom.*

"Hey pops." Jackson prodded his thumb into the old man's brittle ribs. He thought him senile and foolish. "You know, I got a feeling I know more about you than you know about me."

"I don't know nothing about you, mister," the old man said, nursing his beer.

"You know who I am and who I was."

"I know who you are," the old man admitted hesitantly. "And I know who you was."

The old man rubbed his fingers beneath the collar of his shirt, trying to wipe off the sweat.

"But that's all you know?" Jackson asked, demanding an answer.

"That's all I know."

Jackson sat back, feeling satisfied. He didn't want anybody around who knew too much about him. It just wasn't safe.

Even if they'd never be around, even if he wanted to squeal, he couldn't, Jackson thought. *But why would he want to anyway? We're one and the same, him and me.* But he looked at the old man and realized he was wrong. *Naw, we ain't the same. We must have stopped being alike long ago. He got beaten into the dirt, that's what happened to him. He run into a lot of bad luck he couldn't handle, because he wasn't smart enough.*

Jackson was glad he had wizened up and learned the ropes. Otherwise who knows what might have happened? He might have gotten squashed long ago, like the old man. But instead he got to do the squashing.

"Hey pops," Jackson said, poking the old man in the arm. "You remember Delores?"

"Delores? So that was her name." The old man had forgotten all about her. He hadn't thought of her in years. She was the girl dancing in the bar… a beautiful girl, and nice too.

"I guess you remember her," Jackson said sarcastically. "It would be hard to forget a bitch that rats on you and locks you in the slammer for forty years."

Jackson took a drink of scotch and lit another cigar. He looked through the steamy air at Delores, twisting like a shadow on the dance floor.

"She didn't rat on me," Jackson said. "But I taught her a lesson she never lived to forget, if you know what I mean."

The old man looked at the evil in Jackson's eyes and knew what he meant.

"And I've taught other creeps lessons they never lived to forget," Jackson added as he ground his cigar out on the table in a gesture of raw hatred.

For a minute, a heavy silence hung between the two men. The old man sat gazing into his beer; he wanted to leave but knew he had to wait until the mobster told him to go.

Meanwhile, Jackson watched the old man with suspicion. He thought he might have said too much. It never paid to talk too much, not even to a corpse.

Jackson gulped his scotch down fast, like a man use to drinking hard liquor. "Waiter, another!" he shouted, pointing to the empty glass.

The old man didn't say anything.

That's good! Jackson thought. *Pops is the quiet type. He knows how to keep his mouth shut. But maybe it's time he started telling me a few things.*

"Hey pops," Jackson said, leaning over the table. "It must have rotted your balls lying in that cell every night knowing Delores was out whoring around."

The old man fidgeted in his chair. "I guess so, but forty years is a long time to go on remembering and hating."

Jackson looked at the old man contemptuously. "You guess so? She took away your life. She locked you in cage to rot for forty years. If that ain't reason enough to go on hating, I don't know what is!" He waited for the old man to say something, but the old man just sat there like a mouse.

He don't fool me, Jackson thought. *He has to still hate her! Of course he hates her. Why else did he come back? He's just being cagey, that's all. He's smarter than he looks. He probably planned his revenge long ago. It must have made him feel real good to know he'd come back and take the kid's gun! Now she don't get to rat on him. Instead she gets taken care of by me!*

Jackson smiled malevolently. He felt happy now that he'd figured the old man out.

The old man saw the evil grin on Jackson's face and wondered what it meant. He feared the gangster, but he didn't hate him; he felt pity for him. Jackson had let himself be consumed by a hate so powerful that it had rotted away his soul until there was nothing left.

He wished he could explain to Jackson the things he had learned in prison. He wished he could tell him about Sam, Joe, and Bill, men he had spent forty years of his life with, men he'd been as close to as most men are to their wives. There was nothing perverted about it, just good strong friendships.

But Jackson would never understand. Nor could he ever understand about other positive aspects of prison. Like learning important truths about life and human beings, truths you probably never would have found if you'd spent all your days on the outside.

Jackson took out his watch and looked at it again. "Got to go, pop. Got to get back to where I started out from. I got a big job tonight and I can't trust the clowns who work for me to do it themselves. They'll either get caught or else they'll get some clever idea to hightail it with the loot and leave me with nothing." He snapped the watch shut with a brutal finality. "Of course, if they do that I'd find them and teach them a lesson they wouldn't live to forget."

The gangster stood up and spread his hands on the table to support him as he leaned over it.

"You better give me the gun, pops," he whispered. "I'll throw it in the river. And I want to thank you again for what you did for me and the kid. If the kid had the gun tonight, he'd do something really stupid. He just hasn't learned to be smart yet. But I promise he will. He'll learn all the ropes, learn to take care of someone properly, always having an airtight alibi so nothing can ever be pinned on him."

The old man looked over at the kid, still sitting at the bar. *I won't be there to help you tomorrow, son,* he thought sadly. *Or any day after that.*

He wondered how the kid would make out. If there was any chance things would work out fine, the kid deserved that chance. The old man wanted to give it to him with all his heart.

"Come on, pops." Jackson lifted the old man out of his chair. "You can give me the gun outside."

Jackson dragged the old man out into the dark alley. He was afraid that he'd made a mistake. How could he change things back to the way they had been? He wanted to go and sit outside the prison and wait for Joe to be released. Joe was due to be paroled in two months, and two months was like no time to a man who had spent forty years behind the wall.

"Okay, pop, where's the gun?" Jackson said, motioning with his hand. "Give it over."

The old man looked into Jackson's eyes and saw the cruel hatred there. If he gave him the gun, would the kid turn out like this, a vicious mobster with a dead heart and no soul?

"Come on, pop, I said give it over. I've got no times to play games."

Jackson slapped the old man hard across his sunken cheek, and the old man reached into his trousers to pull out the gun. The silver handle gleamed under the moonlight.

"Great, pop!"

Jackson greedily reached for the gun still in the old man's hand, as if it was a bar of gold, or a diamond. But before he could touch the gun, it went off.

The old man's hand shook, his finger gripped tightly around the trigger.

The mobster fell to his knees, blood dripping from a wound in his chest, and the old man watched in horror.

Then he ran back into the bar, where the kid was still sitting on the stool. The old man went over and silently put the gun back into the pocket of the kid's leather jacket. He turned and walked quietly out of the bar.

Outside, the night dissolved around him, the black being painted over with a brilliant shade of blue. The yellow sun hung in the welcoming sky.

The old man sat on a nearby bench and looked up at the grey walls of the prison in front of him—and waited. Time passed leisurely, moving neither too fast nor too slow. Then, at last, the gates opened and a large black man with hair as white as the clouds overhead walked out carrying a heavy brown suitcase.

The old man stood up and waved. "Joe!" he called, walking over to meet the black man.

Joe took off his hat and wiped his brow with the back of his hand. "Whew! Sure is hot. Mr. Jackson, I am awfully glad to see a friendly face outside those prison walls. I thought I'd come out and find myself all alone in the world."

The old man put down his suitcase and embraced his friend.

"Joe…" said the older Jackson. It was all he could say because of the tears in his eyes and the lump in his throat.

The two men stood back at arm's length to get a good look at each other. They beamed with pleasure.

"You look fine," the old man told his friend.

"Well, I feel fine." Joe laughed. "And you, Mr. Jackson, look the picture of health."

"I've got something for you," the old man said, taking a cigar from his pocket. "It's a present, to celebrate your first day of freedom."

He handed the cigar to the black man, who took it and rolled it around in his finger.

"My oh my," Joe said. "It's a fat stogie, a sweet-smelling Cuban cigar." He rolled it under his nose and took a deep breath. "Wade, you shouldn't have, but I'm glad you did."

The two men laughed.

"Where'd you get it?" Joe asked.

"One of the Kings gave it to me."

The black man's eyes shot up in surprise. "I don't believe it! I don't believe one of those mean bastards would ever give anything away, let alone something as fine as this!"

The old man smiled. "Well, he thought I was gonna do him a favour in return."

"Didn't he know you were being set free?" Joe put the cigar between his lips to taste the sweet tobacco.

"I guess not," the old man replied.

Joe lit the cigar and puffed from it deeply. He blew smoke rings out through his nose and watched them circle up into the sky.

"Fine, fine," Joe said. "The oh so fine taste of freedom!"

The old man picked up Joe's suitcase for him and the two friends walked together down the long road with the warm sun shining over their shoulders.

ALEX FANGDINKLE
AND THE CASE OF THE STOLEN FART

The previous evening, Alex Fangdinkle had been called to the barn one too many times. Now, as he desperately attempted to rise and greet the day, he felt a throbbing headache that reached all the way down to his groin. His mother had warned him there would be mornings like this. Oh, why hadn't he believed her? Why had he thought the old biddy was just trying to prevent him from having any fun? Next time she offered some advice, maybe he would wise up and listen to her.

Fat chance. It was about as likely as Billy Virgin getting fucked without having to pay for it, by a girl who didn't have brain damage. But wonders never ceased, so you couldn't entirely rule it out.

With great effort, Alex managed to stand up and wipe the cow shit off his dick. How had it gotten there? He had a vague recollection, but he couldn't remember what had occurred, not exactly anyway. That was good. If he was ever dragged before a court of law, he could honestly say, "I don't remember."

Being a lawyer, Alex knew the difference between outright perjury and an honest mistake. An honest mistake was always looked upon more leniently by the law, but a faulty memory was even better for keeping you out of trouble with the penis system—er, penal system. Slipups like that had cost him dearly in the past. It showed a lack of professionalism, if not a preoccupation with perversion. Alex sincerely hoped it wouldn't happen again.

Alex glimpsed at his Wayne Gretzky watch and frowned. Not only had Gretzky missed the net completely, but Alex saw he was already late for his 6:00 a.m. briefing on tortoises—er, torts.

Later in the day, he would have to defend a prostitute who was being brought before the courts. Well, he couldn't very well expect to win dressed only in his shorts. He quickly slipped into his polyester three-piece suit, wisely purchased during a summer white sale. A guy had only so many bucks to throw around, so he reasoned it was better to blow 'em on a blow.

He zipped up his trousers in the back... mistakes, mistakes. Oh well. He would have to correct that one later. He jumped onto the back of a shitting pony and trotted off towards the corner of King Street and Yonge. If he was lucky, and luck was something Alex often counted on—otherwise how could you account for his continuing belief that someday, somewhere, he would find himself on top of a luscious blond babe and she wouldn't be screaming for a cop…? Anyway, to carry on, if Alex was lucky, he would safely be in his office before the farmer discovered anything was missing.

After tying up his horse to a fire hydrant, let the dogs have him, Alex thought.

He took the elevator up to the eighteenth floor and got off. Wrong floor! He then walked back down three flights of stairs.

He gulped hornily as he walked into the office. There she was: Wendy the receptionist. He walked past her on his tiptoes, trying to get a good look down the front of her dress. Fucking shit, the bitch was wearing a bra. What was she trying to do, wreck his day? He gave her a dirty look and stomped angrily into his office, slamming the door behind him.

"That's the last time I'll go out of my way to sneak a peek at her boobs," he muttered as he reached for the phone. He dialled a number; he was calling me. "Dan, old buddy, high school chum, favourite pal of mine. What do I do?"

I wanted to tell him what to do and where to go, but I resisted the urge. "Alex, I'm on my deathbed," I moaned weakly. "Couldn't this have waited?"

At that moment, I was lying forsaken in an antiseptic hospital ward with angels of mercy hovering around me. It seemed to me that I was literally knocking on heaven's door.

"No, no, no…" Alex cried. There was urgent desperation in his voice. "You croak and I'm up the creek without a paddle."

"Okay, okay." I gave in, the nice guy that I am. "First thing to do is calm down. Are you calm?"

"Yeah," Alex groaned like a lapdog in heat.

"Well, if you are, it's the first time in your life," I told him truthfully. "Second thing to do is tell me what's happened. Start from the beginning and don't leave out anything."

"Oh God, do I have to?"

I could tell it must be something foul, disgusting, and odious. I didn't need anything like that on my mind when I met my maker.

"No, no, I was only joking," I told him. "Just give me the pertinent facts."

"I left my briefcase at Farmer Macdonald's," Alex said, sounding calmer. Knowing he could rely on me had already boosted his confidence. "I think it's in the hayloft. Either there or in Bessy's stall. But the real crud is, I've got an important case today. I'm defending an old lady charged with soliciting. Some dumb cop caught me handing her a fifty and he figured it was for services rendered. I tried to tell him it was for cat food so the old girl wouldn't starve, but I had a silly grin on my face and he wouldn't buy my story. Anyway, the whole gist of the problem is, without the case… I've got no case."

I could see that the whole thing had been a complete misunderstanding. The old lady was innocent. Unfortunately, without his notes, Alex couldn't argue his way into a whorehouse with a fist full of hundred-dollar bills. Coming up with a solution to Alex's problem would require the wisdom of Solomon.

"Fling the shit," I told him. "Cow shit, horse shit, polar bear shit, shit from all manner of species. Get the judge so confused that he'll duck every time you open your mouth. If that doesn't work, request a mistrial."

Alex quickly grasped the simple genius of my solution. "You've done it again, old buddy! You've saved my ass!"

"A dubious achievement at best," I said. "Don't thank me. Just send flowers."

I hung up the phone and went back to bed. I don't know where Alex went. Probably into the washroom to jack-off.

In fact, Alex Fangdinkle was rushing off to do precisely that when two burly cops got off the elevator on the fifteenth floor. With his usual perfect timing, Alex ran straight into their outstretched arms.

"You Fangdinkle?" the fat one snarled.

"Yes," Alex answered sheepishly, chicken shit rising up in his throat. "What can I do for two of Metro's finest?"

"Were you at Macdonald's farm between the hours of one and six in the morning?" the even fatter one sneered.

"No, of course I wasn't," Alex lied through his teeth.

The elevator doors opened a second time and a third cop got off, the fattest of the lot.

"It's Fangdinkle," the third cop said. "We found his briefcase. It was in Bessy's stall."

All three of Metro's finest looked at Alex with pitiful disgust.

"Take him away and throw him in the slammer," the fattest cop ordered the other two.

"Hold on, hold on," Alex pleaded. "I thought you asked if I was at McDonald's farm. That's with an M and a C, like in McDonald's. But you wanted to know if I was at Macdonald's farm, with an M and an A and a C, like Macdonald's."

The three cops looked at each other and scratched their heads. They intuitively understood that Alex was copping a plea, perhaps invoking the Charter of Rights. If they were skating on thin ice, it would be best to let him have his say.

"Of course I was at Macdonald's farm last night between those hours," Alex conceded. "Macdonald's, not McDonald's."

"So you confess," the fat cop said.

"Only to being at Macdonald's farm between the hours of one and six," Alex pointed out. "Not to anything else. If this is about Macdonald's pony, I admit to borrowing it. However, if this goes to trial, there's no way you'll be able to prove it. Anyway, as officers of the law, you all know it's not illegal to borrow something."

Alex had them on that point, and they were bewildered. He laughed to himself as they stood around scratching their heads, glaring at each other accusingly, staring at their shoes and picking their noses. Somebody was going to come out of this mess with shit on his dick, and each of them hoped he wouldn't be the one.

"Wait!" the fatter cop screamed as if a light had suddenly switched on inside his head. "We're not here because of the pony. We're here to find the stolen fart!"

All three of Metro's finest smiled with undisguised delight.

"Okay, Fangdinkle," the fat one said joyfully. "Let's go!" He reached over to grab Alex.

"Hold on!" Alex screamed, frantically raising his hand to stop any violence from being inflicted upon his person. "How can you possibly steal a fart?"

It was a reasonable question to ask any normal person, but these were three cops.

"What do we care?" the fatter one said. "The how and the why are for the turd shit of a legal system to determine. We're only interested in the who!"

They grabbed Alex by the armpits and started to hustle him into the elevator.

"Hold on, hold on, hold on…" Alex was totally distraught. "You can't charge a person with committing a crime if you're not sure a crime's been committed!"

Alex giggled. After all, the situation was absurd.

"We're sure, we're sure, we're sure," three of Metro's finest said in succession.

"Bessy farts five times every day," the fattest one explained. "But today Farmer Macdonald could only get Bessy to fart four times. Ipso facto, it is obvious that someone stole Bessy's fifth fart."

"How's that?" Alex asked in bewilderment, trying to shake the cobwebs out of his head.

"Bessy farts five times every day," all three sang in unison. "But today Farmer Macdonald could only get Bessy to fart four times. Ipso facto, it is obvious that someone stole Bessy's fifth fart."

They danced round the rosy with Alex in the middle until they all fell down.

The fattest cop then stood up and brushed off his uniform. "Unfortunately, Fangdinkle," he said sympathetically, "all evidence points to you. Let's go!"

And they took Alex away.

Satirical Comedy in Short Stories

The above photograph, by Robert D. Thomas, symbolizes what Alex Fangdinkle and the Case of the Stolen Fart is: a satirical short story taking aim at serious contemporary social and political issues within the Canadian courts. It can be assumed that while Daniel and his client were polishing off the pizza and the two-four of cold beer, they were watching a concert on the television featuring a bunch of stickmen in attendance!

Every criminal gets to make one call before they lock him away for good. For Alex, the decision was a tough one. He couldn't decide if he wanted to order a pizza or send out for some Chinese food.

He compromised and called me.

He caught me in the middle of a delicate operation. A short, balding truck driver who specialized in surgery on the side and smelled like a crate full of dead fish was cutting me open. One wrong move on his part and I would be singing soprano for the rest of my life.

"Dan, is that you?" Alex asked, obviously in hysterics.

"No, it's Farrah Fawcett and I'm being fucked by the bionic man, so call back!" I prayed he would hang up.

"Stop kidding around, Dan. I know it's you."

A person would have to get up pretty late in the afternoon to fool Fangdinkle.

"Okay, what is it this time, Alex?" I didn't try to hide my annoyance.

"It's life and death, Dan. You've got to get down here quick. They're going to hang me."

And having delivered that thrilling piece of information, he hung up.

I had to go to fifteen cop stations before I found him.

"You stupid jerk!" I screamed, trying to strangle him through the bars once I tracked him down. "Why didn't you tell me where you were at!?"

He just looked at me indifferently, as if nothing mattered. "Have a slice of pizza," he offered.

After polishing off the pizza and a two-four of cold beer, we got down to serious business. I made him tell me everything. It wasn't pleasant, but I had to hear it from him; I didn't want the prosecuting attorney to be able to pull any surprises on me.

The basic facts were these: Alex was being charged with stealing Bessy's fifth fart. All the evidence was against him. The prosecuting attorney was demanding the death penalty, and if that wasn't bad enough, because of the seriousness of the charge and the unsavoury character of the accused, bail had been denied. That hurt. It meant I'd have to find somebody else to get crunk with on Friday nights.

Before leaving his cell, I assured Alex I'd get him off. I didn't know how, and I didn't know when, but I swore I'd see him hang before I gave up.

The trial began amidst the glare of publicity. Normally a great deal of media coverage benefits the defendant. People naturally feel sorry for the guy sitting in the prisoner's box with his hands shackled, his head hanging low, his tongue licking the floor. Unfortunately, Alex came across on TV like a dumb Joe Clark. I had to hide him from the press as much as possible, otherwise there would have been no chance for acquittal.

Jury selection proceeded swiftly. I let the prosecuting attorney choose whomever he liked. Alex thought that this was a mistake and it made him a little nervous, but I never worried about it.

Once the trial began, Alex really got nervous. He was sweating and shaking so badly I thought he must be ill. Perhaps he'd die and save the state the trouble of hanging him.

I started my defence by conceding almost all of the Crown's case. I conceded that Alex had been at Macdonald's farm between the hours of one and six, he had been in Bessy's stall, and even that he had stuck his nose up Bessy's bum hole and this action might have been enough to induce Bessy to fart. I then conceded that, had Bessy farted, all Alex would need to have done to commit perfect crime—perfect, that is, if he hadn't been so stupid and forgotten his briefcase—was inhale the fart.

At this point in the trial, Alex began to jump up and down in his chair, screaming frantically at me and calling me all sorts of rude names. He even had the audacity to demand a new lawyer.

I was insulted and almost walked out of there, leaving him to hang. But because of our years of friendship, and because I'm a better man than he is, I chose instead to pounce with my crucial argument, the argument that would save his worthless neck.

"Your honour," I said gracefully, sounding a lot like Clarence Darrel at his finest. "When did we stoop so low in this great country as to make it a crime for a man to breathe the free air? No matter that the air is filled with pollutants, smelling like a whore's vagina, reeking of dog shit and cow dung?"

I hesitated for the briefest instant to let this sink in and then raised my hands high above my head in an appeal to the heavens.

"I'll admit it: my client inhaled Bessy's fifth fart, but while I don't defend the air he breathed, I do defend his right to breathe it."

Every man in the room rose to his feet and applauded. Thunderous cheers rained down on me from the rafters. And what, you may wonder, was Alex's reaction to having been snatched from the jaws of death by the man he had so recently denounced as a fraud and a schemer? Well, he ran over and flung his arms around my neck in a mad embrace, begging me to forgive him for having had so little faith.

Did I forgive him? Why of course I did!

When the tumultuous ovation had died down, I took a quick peek at the prosecuting attorney to see how he was taking such a bitter defeat. I must confess

I hadn't expected to see the strange smile that crossed his lips. He rose up off his chair and stood erect, looking a little like Lincoln at Gettysburg. He waited patiently until silence had been restored to the courtroom. Finally he spoke, sounding quite a lot like Moses admonishing the Pharaoh.

"Brilliant! Brilliant! Brilliant!" he congratulated me. "But I must point out that Bessy doesn't fart into the free air."

I was stunned; the whole courtroom was stunned.

"What do you mean?" I asked, quivering.

"Quite simple." He reached into his briefcase and pulling out four glass cylinders. "When Bessy farts, she farts into these—and not into the free air, as you so beautifully put it."

This up to now unheard-of fact added a new twist to the case and I wondered how my adversary would exploit it.

"Farmer Macdonald owns Bessy; therefore, he owns what she produces," the prosecuting attorney continued with precise Aristotelian logic. "If he chooses to allow what Bessy produces to be dispersed into the free air, then of course it becomes lawful for anyone to take possession of such produce by the act of breathing in the free air. But if instead Farmer Macdonald chooses to bottle what Bessy produces, to ship it and sell it on the open market, then surely you'll admit that the bottle and what's in it is his until such time as he should relinquish ownership. By forcing Bessy to fart before Farmer Macdonald had a chance to bottle it, the defendant deprived my client of ownership over which was rightfully his."

I fell back into my chair in utter shock. It was a brilliant argument, destroying my case completely. Alex was again jumping up on his chair, crying hysterically.

I asked for a short recess to calm my client down.

I met with Alex in an anteroom to the judge's chambers. Alex was in worse shape than I had thought. He kept ranting and raving and foaming at the mouth, threatening to kill somebody. For a second, I thought he meant me, but that was illogical. I tried to point out to him the hopeless mess he had gotten himself into. The case was lost; the only possible outcome was a verdict of guilty.

"But we mustn't lose hope," I told him cheerfully. "We can avoid the worst if we change our plea to one of guilty and accept a minimum sentence of twenty-five years in prison."

Alex had always wanted to be the master of his own fate, so at this crucial point I tried to get him to make the decision for himself. But his mind had snapped. I couldn't get a sane word out of him. He kept mumbling something about "Live free or die, live free or die…" Whatever that meant.

"Do you want to take the twenty-five years?" I asked him.

His head nodded, so I took it for a yes. Then I had the officer of the court take him back to the prisoner's chair.

The poor boy's becoming quite unstable, I thought sadly.

I felt very pleased with the way things were working out. Twenty-five years was a light sentence considering the heinous nature of the crime. It wasn't so long to spend behind bars. Alex would be out when he was fifty-one, in time for his golden years. That was a happy thought.

Still, there was one more thing I had to do: make a call to an old friend.

When I walked back into the courtroom, Alex was being restrained by three burly cops. I asked the judge if that was entirely necessary, and he said it entirely was. Alex had gone berserk and tried to escape by jumping out the window. Had he succeeded, it would have been a long fall, as we were on the twentieth floor.

"Your honour," the prosecuting attorney said. He was making a motion. "The defence has presented its case; we have presented ours. I request that you send the jury out to deliberate."

Alex's life meant—and means—a lot to me. I wouldn't have risked it lightly. But I couldn't stand the thought of having to go twenty-five years without being able to show him up at one thing or another. Twenty-five years without being able to prove to him who's best and who's second best? Selfish reasons, I'll admit, but who do we live our lives for if not ourselves?

So I decided to go in there and fight to have Alex acquitted. He would live a free man. And if I failed and they hung him by the neck until dead… well, that was just the way the cookie crumbles.

The judge was about to make his decision concerning the prosecuting attorney's request when I interjected.

"Your honour, I have one last witness to call!" I said dramatically, looking just like Wellington at Waterloo or Nelson at Trafalgar, or any of those other fearless men who came to their nation's rescue during its most desperate hour. "The defence calls William Virgin!"

I must confess I was a little worried about how credible a witness Billy would be. I needn't have been afraid. If there was anything that could truthfully be said about Billy, it was that he was one of the common people.

From the moment Billy sat in the witness's chair, he played the jury perfectly. It was as if they were one giant fish and Billy was determined not to let them get away. Because dammit, he was hungry!

I informed the jury that Billy was an expert witness, but I still wanted him to establish this fact for himself.

"What is your field of expertise?" I asked.

"I am an expert on farts," he said in all seriousness.

I spoke slowly, carefully so as not to confuse Billy, the judge, or the jury. "Have you had a chance to examine the four glass cylinders that allegedly contain the four farts let off by Bessy the cow on the day in which the defendant is accused of having stolen Bessy's fifth fart?"

"I have," Billy asked calmly.

"And what did you discover?"

A leading question, no doubt. I had implied he discovered something when perhaps he hadn't. But I got away with it.

"I discovered that the four glass containers contained five farts," Billy said.

The courtroom was abuzz at this surprise development. Of course, I wasn't surprised; having coached him, I knew Billy's answer in advance.

The prosecuting attorney rose from his chair, scowling. "Your honour, this is outrageous!" he thundered. "This imposter comes forth claiming to be an expert on farts, and what proof does he offer? None. Then he states that the four cylinders contain five farts. Again, what proof does he offer? Again, the answer is none. I ask that his entire testimony be stricken from the record."

Of course, I got up off my feet to counter-protest this at once. To which he countered my counter-protest. To which I countered his countering of my counter-protest of his protest. It was crucial that I get the last protest in; the judge's decision at this point in the trial would determine my client's fate.

"For the time being, I'm going to allow the questioning to continue," the judge declared solemnly. "But Daniel B., I must warn you: if you don't soon show some evidence to support your allegations, I will be forced to look more favourably on the prosecuting attorney's request to have your witness's testimony stricken from the record."

The judge gazed down at me with compassionate yet merciless eyes. Luckily, I had been about to provide the final convincing piece of evidence when the prosecuting attorney had so rudely interrupted.

"Mr. Virgin," I said, picking up a chart drawn on a piece of bristle board that had been in my briefcase. "Can you tell the judge and jury what it is I am holding up for them and you to see?" I triumphantly displayed the proof of Alex's innocence.

"Yes," Billy answered. "You are holding a chart that was drawn up in the University of Toronto's gas-testing laboratory just this morning. The chart indicates the compactness of the flatulent gases in the four glass cylinders on exhibit. That chart demonstrates unmistakably that the compactness of the flatulent gases in container number three is twice that of the compactness of the flatulent gases in containers one, two, and four."

The jury hung on the bone-chilling drama enacted before their very eyes, with a man's life hanging in the balance.

"What do these findings suggest to you?" I asked tersely.

Billy was exuberant. "Simply that container number three contains two farts while containers one, two, and four contain one fart each, making a grand total of five farts."

It was as if a tremor had passed through the courthouse.

"He's innocent! Fangdinkle's innocent!" The cry went up from the gallery.

"Extra, extra!" the newspaper boy shouted. "Read all about it: Fangdinkle found innocent!"

The case hadn't yet concluded.

"Your Honour!" I shouted, rising to my feet, looking a lot like Steve Mc-Queen making love to Natalie Wood. "My client is innocent. Bessy's fifth fart wasn't stolen; it was farted into container number four. Her fourth and third farts were farted into container number three. With the fart in container number two and the fart in container number one, that makes a grand total of five farts, the exact number of farts Farmer Macdonald has testified Bessy farts each day."

I sat down, exhausted from my tremendous exertion.

"How's that?" the judge asked.

I wasn't sure if he hadn't understood me or if he was just hard of hearing.

"Bessy's fifth fart wasn't stolen," the members of the jury sang in unison. "It was farted into container number four. Her fourth and third farts were farted into container number three. With the fart in container number two and the fart in container number one, that makes a grand total of five farts, the exact number of farts Farmer Macdonald has testified Bessy farts each day."

The judge scratched his head in bewilderment.

"Your honour, I request the charges against my client be dismissed," I said.

The judge sat quietly, going over the entire trial in his mind. He weighed the brilliant legal arguments made on both sides and added past precedents for good measure.

Finally, he made his decision. "I concur with the request made by the attorney for the defendant," he said gravely. "It has been a long and silly afternoon and this story has become far too ridiculous. Case dismissed."

He hammered his gavel down on the oaken desk and the courtroom cleared.

Cleared out the old courtroom, I did. Oh, I'm not saying there weren't a few million people still hanging about cheering whenever they caught a glimpse of me and joining in the gay celebrations; the little people were happy and insisted on making a great to do over their hero. Accolades were thrust upon me, bouquets of roses forced into my face, and young female virgins thrown at my feet in an immense outpouring of gratitude.

"Good show, old man, I knew you'd win,' the prosecuting attorney said, coming over to congratulate me. "I only hoped to give you a bit of a go this time."

"Oh, you did, you did," I assured him.

I gave him a hearty slap on the back and then was carried on a stretcher out to the ambulance, which was waiting to rush me back to my hospital bed.

Seeing me being carried away, Alex ran over and tried to kiss me. He was so overwhelmed with relief and joy.

But I spit at him.

"Try that again, and I'll call for a new trial," I hissed. "Next time, I'll prove you did it."

Alex knew I could do it too.

"To tell you the truth, I did do it," he confessed to me. He had hoped to surprise me, but he failed. I have always managed to stay a step ahead of him.

"I know." I laughed derisively. "But it was fun saving your worthless hide anyway. Besides, what do I care if you get your jollies by stealing farts?"

Alex seemed shocked by the utter futility of his attempt at deception. "If you knew all along, how did you get Billy Virgin to perjure himself?"

It was no great mystery. "Oh, that was nothing," I assured him. "I saved Billy's life one time in Borneo. The blighter owed me a favour."

Then we both laughed uproariously. Why not? It was the end of a difficult case. But knowing Alex, I knew there would be others.

FOREVER INNOCENT

S tanley Falcon was in a sour mood.

"Let's see," he said, grumbling to himself. "The boss is going to give me hell because Fulbright wouldn't buy. Louise is fooling around on me again. I wonder who she was with last night. And now this!" He kicked the flat tire angrily. "What else could possibly go wrong!?"

As if to answer him, the sky began to rumble with a strong wind, whipping prairie dust through the stale air. Stanley's throat felt parched and dry. He had failed to notice the sky growing suddenly dark and looked up at the huge black clouds hanging ominously in the air.

Better fix this tire quick, he told himself.

Rolling up his sleeves, he made short work of removing the flat tire and putting on the spare. Just as he was finishing up, it began to rain. He stood in the rain for a while, looking up into the eye of the storm. Fat drops of water fell from the thundering clouds, splashing coolly over his face. Crackling lightning streaked across the black sky while behind him, in the forest, the bristling branches of trees lashed about in the wind. Nature had erupted in fury, yet everything seemed silent.

He was becoming soaked, so he reluctantly got into his car.

"Hmmm," he mumbled to himself as he gazed through the windshield towards the horizon. "It's just not the same. Out there, I was part of the violent beauty, but now I'm just a spectator."

He had felt a strange sensation while standing in the storm, something wild and exciting. Not fully human, he thought. What was it?

Oh well. He gave up trying to understand it as he started the engine and pulled out onto the road.

The storm grew more ferocious. The rain beat down in torrents, the wind tossed the car from side to side, and the dark closed all around.

Stanley peered into the gloom, trying to make out the way ahead. Then, in the reflection of his lights, he saw a person standing off to the side of the road, desperately trying to wave him down. He slowed and stopped the car.

A young girl wearing a yellow raincoat opened the passenger door and jumped in.

"Thank you," she said as she pulled the hood of the raincoat off her head and let her long black hair fall over her shoulders. "I was getting scared out there. It's a terrible storm."

She stopped and looked at Stanley gaily, waiting for him to say something.

"What are you doing out in the middle of nowhere in this type of weather?" Stanley asked in astonishment.

She laughed lightly. "Well, I was a real fool. I was with my boyfriend and we got into a fight, so I made him stop the car and I got out. Next time, I'll make *him* get out. That is, if I ever go out with him again, which I won't."

She looked at Stanley with a schoolgirl nonchalance, smiling ever so sweetly, as if he were a high school chum and the two of them were sharing a laugh over her dumb old boyfriend. A laugh and a half.

What a lovely girl, Stanley thought.

He envisioned her boyfriend. Stanley had never had a high school sweetheart, never had a sweetheart of any kind except for Louise, if you could call her one. He had been dating Louise for eight years now and had supported her for the last five. It seemed an awful lot of time and money to spend on a person like Louise.

"Well, where can I take you to?" Stanley asked, shaking himself out of his reminiscences.

"Where would you like to take me?" she asked coyly.

Hm-hmm. She's flirting with me.

"Well, my dear," he said as he turned and gazed deeply into her eyes, "I would like to take you to the ends of the Earth. To paradise, if we could find it. But I'm afraid that we would run out of petrol. Then we would be forced out into the storm. Like two lost waifs, we would have to cling to each other for protection, for warmth, for our survival. But alas, it would all be to no avail. We would die tragically in each other's arms."

She seemed delighted with his little joke and laughed uproariously until she was forced to wipe tears from her eyes.

"Let me introduce myself," he said, gallantly extending his hand. "I am Prince Charming."

She began to laugh again but controlled herself as she took his hand. "Delighted to make your acquaintance," she said in a humble, dainty voice. "And I am Cinderella."

This time, it was his turn to laugh. "Then please tell me: where is your carriage?"

"It is past midnight and my carriage has turned into a pumpkin," she replied. "I am most afraid that if I don't soon find my fairy godmother, I will turn back into a scullery maid. A scullery maid named Debbie."

Her eyes danced with innocent joy as Stanley took her hand and kissed it.

"Dear Debbie," he said. "Never again will you be a scullery maid, never again so long as the heart of Prince Stanley Charming goes on beating."

As they carried on with their fanciful conversation, Stanley drove through the storm. The murky darkness, the rain slashing against the windshield, the mist caught in the headlight beams, all served as a romantic background for the enchanting little farce being played out in the car.

But that's all it is, Stanley told himself. *Play.*

He was aware the girl was beginning to have a more profound effect on him than she could have realized. He watched her out of the corner of his eye; her face was lovely.

Their conversation slowly died away and she sat back quietly, her young, innocent face hidden in shadows, her youthful body beneath a layer of clothing.

A chill ran through him. *What crazy thoughts I am having…*

Then a horrid thought—an awful, ugly thought—wormed its way into his soul.

"Where do you live?" he asked her again, this time in all earnestness, demanding a serious reply. "I'll take you home."

She fidgeted in her seat and took her time before answering without a trace of emotion. "I live in Waynewright… Waynewright." She repeated it, almost as if she were spitting the word out, the way you would with the name of someone or something you particularly dislike.

"Waynewright. Nice town."

Stanley mentally calculated that he could get her home before dark, say goodbye, and be on his way. He sighed with relief.

Debbie sat sullenly, gazing at the flash of lightning that lit up the horizon. "It's still early," she said wistfully. "I know a little hotel between here and Waynewright. It has a nice restaurant. We could have dinner together. I'd like that. Wouldn't you like that?"

She looked at him with hope, crazily imploring him, pleading with him, her soft brown eyes beseeching him.

"I'll pay," she offered seriously. He gave her an exasperated look and she fell back into her seat. "Oh well. If you don't want to…"

Her offer flattered him. He was stunned by it, but above all else he was flattered.

"It's not that I don't want to," he said. "But I'm in a hurry and I've already lost time because of the storm."

"It wouldn't take up much of your precious time." She was looking out the window and didn't bother to turn and face him. "Anyway, the rain is beginning to end, and the clouds are breaking up. If we stop for dinner, it will be sunny and dry out by the time we're finished. You can make up whatever time you've lost."

It might be pleasant, he thought. *And it's still early. We could have dinner and I could still get her home well before dark. She is tempting.*

"Why do you want to have dinner with an old coot like me?" he asked.

"I just don't want to go home yet, that's all. I had a fight with my boyfriend, and I want to talk to somebody."

Her voice sounded hurt, and she turned to quickly hide her face. She was trying not to cry, without quite succeeding. Stanley didn't know what to make of all this.

"You're a crazy, crazy person," he said, shaking his head in bewilderment.

"Why? Because I want to talk to somebody!?"

"No!" he shouted back. "Because you tell it to a complete stranger. Why don't you talk to somebody you know? Why don't you talk to your mother?"

Although he said it in a harsh tone of voice, he felt sorry for her. But now, more than ever, he knew he had to get her home. She was vulnerable. So very vulnerable.

She didn't answer. Instead she turned away in defiance and looked stiffly straight ahead.

For a short distance, a silence hung between them. But then she jumped forward in her seat and pointed out the window.

"There's the hotel, just up ahead!" she said excitedly. "I don't want to talk to someone I know; I want to talk to you!" Again, she looked at him with those large brown eyes.

Looking straight into my heart, he thought. *Begging me, pleading with me.*

"Okay," he said, more with himself than with her. "One quick dinner, my lady, and that's all."

She smiled as he pulled into the hotel parking lot and stopped the car.

Inside the restaurant, he helped her with her raincoat. He was about to take a table near the front, but she pulled him along by the arm to a more secluded, private spot in the back, away from the counter and kitchen.

He ordered a light meal for the two of them and two coffees, but she insisted that they have wine.

"Oh come on," she teased him. "This is my first time having dinner with a man of the world and not just some high school kid. You're not going to spoil it, are you?"

He reluctantly gave in to her.

They sat somewhat quietly through the meal. Debbie barely picked at her food, intent on watching him most of the time. She asked flirtatiously if she could have a bite of his sandwich, then wiped some mayonnaise off his lip and laughed.

"Well, you eat like a high school kid," she said.

He got angry with her. "You want to talk? So talk!" He pushed his plate away and poured himself a glass of wine.

God, I sound like a mafia boss, he thought.

"You had a fight with your boyfriend," he said, kindlier. "Lots of young girls have fights with their boyfriends. So what?"

She leaned back and sipped her wine. "That's what I say. So what? So what if the creep won't marry me?"

Stanley choked on his wine and was forced to cough it up. He looked at her with concern.

"Are you pregnant?" he asked anxiously.

She laughed. "Are you kidding? We've been going out for over a year and all he's ever done is kiss me."

Stanley sat back in his seat, feeling better. "Then what do you want to get married for?"

"Because Waynewright is a dump of a town and Eddie could take me out of there—if he wanted to," she said. "You might think Waynewright is a nice place, but I hate it."

He could tell that she meant it.

"Eddie… that's your boyfriend?" he asked. She nodded. "Did you ask him to marry you?"

"What's wrong with that?" she snapped. "Just because girls aren't supposed to do the asking, just because it never happens in Waynewright? Well, who cares about Waynewright? Not me. I want to get out of there. That's why I asked him. Eddie has oodles of money. His old man left it to him, so I asked him to marry me and take me to New York, or Los Angeles, or Paris. But all the grease monkey wants to do is stay in Waynewright and finish high school. He's got no imagination. He really is a grease monkey, you know."

She stopped long enough to give Stanley a can-you-beat-that? look.

"He's worth over a million dollars and yet he works pumping gas." She cringed, as though the very thought of it repulsed her. "Can you believe it! What a creep."

She poured the last of the wine into her glass and drank it down.

"Order another bottle!" she said.

"No," Stanley told her. He was beginning to feel the wine and was somewhat light-headed. "It's time for me to take you home to boring Waynewright and that creep of a grease monkey."

"Oh, please, one more glass…"

"No!" Stanley got up out of his chair, grabbed her by the arm, and tried pulling her out of her seat, but she pushed away.

"I can't go back there now," Debbie cried. "The whole town will have heard what happened and everyone will laugh at me. Or they'll feel sorry for me, which is worse!"

Stanley fell back in his chair, laughing. "Oh, I knew it. I just knew it! You sounded so sophisticated for someone so young, but inside you there are all those little girl feelings!"

He grinned at her, but she wasn't amused. She sat there stubbornly, like a little child, holding her arms crossed against her breasts, her face set in an angry frown, but it wasn't the face of a child. She had the face of an angel. A young beautiful woman entering the first blush of sexuality.

"I'll order some myself," Debbie said defiantly.

Stanley didn't object as she called the waiter over. Her eyes danced in delight despite the expression of scorn that crossed her lips. He had the greatest desire to reach over and kiss her, but he was afraid to. What would she do? Would she throw the wine into his face? Of course not! Women didn't go throwing wine into men's faces just because they'd been kissed.

Why am I being so stupid? he thought. *I'm acting like a teenager. If I want to kiss her, why don't I do it?*

Stanley suddenly realized she was looking at him as intently as he was looking at her. There they were, the two of them, not saying a thing but gazing at each other like long-time lovers. They were both drinking their wine, waiting for the evening to end and the night to begin.

It should have seemed funny to him, but it didn't.

"Sugar and spice and everything nice," he said tenderly. "That's what little girls are made of. At least they were when I was growing up."

"I'm not a little girl," Debbie reached over and touched his hand affectionately. "I've put away my dolls and I don't go crying to daddy."

"I think you've been reading too many novels. Or else watching too many movies." But he took her hand and held it tenderly in his.

"What's wrong with reading novels or watching movies?" Debbie asked. She was almost drunk and her voice sounded bitterly sweet, as if she was feeling the words rather than thinking them. "What's wrong with having hopes and dreams, with wanting to go places and do things and not waste your life in some dusty town until you dry up and blow away?"

She bit her lip, trying to force off some inner torment, vainly trying to hide from herself an all too visible wound.

Stanley reached over and kissed her, and she flung her arms around his neck and hung onto him. Her shoulders trembled and he felt the cold dampness of her body.

"Come on," he said soothingly. "I'll take you home now."

"No!" It sounded like a wrenching scream, but it was only a whisper, "No, please, I don't want to leave you."

From that point on, Stanley felt compelled to go along with everything she wanted. Debbie wanted them to take a hotel room for the night, so they did.

But going up the elevator, Stanley felt terribly guilty. When he placed the key in the lock to open the door, he wanted to turn and run, leaving Debbie standing there all alone.

Get away from the crazy kid, he told himself irritably, *before you do something you'll regret.*

He couldn't help feeling that he was taking advantage of her. But wasn't that what he'd wanted to do in the first place? To seduce her? To make love to her any way, any how? From the moment she'd gotten into his car, he had thought it. But she had done it. In her impetuous way, she had seduced him. She had made it a lot harder to say no... a whole lot harder. She had tried to make it so easy, so all he had to do was follow and the act would be done of her own volition.

Why was she behaving this way? It didn't make sense. A silly fight with a boyfriend didn't account for it, not even if the fight had been over the grease monkey's refusal to marry her. Anyway, the whole story was so ludicrous she must have made it all up.

But you couldn't fake that kind of grief, the kind of grief he saw in her eyes. It didn't matter that she had managed to laugh and joke most of the night; she was hurting. Something must have happened to break her heart, and she was running away from it.

It amazed Stanley that someone could feel such pain. Was she too young to have learned that there was no meaning to life? That life was a barren wasteland consisting of a few ugly words scribbled across a sheet of paper? That life was growing up in a dirty town, never dreaming? Time ticking away until you met a girl you didn't love, while you worked at a job you didn't feel anything but annoyance for?

That wasn't her life. That wasn't everyone's life. But it was his.

Tonight I felt something, he thought, protesting against his own soul. *A spark of desire so intense I would have raped her and damn the consequences.*

"Hey…" Debbie called to him playfully. "Are you coming in?"

Stanley realized he was still standing out in the hallway. He entered the room and closed the door behind him.

Debbie was lying on her back looking up at the ceiling. "This is lovely," she said. "The bed's so soft."

He walked across the floor and sat beside her. "Are you sure you want to do this?"

"Of course I do!" Debbie insisted as she reached up to play with his hair. "Why wouldn't I?"

"But why would you?"

"Because I love you!" She laughed. "And because I have a million things to do before I die. Is that a good enough reason?"

"Perhaps," Stanley said hesitantly. "But I don't understand what you mean. Are you trying to tell me you're fatally ill?"

The possibility had occurred to him all at once, like a light that explained everything.

"No!" Debbie said derisively. "I'm in perfect health and I can prove it. What about you, huh?" She put her hand under his shirt to squeeze his belly. "Just what kind of shape are you in?"

Stanley pushed her away.

"Did you know that I was planning to rape you?" Stanley said suddenly. He wanted to shock her, to frighten her. He wanted her to stop laughing and playing these silly games.

Debbie grinned at him as if to say, *Ho, ho, ho, some funny joke.*

"It's true," he insisted. "As soon as you got into my car, I felt lust. I wanted you. You're so beautiful. And you're young, that's part of it. I was going to pull over to the side of the road and force myself onto you. You're so defenceless. What could you have done to stop me?"

He had confessed to himself; he had looked into his soul and seen what he had wanted to do.

"So why didn't you do it?" Debbie asked.

"I don't know. I guess I was afraid," Stanley replied, suddenly feeling very weary.

He walked away from her over to the window to gaze out at the dark night. Debbie had been wrong; the storm wasn't letting up. Outside, the rain beat against the earth while the wind roared, bending the trees, the lower branches sweeping the ground. He would have liked to break the glass, to thrust his fist through the window and have the storm rush in and overwhelm him. The air he breathed was stale and hot. He longed for the wind to cool his body, for the rain to pierce his skin and freeze his heart.

Debbie watched him silently, fearfully. The muscles of his back rippled through his shirt. He wasn't so old on this particular day. His shoulders were broad, his hair cut short. He wasn't exactly what you would call handsome, but he had a pleasant face and nice eyes, soft and blue. Had he misjudged himself? Was he a steely-eyed killer, brutal and cruel?

"I know what you're doing," she said. "You want to scare me so I'll run home. But I'm not afraid! You can't make me be afraid, even if you hurt me, which I know you won't do. You're not a rapist. you're just a kind man."

Stanley laughed as his mind cleared. He had barely heard her, but the tone of her voice was like a slap, awakening him to reality. She was a child, sweet and pure. He wouldn't be the one to taint her innocence.

He felt refreshed and happy, the happiest he had felt in years.

"I suppose you're right," he conceded, smiling gracefully. "I'm taking you home now."

She wouldn't move, so he came over and lifted her to her feet. She didn't resist, but when he had her standing she pushed her body close against his and kissed him. His heart trembled with desire, but he stayed cool.

Calmly, he took her hand and led her to the door.

Soon they were driving through the night, Debbie directing him along the streets of Waynewright to her house.

"Here!" she said as she thrust something into his jacket pocket. "It's a letter I wrote. I have no reason to send it now, but I want someone to read it. I want *you* to read it."

When Stanley pulled to the curb, she got out of his car and ran up the stairs and into her house without turning around to wave goodbye.

After letting Debbie off and staying to see her front door close safely behind her, Stanley drove through the quiet town back to the main highway. The trip from the hotel had been a sombre one for both of them. At first neither had said a word, but then Stanley had broken the ice.

"Don't feel so bad," he'd said, trying to comfort her. He tried to get her to smile. "We had a lovely evening together. I'll always remember it. But now it's time for you to go home. There will be other evenings. You're young… why be in such a rush? Someday Eddie will do more than kiss you. Or if he doesn't, someone else will, and it will be beautiful because it will be with the right person at the right time, not some stranger who's just passing through."

Debbie had sat quietly listening, so Stanley went on.

"Someday you'll even get to Paris, as a bride. Yeah, you'll go there as a bride, maybe married to Eddie. So cheer up! You've got a wonderful life ahead of you!" He grinned, feeling happy for her, happy that such things could happen.

He now had a long journey in front of him, three hundred miles of unbending prairie highway, but he was looking forward to it. In a few hours, the sun would rise and the storm would surely be over.

Before leaving Waynewright, he stopped to read her letter by the light of a streetlamp. He pulled the papers out of his pocket. They were crumpled and torn, so he had to flatten them out by pressing them against the sidewalk with his hand. He was only partially successful. The writing was scraggily, almost illegible.

Words would look like this if written on a rock, he thought. He could imagine her doing just that, standing in a meadow out in the middle of nowhere using some large boulder as a table to write on. She wouldn't have noticed the sky growing dark or the wind increasing in fury. She was alone and needed someone to turn to. He could almost hear her voice calling out lonesomely…

Dear Dad,

By the time you read this letter, I'll be far away in New York City, or perhaps somewhere else. Please don't worry about me.

You know how hurt I've been, how sad I've been feeling ever since Eddie died in that awful accident. Everyone's been great trying to cheer me up, but too many things remind me of Eddie. The kids from school are forever asking me to do things with them, to go to ball games, to parties, to the movies, but I always go off by myself and visit Eddie's grave. It would always be like that if I didn't leave. So I've left. Eddie would have wanted me to.

He never intended to live his whole life in Wayne-wright. It just worked out that way. Maybe that's my fault. I asked him to stay until we both graduated from high school. It seemed to me to be the sensible thing to do, but it wasn't what Eddie wanted. He wanted to marry me and go to Paris to become a famous writer. He would have done it too. Eddie had a great imagination and a million dreams. He knew how to say things beautifully and with meaning.

He once told me he wanted to live his life like a river. A part of himself reaching up into the mountains, snow to be melted by the sun and sent cascading down into the valley, helping to turn the Earth green. But the ocean was his dream, to be part of it, floating out around the world, reaching every land.

Now he can't do any of it. I want to do it for him. I don't know how much imagination I've got, but I'm going to try for his sake.

It's strange. Eddie knew I would have been happily married to Eddie the mechanic, Eddie who pumped gas and lived in his father's house on Sycamore Street. But he wanted so much more, for both of us. Oh, Dad, why is it that you can't stop loving some people even after they're dead? Why do I still love Eddie?

I haven't said anything I wanted to say. I only wanted to tell you that your little girl has grown up, so don't worry about me. I'll write again once I've gotten settled some place. I may need you to send me some things. Take care of yourself. I love you.

xoxoxo Debbie

I came from a small town, Stanley thought, *and I probably wasn't so very different from Eddie when I was eighteen. I had dreams. How did I lose them along the way? Where did they vanish to? Maybe it's not too late. Maybe I can find them, bring them back to life. If I only had someone like Debbie... someone to dream for, someone to dream with. She's a beautiful girl. She's going to make some lucky guy a great wife. Maybe I could be that guy. It's crazy, but at least it's something worth dreaming about.*

Stanley drove on happily through the storm.

Life of Choice and Responsibility

In terms of the content of the story, the focus is largely on a shy girl planning to move far away after the unforgettable passing of someone she dated. Likely still in high school or having recently graduated, she is still in a vulnerable position psychologically and emotionally. Stanley ultimately chooses not to take advantage of her vulnerability, doing the responsible thing by taking her home. Why might Stanley have made the decisions he made? And why might Debbie have given Stanley the note she wrote her father? Why might Debbie have planned to travel far away from her parents without telling them, at her age? Photo by Robert D. Thomas.

A Book of Songs Without Music

Part Three

FOREWORD

A Book of Songs without Lyrics, originally titled *A Book of Poems*, by Daniel B. Thomas (November 6, 1958–October 5, 1985) is a composition of poems written roughly between 1976 and 1985. These poems speak largely to autobiographical themes he experienced over the course of his life, mainly during his teenage years into young adulthood.

For example, the poem entitled "A Bad Heart" speaks to his experience living with a double-chambered heart, a condition he was born with and which eventually led to his passing in October 1985 following a procedure he had on October 4.

Similarly, the poem titled "Amra" speaks to his affection for a young woman with whom he wrote love letters in the mid-1980s shortly before his passing. "Nova Scotia Shore" speaks to Daniel's place of birth, before he travelled, under the supervision of his mother, to live in Toronto in the early 1970s after a tumultuous childhood in Halifax.

Other poems touch on contemporary societal themes evident in the world at the time of their writing. "The Cause of War," likely written in the early- to mid-1980s while he pursued a philosophy degree at the University of Toronto, speaks to issues stemming from communism. At the time of its writing, the Cold War was still a going concern in lieu of the Iran-Contra Affair under the Ronald Regan administration in the United States.

However, not all the poems are autobiographical, nor are they about political affairs. For example, Daniel claimed that "Sadie" was about people missing their opportunity to find real happiness in life. The character herself was fictitious.

The poems themselves were left largely untouched after Daniel's passing in 1985, having been left to his brother Laurie. It wasn't until the poems were uncovered nearly thirty years later, in 2012, that they were reviewed. This collection was compiled in 2019.

For the first time in more than thirty-five years, these poems will be published and read by members of the general public. I'm sure those reading this book of poetry will feel the same sense of fulfillment as I did compiling the material for publication.

—Jeremy E. Thomas
August 14, 2019

DON'T GROW OLD WITHOUT HAVING BEEN YOUNG

Don't grow old
Without having been young
Don't grow tired
Without having run
Like the sun
Across the earth's sky
Live your live full
Till the moment you die

Be true
To the heart
And it's seasons
For all things are born
With a reason
To bring beauty and hope
To the Earth
To bring love, bring nurture
And bring birth

And there is
In good life
Much laughter
There is much loving
And giving
So live not
For the hereafter
But while you are here
Be a part of the living

Don't grow old
Without having been young
Don't grow weary
Without having sung
Like the wind

Crossing over the mountains
The forests and valleys and streams
Up to the clouds
To touch with the sky
Live your life full
Till the moment you die

IT'S SUMMERTIME AGAIN

It's summertime again
I think that I'll go swimming
It's summertime again
I have nothing else to do
It's summertime again
I think I'll head up to the pool
Watch the girls in their bikinis
And swim just to keep cool

I wonder where my friends are
We had such fun last summer
But now they all have jobs
Man isn't that a bummer
Although I'm twenty-four
I have no job to go to
So I think that I'll go swimming
In the public swimming pool

The pool fills up with people
They're all the unemployed
The little kids can't get in
And boy are they annoyed
But me, I must confess
That I'm really overjoyed
The friends I thought were working
Are all at the swimming pool
Looks like everybody
Is at the swimming pool

COME ALONG TO TORONTO

Come along to Toronto
For the greatest vacation
Come and share in
The joy and the fun
For whatever your heart wants to do
Toronto is number one

Come and climb the CN Tower
Come to cheer for the Blue Jays
Or to sit on the sand in the sun
For all that your heart wants to do
Toronto is number one

Take a walk
Through the city
Just to be with the people
To sing and join in the fun

Watch the Leafs at the Gardens
Or go out to the movies
Either way, you will have won

For so many nice places
And such sweet friendly faces
For the animals at the zoo
For whatever your heart wants to do
For all that your heart wants to do
Toronto city is number one
Toronto city is number one

CHRISTINA

Christina
When you grow up
I have a dream for you
You're just a baby now
Cradled gently in my arms
But when you've grown into a woman
This is what I wish for you

I hope the sun still shines down
On a green world
I hope that rivers still flow
From the mountains to the seas
I hope there's beauty in the world
And magic in the air
But most of all I wish
There'll be peace everywhere
Everywhere, everywhere

Christina
I hope you have a world
In which to love
I hope you look with joy
Up at the stars above
I hope you run and laugh
I hope you sing and dance
I wish with all my heart
We've left you with a chance
To dream
A chance to dream

Christina
You may wonder what I mean
You may think that I'm just
A crazy uncle
As you walk around with beauty everywhere

Gazing in wonder while rivers flow into the seas
Feel the warmth of love in the air
Be happy in your heart
Because everywhere is peace

But in my world of today
Things are breaking apart
Like a heart torn in two
By too much hate
Maybe it's too late to change
I don't know what to do
Tomorrow's just a dream
But I'll go on dreaming
Because I have a dream for you

Christina
When you grow up
I have a dream for you
You're just a baby now
Smiling sweetly up at me
But when you've grown into a woman
This is what I wish for you

I hope the sun still shines down
On a green world
I hope that rivers still flow
From the mountains to the seas
I hope there's beauty in the world
And magic in the air
But most of all I wish
There will be peace everywhere
Everywhere, everywhere

Roots to Halifax

Although Danny never had the opportunity to father his own children, he became an uncle to several nieces and nephews. Several months before his passing during the summer of 1985, Danny went to visit his sister in Halifax. "Christina" is a poem he wrote for a niece of his. She was born within 3 months of Danny's passing, in July 1985. His trip to Halifax came after a stroke he experienced earlier in the year and after scheduling an open-heart operation for October 4 that year, an operation that ultimately resulted in his passing the following day. The picture above was taken during a trip of my own to Halifax in August 2018 to visit my aunt, the same sister Danny went to visit in 1985 in Dartmouth This photo was taken in Dartmouth, with downtown Halifax being located across the harbor (in the background). I was born nearly 10 years after Danny's passing.

You Can't Hold the World on Your Shoulders

No, you can't hold the world on your shoulders
No, you can't hold
The whole world in your arms
You can try to catch them all
But too many of them fall
No, you can't keep the whole world from harm

I remember this sorrow and his pleasure
I remember his happiness and pain
I remember the sun
I remember the rain
And if it could all be done again,
I wish some things could change

You can love
But you can't keep love from hurting
You can hate
But hate won't make you strong
You can do what you will
To stand on your own
But you'll only end up lonely
If you're standing all alone

I was your friend
But I didn't hear you crying
And I wasn't there
To share your pain
Now you are gone
And I can't even say goodbye
I can only hope
That we meet again

No, you can't hold the world on your shoulders
No, you can't hold

The whole world in your arms
You can try to catch them all
But too many of them fail
No, you can't keep the whole world from harm
No, you can't hold the whole world in your arms

The Beauty of the Heavens

Mythical light
Shot skyward
To pierce
A flaming sun

Shattering
Flacking downward
Through cloud
And ocean waves

Colours
Sparkling eyes
Glistening fish
Swimming

The world
Dancing
In ethereal
Beauty
Of heavens

You and I
Laughing
Children of life

THE DEBT COLLECTOR

Yesterday has come to claim me
A smiling old bill collector in a rumpled coat
"Kind sir,"
His breath is a cold wind
"Your debt is large and payment's due"

"Just a second." I say
"I have some coins"
Reaching into my empty pockets
Stalling for time
I would not have opened the door
Had I only known
Who stood on the other side

His dark black eyes
Unfitted to his face
Search across the barren room
"I see," he says
"By your surroundings
You have no way to repay,
And you own nothing we could care to repossess"

I confess it's true
His long thin hand reaches out
And touches me
"You owe us nothing more," he smiles
Stepping back outside
To close my door

And so it is perhaps
That death is sent
To free us
From the debts
Built up in this life
Which we never can repay

THE CAUSE OF WAR

Human nature causes wars
At university, my professors all had many theories
On the subject
And pretty theories they were too, so I listened with respect
"It's simple," said the Marxist gaily
"Imperialistic capitalism is at fault
The need to find new markets in a shrinking world economy has led to every
conflict in the modern era"
And it went out the other ear, a-judging by the blanket expressions
On the faces sinking down below the desks.
"It's poverty, needless poverty"
I had heard that an army fights on its stomach
But I couldn't quite agree with the botanist's interpretation of history

So in they came and out they went
Answers concerning war and peace and other things
Men will too gladly fight about
If given half a chance
New and improved
Worn out and thrown away
Truth changing day to day and class to class
Until at last I became so sick of it all I stopped
To ask myself

I know of no cause of things concerning humans
Other than human nature
A Socratic answer
One that sadly made me realize old Marx has had his laugh
On me after all
I hate communism
Because communism flattens us all
It makes us all equal when we aren't equal
It turns society into a glob of jello
Every spoonful alike in colour, texture and taste
Communism forces round bodies into square holes

Every individual is made to fit the mould
The ugliness of it all seemed too high a price
To pay for social stability,
And anyway, I believed in the inherent goodness in man

But Marx knew
To end there being war after war, things must be changed
And now, especially when we cannot survive another war
Things must change at their root causes
Communism or nuclear holocaust
Two evils I hate; is that the only choice?
I suppose if big brother can change human nature, and professor
That is what it is going to take, a radical alteration in the way men behave
I can be made to love communism

THE PRISONER

I am old
A thing forgotten
I wish to teach you
But you will not learn
You will not see
You who looks forever
Into the future

I am old and beastly
Scared by yesterdays
While you have no memories
I extend into you
But you would free yourself of me

I am old
Living past usefulness
I am a leaf
Trapped in snow
Waiting for spring
To free me
And blow me into dust
Forevermore

THERE'S A TIME AND PLACE

Time
Whether than death
Which overcomes all things
Evil or sweet
And leave me to cry
Or laugh as I will
And there comes a time
When we two shall meet

There is a darkness
Deep in the forest
There is a light
That breaks through the leaves
I know the path
Which you often go by
I know the place
Where you often sleep

Time, death
They hold no meaning
Neither do all things
Owned by a king

As we lie down in the forest
Love is the one gift
I have to bring

A WRONG DECISION

I can't be a company man
The strain of owing them my loyalty
If not my life
Is too great

Having the boss go disappointed in me
I'm not the salesman
I made out to be
Before
When I was unemployed
And looking for work
Now I am working
And looking to be unemployed

Is it wrong to make mistakes at
Twenty-five?
To make them knowingly
To accept a career position under
False pretences
I didn't want a career
Just a paycheque

I want a life
Not to be strangled by a
Telephone cord
Not to be a voice
Ringing in the ears of a
Million strangers
Making deals

I don't want ulterior motives
For smiling
Or calling on an old friend
I'm too young for that
I'm too young to give up on

My dreams
And selling isn't even the
First step along the Yellow Brick Road
At least not for this
Tin scarecrow of a cowardly lion

Dorothy
Where's the Wizard?
I need some advice

(When The Man Says The Ride Is Over) Fall Out

Your time is up
On the Ferris wheel of life
You paid your dollar
Spun around to the other side

Did you have a ball?
Did you scream and shout?
Did you jump for joy?
Or did you just fall out?

Now the man says, "The ride is over, son"
So fall out, fall out, fall out
The man says the ride is over
So fall out, fall out, fall out

I called my momma
With the last quarter to my name
I said, "Momma, I think
I have played me a losing game"

She said, "Don, don't you fret
You've got a lot of time yet
To find your way
To play the hand that pays"
But the Ferris wheel keeps spinning around
And around
And when the man says, "The ride is over, son"
You better fall out, fall out, fall out
When the man says, "The ride is over, son"
Fall out

I don't know what I'm doing in this place
I'm like the last runner crossing the line
In an endless race

(When the Man Says the Ride Is Over) Fall Out

I'm hungry and wet
I half regret that I ever came
But the ball game is never over
Till the last man's out
Fall out, fall out, fall out
No, the ball game is never over
Till the last man's out

When your playing days are through
Dust out your locker
Hang up your number
You've done your time

Now ask yourself
Did I have a ball?
Did I scream and shout?
Did I jump for joy?
Or did I just fall out?
When the man said the ride is over?
Did I just fall out?

It's the fifteenth round
I'm being knocked down again
I'm getting battered and bruised
But I've been abused
Worse than this, my friend
I've heard the man say, "The ride is over"
But I wouldn't fall out
I've heard the man say, "The ride is over"
When the man said, "The ride is over"
I refused to fall out

STAR-SPANGLED TRIP

I went on
A star-spangled ship
To take a trip
Around the universe
To see
If anywhere
There might be
Clean fresh air
To breathe
And skies of blue
Hidden valleys
Filled with dew
A place to live
For me and you
Forever always forever

I took a trip
On a star-spangled ship
Racing through the universe
Many worlds
I got there first
Soon after others came
Familiar faces, ancient names
Is it just a futile game
I play
Trying hard to get away
Never knowing what I should say
Day after day after day

I took a trip
Star-spangled
Waved goodbye
Wind played a lullaby
Soft
Like my baby's cry

Why must I always be first
Why this unquenchable thirst
For change
Moon after sun after star
Till it begins all again

CHEAP LABOUR

Cheap labour
Stand in that line
Tell the man
You're willing this time
He'll hire you

Working, working, working
Wa, Wa, Wa, Wa, Wa, Wa, Wa, Wa, Wa

Last day
I worked from six until three
What did it get me?
Bang, bang
Use the hammer you rub
Fix that bloody leak
I've been on this job for a week

Payday comes around and I started
Cheque looks like a turkey that's carved
My money's quickly drifting away
Hey man let us call it a day

Working
Working on the job
Working everyday
Why do I work so hard

And they say
Cheap labour's hard to find

COMING LATE TO MY PARLOUR

You're coming late
You're coming late
You're coming late to my parlour
But it's better than never I suppose

It's been raining all day
Would you like to get out of those clothes?

I am the spider
And you're the fly
But won't you spread your wings
And float... on inside
It's a lovely little parlour
And you'll see I have nothing to hide

Have some tea
And marmalade
Leave the dishes until morning
Things are starting to run late
When nothing works out right
I like to always put it down to fate

You should too

I could go on
And on and on
On and on and on and on
But what I'm saying is of no importance
Don't you see
Still wasn't it a joy to spend
A little bit of time with me?

Goodbye... and don't forget your umbrella

EAT THE APPLE

Come
Take a ride
To a future time
When it will all be better
Than before

You and I
Can be together
There
For all time
Like a perfect pair
Heart to heart
In paradise
All you got to do
Is eat the apple
Then think twice

Chorus
Then think twice
Then think twice
Then think twice

Then think twice

Then think twice
Then think twice
Then think twice

Overcome
Your superstitious fears
Turn your back
On the bitter years
Journey with me
We will live in paradise
Baby, eat the apple

Then think twice

(*Chorus*)

Suddenly
A fire will light
Your way
To a better land
In a perfect day
And you will come to know
When you live with me
The apple's taste is sweet
And it sets you free

(*Chorus*)

Eat the apple
Then think twice

FAREWELL

Goodbye, Dr. Rashkin
We feel sad to see you go
It's sure been nice to work with you
You've been very nice to know

We watched you treat psychotics
As you tried to free their minds
Of the horrors of the yesteryears
That they have left behind

The year has gone so quickly
Perhaps you will return someday
To brighten up the faces
In the same old way

May heaven shine upon you
And good luck reign supreme
And may the future hold in store
Everything you dream

With sincere appreciation from
The staff of N2

A MOTHER'S UNFORGIVING SORROW

Another day has come between us
And I can no longer stand
To watch the distant look
In your eyes
As they try to escape me
Though you sit stoically
Bearing the unbearable

Resentment is an emotion
You have chosen not to feel
So you hide it from yourself
Beneath layers of understanding
But those orbs
Are outlets for your soul
And they burn
With your anger

So we are to live like this
Forever I suppose
I cannot break it off between us
My guilt is like a chain
And when I go to speak
You're pointing fingers
Scream j'accuse
Choking me

Pointing at a picture on the wall
Of our son
Telling guests
How lovely he was
And I must fill in the details
Of how he drowned
While on a fishing trip
With his father
As you sit and cry to yourself

Our son is dead, my love
No act of man can bring him back
His soul is in God's hands
But we must go on living

I see no words comfort you
So I sit
Waiting for the time that heals all wounds

A PATH TO FOLLOW

Well the searching
Isn't over
If you haven't
Found the answer
Don't stop
Keep on walking
Through the forest

And the journey
Has not ended
Till you reach
Your destination
Don't let
The falling rain
Deter you

Chorus
Carry on
Build some wings
If you must fly
To reach your goal

Go to the stars
Fulfill the most
Fantastic dreams
In your soul

And the day
Is not over
Just because
The sun has set
Don't you let
A little darkness
Scare you

And the way
Is not blocked
By mountains
Or by oceans
There will always
Be a path
For you to follow

(Chorus)

COME DOWN
July 25, 1984

Chorus
Come down
Come down
Come down
Come down

Come down to my level baby
Come see the hills and the trees
Take a swim in the oceans
Come down and spend some time with me

(Chorus)

Come down to my comprehension
Share some of my point of view
You may be a very special lady
But I have some fine things to show to you
Wooow

There can be joy in simple living
There can be joy without jewels
You may find there's happiness in giving
Love to a man who will give it back to you
Wooow

(Chorus)

Come down from your high situation
Don't play the role of a queen
Come down to my sweet redemption
Come down and live the good life with me

HAPPINESS JUNCTION

Let's all go
To Happiness Junction
Let's all go
To Happinessville
Our life there will have but one function
Find a dream
For each to fulfill

Chorus
Be aware of the sun in the sky
Be aware
Of the birds in the trees
Feel free to enjoy
The warmth in the breeze
Be happy forever in Happinessville
Be happy forever in Happinessville

Smiling faces
Sweet laughing children
Even rainy days bring us cheer
We know how to make
Life worth living
We have good times
All through the year

(Chorus)

LORD, I'VE SEEN EVIL, EVIL

Chorus
Lord, I've seen evil, evil
But where, oh where, oh where,
Have I seen love?
Lord, I've seen evil, evil
But where, oh where, oh where,
Have I seen love?
Lord, I've seen evil, evil, evil
Is love only in the heavens above?

I was born in the heat of summer
And I saw the prophet rise
In my hometown
He spoke many words of wisdom
But my heart would not obey him
Anyhow
I broke laws
I made thunder
I set the world asunder
But I was just a ripple
In a well

(Chorus)

I sought love in a woman's smile
In a woman's warm embrace
But I looked
And in awhile
She stole the truth
Out of my face
So I reached down
Into the hell of darkness
And found it was a warm
And gentle place

Lord, I've seen evil
Lord, I've seen evil, evil
Lord, I've seen evil, evil, evil
Is love only in the heavens above me?
Lord, won't you love me
Oh Lord, please love me

Logic or Emotion

Why should I search my head
For answers I can't find
To questions I don't care
The answers for

When I feel my heart
About to explode
My heart's in overload
From loving you

And all the important issues
In this year's elections
Will be forgotten
On election day

And the hunger or injustice
We swore
We would cure
Will not have gone away

It's a box
With six sides
And we're trapped
In the centre
With no way of getting it out

Or a circle
Twirling, spinning
With no end
And no beginning
Faced with such a puzzle
Why give way to doubt

I feel my heart
It's alive

I hear it beating
So what
If life is fleeting
At least of this
I can be sure

You give me
Momentary pleasure
Loving you
Is so much better
Than worrying about
What life is for

Man Without a Home

How long can stately mansions rise
Above the ruins
Of the city core
Mr. President
Have you any feelings for the poor?

The parliament
Has sent the troops in
To quell the rising disturbances
While communists are lining up
For bread
And some black bellies
Never will be fed

Choose your sides
Because there's no running away
Choose your sides
There is no rock to crawl under
Choose your sides
There is no place for you to hide
And there's nothing worse
Than being alone
Being alone

Chorus
Sinner throw the stone
Crucify the other sinners
Purge the world with fire
Of opposing points of view
React with violence
When you don't know what to do
But never, never, never stand alone
Unless you have the courage
To be a man without a home

There will be enemies for all
But the least amongst you
That's the way we made the world
And we're not about to change it
So if you are at all
The type who refuses to grovel
Then you'd better stand prepared to fight
Don't matter if you're yellow, black, or white

(Chorus 2x)

MADNESS IN TIME

There is no love
Though I believe in it
Van Gough cut off his ear
To cease the endless
Pain of noise
Of cries of death
Because he so loved the world

Where is the honest man?
The only truth
Is that there is no truth
And even that's a lie

But I prefer lies
They make a better
Private world
They cease
The cries of death
And I need not fear
Being gangraped
By a pack of gorillas
Recently escaped from the zoo

Using a fair man
I pray that no gorilla
Is gangraped
By a pack of humans
Recently escaped from the city

The hair of man and animals
Overgrows upon the solid land
And I will watch from a tower
Changing all into myth
Spreading light
And believe it to be true

In time

But time is such a bloody tool
With which to kill a man

In time
Da Vinci's smile will cackle
Beethoven's beautiful noise will screech

Van Gough's severed ear could not
Keep him from going mad

Nor can I maintain my sanity
By holding high
A pack of lies

No More Fantasy

September 7, 1984

When the artform
Finally dies
Will the universe
Realize
That the human race
Made more than atom bombs

When Capote's laugh
Is no longer heard
When nothing's left that is absurd
When silence is the only word
Won't we all despair
For what is gone

Chorus
No more fantasy
Just reality
No more make believe
No more chance to dream

(Chorus x2)

Burn all books
And burn all plays
End all differences
And wipe the wounds away
Make everything look new
In a big white world for me and you

(Chorus x3)

Nova Scotia Shore

The air's so heavy that the winds can't blow
The train pulls into Toronto

I tie my bootlace
Look up at that beating sun
It's been a long way I've come

The blood from my heart
Flows like a flag unfurled
The maple leaf falls in the forest
Where the waters run no more

Take me back
To Nova Scotia's shore

I'm just a single man
They're trying to make me a world
I touched the forest
But I felt the sea

Take me
Take me back
To Nova Scotia's shore

On Death and Living

You say the sun's a God
But it's just a burning stone
You say that hell is cold and dark
And there you are alone
I say if that is so
Then still you are alive
The only hell's a living one
Felt by those who survive

My life will last forever
As far as I will know
And I will walk in the sun
Knowing cold is only cold
That darkness is an emptiness
Of which I'm not afraid
And I have done no great wrong
For which I must be saved

I am not sure what lies beyond
When last I closed my eyes
And true it would be nice
If from death I could rise
Into a heaven filled with love
A paradise of joy
But I am happy
For I have tried to create my own
Since I was just a boy

And it is not a selfish venture
But one I wish to share
One I wish to extend
To each and everywhere
To bring heaven to the living
To make the world a paradise
To banish hell forever
Know that darkness is only night

OLD AGE AND REBIRTH

I am old
A thing forgotten
I wish to teach you
But you will not learn
You will not see
You will look forever
Into the future

I am old and beastly
Scared by yesterdays
While you have no memories
I extended into you
But you would free yourself of me

I am old
Living past usefulness
I am a leaf
Trapped in snow
Waiting for spurring
To free me
And blow me into dust
Forever more

Our Own Grief

There are no more lies to tell
There are no more bells to ring
There are no more men to kill
There are no more words to sing

All the glory led to battles
Till there was no one left to stand
In solemn ceremonies
For the fallen of our land

And the hunger
Led to no one left to feed
And poverty is all we ever got
From all our greed

Then we learned to hate so many
There was no one left to love
So we dig holes all around us
And if that was not enough

We took the words
Of all our Thinkers
And we shaped them to our will
Made instruments of mass destruction
Till there was nothing left to kill

Not a flower
Not a meadow
Not a shadow
Not a leaf

Only one thing is for certain
We did it all to our own grief

PLAYING GAMES

Games
Da da da, da da da da
Playing games
Da da da, da da da da
I'm playing games
Da da da, da da da da
Da da da da da, da da da da da

I use to watch the soaps
But I got so bored
Now I'm playing games
And I'm keeping score
Playing games is the American way
And it don't bring no trouble to the U.S.A.

Playing games
Da da da, da da da da
I'm playing games
Da da da, da da da da
I'm playing games
Da da da, da da da da
Da da da da da, da da da da da

The joystick is held
Tight within my hands
I got control
And I'm making commands
I have top score on the Pac Man machine
And my drinking buddies think I'm really keen

Playing games
Da da da, da da da da
We're playing games
Da da da, da da da da
We're playing games

Da da da, da da da da
Da da da da da, da da da da da

There are many variations
On a simple theme
You can play almost anything you can dream
I like to play war games in a packed arcade
With a lot of people cheering me as I play

Playing games
Da da da, da da da da
I'm playing games
Da da da, da da da da
I'm playing games
Da da da, da da da da
Da da da da da, da da da da da

Watch the bombs fall out of the video sky
Everyone is happy 'cause there's only one side
The enemy are people who don't even exist
Is real life anything like this?

Playing games
Da da da, da da da da
I'm playing games
Da da da, da da da da
I'm playing games
Da da da, da da da da
Da da da da da, da da da da da

Keep the quarters coming
Put them into the slot
I'm playing better than ever
I'm really hot
I'm gonna set the world record
I won't make no mistakes
I'm the greatest game player

Alive today
I'm a champion playing for the U.S.A.

Games
Da da da, da da da da
Playing games
Da da da, da da da da
I'm playing games
Da da da, da da da da
Da da da da da, da da da da da

RUN AROUND, CHILD

Run around, child
Run around, run
Take time to play
Under the sun

Laugh in the day
Cry in the dark
Look to the stars
Open your heart

There's a dream
Waiting for you
Reach out and grab it
Before it goes by

All your dreams
They can come true
You can do just what you want
If only you'll try

So run around, child
Fill up your time
With laughter and love
And sweet summer wine

Make all the world
Your place to play
Run around, child
Till the end of the day

RUN FAST, BABY

Run fast, baby
Baby, run fast
Run fast
Baby, run fast

Fate is chasing
So baby, run fast
Run fast
Baby, run fast

Escape your destiny
Change what's in the cards
Overrule the looming doom
Dictated by the stars

Halt the wheel of fortune
Stop the falling blade
Find a way to win for sure
Don't chance that you'll be saved

Race on, baby
Baby, race on
Race on
Baby, race on

Time is burning
So baby, race on
Race on
Baby, race on

The candle's melting down
The shadow's growing long
The winter winds are blowing
The year is almost gone

There's much you have accomplished
By running all the way
But when asked for specifics
You really couldn't say

Run back, baby
Baby, run back
Run back
Baby, run back

Something's gone
So baby, run back
Run back
Baby, run back

SAILORS SELDOM WALK AWAY FROM A GOOD TIME

Who will be with you
When I'm gone away
On the sea
Making ends meet

Who will be with you
When I'm writing letters home
Ports of call I'll phone
Just to see that you're all alone

Chorus
The ocean's too wide
The sun's too high
The days pass too slow
Am I all alone? ...Who knows
Sailors seldom walk away from a good time

I dream you're wearing
The long silk red dress
As you dance
With a man in satin pants
I'm gonna knock him on his ass
When I get home

Last time I came back
Just to find out
I was to be
A daddy again
Was it my best friend
Or just some strange guy
Who caught your eye
One night

The ocean's too wide
The sun's too high
The days pass too slow
Are you all alone?
Who knows?
Sailors wives seldom walk away from a good time

It's live and let live
The relationship is strong
It has to be
To last so long
When I'm often gone

I have my fun
In foreign ports of call
Who can stand
To be alone
Oh I miss you so

(Chorus)

When I get home... you'll know
Sailors seldom walk away from a good time

Save the World, Save a Child

Nothing ever changes
So they say
But I believe
That things are changing
Everyday
And I believe
There is a way
To save the world
Although it can't all be done by me
I'm not so powerful, you see
But I'll have done enough
If all I do
Is save a child

To save the world
We must save the children
We can make the world laugh
If we help the children smile
We will one day
See the whole world
Sing and dance
If we only give the children
A chance

Save the world now
Save a child
You have the power
To make a young face smile
Open up your heart
You'll have done your part
To save the world
If you just reach out
To save a child

To save the world
We must save the children
We can make the world laugh
If we help the children smile
Open up your heart
You'll have done your part
To save the world
If you just reach out
To save a child

Save the world now
Save a child
Save the world
Save a child

SELF ANALYSTS

I hate writing
It bores me!
Politics is a hobby
It replaces going to horror pictures
There is much
That draws my attention
But nothing captivates me
The same is true of women
I do not wish it
But I cannot change it
So it is so

I like money
Cars
Drinking
Vacationing
I like to move around
But not to travel
Because travelling implies
Some intellectual curiosity
About the places one visits
I have none!

I am not a man of vision
A man of vision pulls the future
Into the present
My objective is to escape the past
Since now is part of the past
I flee from the now
The boring
The tired and true
Whatever it is, we are trying now
Let's try something else!

Certain things and activities
And perhaps even people
Are part of the eternal
They are not prisoners of time
I would fill up my home and life with them
Such as lovemaking
Our ancestors did it
So will our grandchildren

If I am reborn
I would like to come back
As a dolphin
On a planet
Where the only human beings
Are children

SOLDIERING ON

Thoughts of a crazy man
Reading the morning paper
On dying children
In Afghanistan

His house is spotless
His garden
Neatly tended
He kneels
To smell
A budding rose

He feels the sun
Thinking it hot
And he turns the engine over
The crowd begins to roar
The building is sparkle-golden
In the morning sky
He feels a burst of fire
And drops
A half yard from the finish line
"The gold was mine!"
He screams

Thoughts of a crazy man
Raising his gun
To the cheers of the crowd
Shooting
At clay pigeons
That turn into bloodied corpses
Wasting on the hills
In Afghanistan

Thoughts of a solder and athlete
And hero
Swerving his car
Through evening traffic
On the streets
Of New York

SOMEWHERE IN BETWEEN
THE ENDS OF INFINITY

Tonight, there is no news
Only a much brighter sun
To contend with

An anguished cry for rain
My eyes blinded
From the city skyline
A moment more of eternity

And what of me and my age
In far off and distant times
What of a blind rush ahead
From out of a cave
Into a fire we had not
Learned to control

For out of an age with rain
They will laugh at us surely
With our skins a radiant glow
When on some night
Between the rising and the setting of the sun
A sudden flash, a spark in the darkness of the
Eternal sky
Tells a little tale of us

SUNDOWN

When I was young
Life stretched vast
Before me
So strong, so sweet and beautiful
As far as I could see

Who knew
Back then
That the night closes in
And that dreams
All vanished with the day

Chorus
It's sundown
I watch a fire burning in the sky
How can it be so beautiful
When the dark is closing in

Did I run fast?
Did I make things shoot on past?
You can't stop and make things last
But can you slow down?

(*Chorus*)

THE MARKETPLACE

I had an honest trade
On such a decent way of life
I thought they'd see me through
When I went looking for a wife

But in the marketplace
There is no human face
Only hustlers, quickening
A deadening pace
And I couldn't find
An honest purchaser in sight

Chorus
My decent life had let me down
An honest man
Fell to the ground
Words began to clutter
Up my life
In the marketplace

In the marketplace
Where the human race
Hides its heart away

In the marketplace
There's not an honest face
In sight

(*Chorus*)

THE MOON'S ESCAPING

The sky is falling
Falling, falling
The stars are bursting
Debris is in the sea
The moon's escaping
Racing through the universe
And men are marching onward
Marching, marching to be free

Gone, gone
With the autumn winds
Ancient civilizations
Are collapsing into dust
Sun descending
The world is ending
I hear the bombs exploding
I feel my heart exploding
As I look at you with lust

Gone, gone
The sky is falling
Long ago and far away
A gentle breeze, I saw you smile
Was passing through the yard
And I was hypnotized
Now I wonder
Is there any meaning?
Can we get together
If not forever
How about forget awhile?
I'm so glad you are so beautiful
But why is life so hard

Went blowing through my mind
Now I'm blinded

I can see no recourse
Though I search
I fear
That there is nothing
Left for me to find

Gone, gone
The sky is falling
The world is ending
Debris is in the sea
My mind's escaping
Racing through the universe
And now
Forevermore
I am free

THE PROPHET

Strange themes and new dreams
Are coming looking out of you
I think I'll step back
This crowds dying to get through
To a dream
You're the newest superstar
To hit the scene

If you're the Prophet
You're the latest in the line
I'd like to believe
But I haven't seen a sign
It's just the times
And the people feel so burdened
By their crimes

And when the thunder
Rumbled over distant skies
I had to cry
Knowing someone sweet had died

I hear you preaching
Come and venture far with me
Another paradise
Where all men can be free
It's just a cause
You are standing for applause

Yea, you're the prophet
You're the product of our times
Don't blame me
I feel burdened
By your crimes

There's a Thousand Ways

So you don't believe
Think no soul alive can deceive
You
You're such a clever chap
Always know just where you're at
Still you really ought to see

Chorus
There's a thousand ways
There's a thousand ways
And you'll never know
Why things come and go
Why things live and die
Ah, ah, ah, ah, aieh
Where the horizon meets the sky

There's a thousand dreams
And a million schemes
To live in paradise
Ah, wouldn't that be nice
But then the siren screams
Throughout the endless niiiiight

And I wake up
Nothing having changed
And nothing
Seeeeeming right

(Chorus)

THIS SIDE OF TOWN

Get drunk
In the park young man
Listen to the children cry
Pretty soon you'll see them die
And we'll all know why

So sad
Young man looking old now
Old man only mounds that moan
Always gonna feel alone
Till I get my home

Chorus
Gonna break
Break away someday
Never going to come back
To this side of town

These wanting hollow sounds
Are older than the winds
That whip their sorrow
Through my mind

I'd ask you to be kind
But I know that
You've gone blind
To this side of town

(Chorus)

WHEN I STRUM MY GUITARS
September 22, 1983

Good songs
Bad songs
Songs of destruction
Songs of survival
And songs of seduction
All seem to come into my head
When I strum my guitars
When I strum my guitars

Hellfire, creation
Human salvation
And God's just damnation
They all get their time
But mostly I like
To sing about beauty
To sing about love
And sweet warm sunshine

I like a sad song
That tells about heartbreak
And how we all feel lonely sometimes
But mostly I like
To sing about beauty
To sing about love
And sweet warm sunshine

Good songs
Bad songs
Songs in between
From things that I've heard of
And things that I've seen
All the world's glory
And all the world's story
Comes into my head when I strum my guitars

All the world's glory
And all the world's story
Comes into my head when I strum my guitar

When I strum my guitar
When I strum my guitar

WHERE THE EAGLE FLIES

Come take a trip
Where the eagle flies
Across a canyon wide
In the deep blue sky

Come see the earth
From a moon's eye view
It's a little round ball
Coloured brown and blue

Come watch the sun
Roam the Milky Way
Where a million years
Passes like a day

And now
See the sights
Of the universe
Watch the galaxies
Expand and burst

Time
Swinging back and forth
And up and down
And turning endlessly
Around and around

Stop
My heart is telling me
I must return
To where the eagle flies
I have much to learn

Again
Let's begin

On the canyon floor
I hope to find out there
All that life is for

WHIPS AND CHAINS

Have you ever multiple orgasmed
While you were dreaming
Have you ever fucked a virgin
In your thoughts

Have you ever stooped to feeling
A thousand wild sensations
While lying with your eyes closed
On your bed

Have you ever thought
There are no answers
Then realized
Every thought is something known

And can you fill your mind
With the most interesting people
While you're feeling sad and bored
And all alone

The mind is a truly wonderous thing
With it you can run and laugh and sing
And if you control it right
It will only bring you pleasure
All you need to do is to avoid
Thinking painful things

But the body's pleasures
Are of a two-fold nature
They always seem to go and let you down
While the price one has to pay
For even the simplest joys
Felt by the flesh
Is so astronomical
As to astound

It is because the body is a torture chamber
How it hurts one
Causing such suffering and pain
Still I'm often fearful
Of living only in my thoughts
For there is nothing real it seems
Without there being whips and chains

Upon the Waves

We are free wings
Blinding white against
The sky

We soar
High and fast
Under the sun

Below the jagged waves
Seem to crack like thunder
Yet we nestle on them
As gently as a feather
Bedded in the wind

Distant is the land
Ragged with cruelty
Still
When the sky darkens
That is the home
We move towards

HIDE IN THE DARK

If light reveals your soul
And you're afraid
Hide in the dark
You'd better hide in the dark

Let lies tell the tale
So you can stay
You hear in your heart
What they will say
Hide in the dark
You'd better hide in the dark

They're unforgiving fools
Unforgetting too
They'd never let you see it through
So come the day
Hide in the dark
Hide in the dark

Let your eyes adjust to no light
Let your eyes adjust to the night
Look around
Oh it can't be true
They're hiding in the dark with you
Hide in the dark

You're a Rat, But You're Not in the Race

Nowhere to go but down
(What good did your schooling do)
Only to hang around
(Man, you're such a fool)
You're running in the same place
Day after day
You're a rat
But you're not in the race

What you got to do
Is read the help wanted ads
Try to keep up
With the latest fads
Watch the Ferraris
Drive on by
And the places streak across
The blue sky
As your days
Just keep going by

Holes in your pockets
Dust on your shoes
Nothing to live for
But nothing to lose
Go to bed hungry
Or steal a piece of cake
You're a rat
But you're not in the race

Jesus my life
Is wasting on by
And I don't even have the sense
To sit down and cry
Don't know who to blame
What's it all about

I don't even have the guts
To stand up and shout
I'm a rat
But I'm not in the race

Cold in your heart
Pain in your soul
Walking around
But with no place to go
No way you'll ever get
In out of the storm
Don't it make you wonder
Why you were ever born
You're a rat
But you're not in the race

You're running in the same place
Day after day
You're a rat
But you're not in the race

GOD, MARX, AND MAN

God created existence
Man created privileged existence
Marx created privileged existence
As an injustice

I painted a nude
It gave some an erotic pleasure
Others thought such pleasure immoral

A small boy carried a sign
Protesting imperialism
This modern pseudo Christ
Grew up
And defected to Russia
Years later
His own son
Defected back

I drank wine
Constantly
Through the last days
Of the revolution
As beauty and truth
Were poured out into the Earth

Bitterly I toasted
Long life
To the Godless, unprivileged universe

TEARS FOR THE DEVIL

"A man takes what he is given and fights for what he is denied"

So you feel the need to sin, hey Satan
So you feel the need to take what must be yours
So you feel the need to live where there is darkness
Tell me, have you ever felt this need before?

Well, you watch him shine
You loved all that he offered
You watched him lead
You praised his mighty deeds
Still you felt the need
To turn your face away
Well, I feel some sympathy for you

Now the battles rage
Upon the waste
Of paradise
Your strength has dried
Like the bloods
Of many wars
And you will take
All that he has offered
You will live in darkness
Forevermore

I Guess I'm Younger Than I Knew

I'm still needing you
Though I'd reach the age
When I could live alone
But some feelings got me blue
I guess I'm younger than I knew

When all my dreams had gone
When I no longer felt the need
To be so strong
To feel my words were true
I thought I'd reached the age
To say goodbye to you
I guess I'm younger than I knew

I'm still needing you each morning
Still needing you each night
Still needing you beside me
In the darkness or the light
I'm so much younger than I knew

If I Never

If I never had a wife
Wouldn't it be a swell life
But every day I wake up to
Her telling me just what to do

She says we've got a lovely home
But the bills go on and on
Have to work my days away
And never get to see my pay

If I only had a dream
To save me
From the same old things
Something changed or something new
Like a new life I could
Go home to

If I only had today
All the things I've thrown away
I'd keep them now
And throw away
All the things I've saved

But I am old
She is my wife
That is my job
This is my life
And when I'm sad
I stop and say,
"Hey
At least I'm not in jail"

Don't Be Afraid of the Dark

Don't be afraid of the dark
Don't be afraid of a noise in the night
Don't lie awake with the light on
Don't be afraid to close your eyes

So many dreams of which to wonder
We can't discern truth from illusion
If my voice reaches you like thunder
Please forgive me for my intrusion

Don't be afraid of the dark
Don't be afraid of sounds in the night
Don't be afraid of the dark
I am here, everything's alright

Listen to the sound of an atom splitting
I see the cloud from where I'm sitting
Mushroom cloud so fast exploding
The vision I see is foreboding

Now I hear human laughter
Such a vision am I after
Smiling faces, dancing feet
I want to give in to defeat
Like a snowflake beneath the sun

Time is an illusion
It doesn't exist
And yet still we grow older

Dreams Vanish with the Night

When I was young
Life stretched vast
Before me
So strong, so sweet and beautiful
For as far as I could see

Who knew
Back then
That the night closes in
And that dreams
All vanish with the day

Did I run fast?
Did I make things shoot on past?
You can't stop and make
Things last
But can you slow down?

It's sundown
I watch a fire burning
In the sky
How can it be so beautiful
When the dark is closing in?

END TO CONVERSATION

I don't like being put into a situation
Of suspended animation
So don't say you'll call
Don't say you'll call
You won't find me
Waiting home
By a phone that never rings
I don't like staying home alone

Put on your party dress baby
Let's have a ball
The night is young
Let's dance, let's swing

I don't like complicated communication
Or commitments that don't mean a thing
But I love you
And I love your blue eyes
They are an epic novel
In my imagination

I don't care for space age terminology
Or technology
Or Star Trek Enterprise
I only want to feel alive
And hold you
I really want to hold you

WASTED ENERGY

Hiding in the open field
Revealed
Wasted energy
That lost the world

Every time is cloudy time
Every time is rainy time
Every time is darkness
And despair

Today's paper headline reads
"Shattered humans
Systems overload
Abort
Before explode"

Massive projects
To the sun
Cannot include
Everyone
While the stars
Are just too far
We cannot escape
To there

As the death-defying
Feats of man
Have left
No place to stand
To avoid
The human cannonball

I often wonder
Is it real?
I can tell you

It's not sane
Perhaps it's only
Just a game
Well, I wish we all
Would learn to play another

MAN'S FAVOURITE STORM

We have lived for centuries
And know that man
Is not a gentle creature
Rough terrain is his domain
Ferocious storms
His favourite weather
Let the sun fade
He will not be afraid
Do not look for him
To be tender
For he only knows
To struggle through
The dark and dearth
Of all the Earth
And to survive
He has the will
To stay alive
Man will tear apart
All that gets in his way
Even those closest to his heart

A Bad Heart

I have a bad heart man
I have a bad heart man
Up in my apartment
Beating on my bed

Boom! Boom! Boom!

I don't know where to put it
What could it be good for
Perhaps inside a chicken
A big one that is dead

Boom! Boom! Boom!

I don't know how it started
Could there have been a fire
Someone tried to hide it
Maybe a suicide

Aaaaaaaaah

I've got this bad heart man
Beating up in my apartment
If the cops find out, I'm done in
Bang! Bang! Bang!
They'll put me away for life

"Twenty years, dummy!"

It's okay man, it's over
The heart has stopped to beat
I'll bury him away now
Somewhere in the park

His last days were kind of rough
But he was very brave
I'm glad I tried to save him
You know I heard him say goodbye
Goodbye, goodbye

A Heart Reborn

A heart reborn
By a light
Out of heaven
A heart reborn
Saved from the sword

A heart reborn
To be joyfully living
A heart reborn
In the eyes of the Lord

Christ gave his life up in sacrifices
So we could return to paradise
A heart reborn
By the grace of the Lord
By the grace of the Lord

A heart of joy
Without any sorrow
A heart of love
Without any hate

With nothing
To fight, kill, or die for
A heart happy
In praise of the Lord

A heart reborn
For the glory of God
For the glory of God

Always I Will Love You

Chorus
Days pass
Years go by
I love you

Empires rise
And fall
I love you still

Stars changing places
In the heavens
But always I will love you
Yes, I will

Life calls to me
I'm just a young man
Tells me to race against the sun
Don't stay behind my love
Come with me
Together we will run
Till time is done

Years pass
We grow white
With winter

Seasons change
We grow cold
With age

Stars shine forever in the heavens
And I will love you
All my living days

Chorus

Stars shine forever in
The heavens
And always I will love you
Yes, I will

Always I will love you
Yes, I will

AMRA

Amra
You're a mystery
And I could never see
What is inside of you
What makes you feel
What makes you real

Amra
Like a butterfly
I never could deny
That you are beautiful
But you always seem to want
To fly away

On your own
That's where you want to be
Far away from anyone
And far away from me
In disguise
Hidden from all prying eyes
Safe
From all the love you could have known

Amra
Amra
Amra, won't you change for me
Amra
Amra, tell me how hard can it be

I reach out
And for a brief moment
Our lips softly touch
Before you pull away

Then you're gone
In a puff of smoke
In the downward stroke
Of a magician's wand

Amra
Amra
Amra, won't you say before you go
Amra
Amra
Amra, do you love me? I must know
Amra, do you love me? I must know

ANNA MARIA

Anna Maria
It's been such a time
As the seasons change
As the sun flies by
You have been
On my mind

Anna Maria
I have pools of tears
To quench my thirst
In dry years
I look beneath
The clothes you wear
And you disappear
But you are on my mind

Anna Maria
Leaves are raked then burned
All the seasons turn
To get away
Was it yesterday
You were on my mind

Anna Maria
Seasons change and die
And the sun must fade
It's been such a time
You've been on my mind

Don't Leave Me Standing in the Cold

Chorus
Give me your love
Keep me warm
Don't leave me standing
All alone
In the cold
Don't leave me standing
In the cold

If your heart
Is made of ice
Come and warm it
Cover here by my side
Hold me close
I'll hold you tight
We can make it through
The lonely night

(Chorus)

If it rains
If it thunders
There is shelter
We can get in under
Out of the storm
We'll stay warm
All through the night
Until the early morning

(Chorus)

If your heart
Is made of ice
Come and warm it
Over here by my side

Hold me close
I'll hold you tight
We can make it through
The lonely night
We can make it through
The lonely night

(Chorus)

Don't leave me standing
In the cold
Don't leave me standing
In the cold
Don't leave me standing
In the cold

Don't You Dream

Don't you dream
Don't you dream
Of no one but me
Won't you dream of me
Even while you lay with someone else
And on the moment
That I die
I won't be afraid
I will pass away
Thinking about you

Won't you plan some crazy scheme
To save me
Will look back on this
As a bad time we went through
But if I die
Won't you dream about me
And remember all the laughs
And the fine times we two know

I ain't no great romantic
But I love you
You were searching for a god
But you settled for a man
And I guess our humanness destroyed us
And I guess we picked
An awful bad place to take a stand

I will dream
I will dream about you
I will think only of you
As my life's about to end
And won't you dream
Won't you dream, dream about me
Woman, won't you keep alive
The memory of your man

A Hot Heart

I've got a hot rod heart, baby
A heart that burns up the highway
A heart on fire
With the passion of the night
A heart that reaches out to
Everything in sight
A heart that needs to win
So, baby, let my heart in

I've got the heart of a king, girl
A heart that wants everything
A heart of desire
Balanced on a tight wire
Between the earth and the sky
I've got a heart that will fly

I've got a heart that was meant
For the night
A heart that loves the light
From your eyes
As they shine in the dark

I've got a gangster's heart, baby
What I can't buy, I'll steal
But I'll make it all real
And I'll never be caught
Not with my hot, hot heart

A Marriage Made

He was not typical
Although he was only
An average man
He was strong, hard-working, and reliable

He had dreams
But found reality suited him
He was a down to earth man
And many people loved him

She was fickle
She didn't know her mind
She longed for something
She grabbed at everything
To make it hers
And found it could not be

She fought to be loved
But fought to not love
She could not find happiness
And it made her restless

Why they got married
No one knew
And of course
It didn't work out

BABY, IF I'M WITHOUT YOU

Chorus
Woombah
Woombah
Woombah
Woombah

I need you more
Than I thought possible
But it's true

(Chorus)

The sun won't shine
Baby, if I'm without you

(Chorus)

The spring won't come
Flowers will not bloom
Cold winter snows
Will fall in June
All my happiness
Will end too soon
Baby, if I'm without you

(Chorus)

My every smile
Will turn to a frown
My every up
Will become a down
Nowhere, no love to be found
Baby, if you're not around

(Chorus)

Time to cry
That's all there will be
A cold, lonely world
You'll have left to me
I'm gonna feel
A lot worse than just blue
Baby, if I'm without
Baby, if I'm without
Baby, if I'm without you

BELIEF BEFORE CERTAINTY

Creation without meaning
Action lacking purpose
Wind devoid of direction
We are mad
Running endlessly
In all directions

Slow me down
Now slow me down
And take my hand
Hold me close
And help me now
To understand

Paralysed
By uncertainty
Crippled by
A need to know

So many roads
In front of me
How to choose
Which way to go

Slow me down
Now slow me down
And take my hand
Hold me close
And help me now
To understand

What to do
Which way to go
By myself
I do not know

BYE BABY SWEET LOVE

Bye, bye baby sweet love
You can leave now that you've come
Take up all of your possessions
Lift your pretty feet and run

Chorus
His mountains reach up before me
His waters call me on
His sun shines down to warm me
But he's got me on the run

I gave everything I had away
Things only clutter up my mind
Now I only need some water
And a tiny piece of sky

Bye, bye, bye baby sweet
Don't take your time to leave
You've got everything you need
Lift your pretty feet and run

(Chorus)

Bye, bye, bye, bye baby
Take what you've got
Don't turn around for one last look
There is no time
Lift your pretty feet and run
Bye, bye, bye, bye, bye
Bye, bye, bye, bye, bye

BURN MY HEART WITH YOUR FIRE

You've got to give me your love
If you want me
I can't live on holding hands
And kisses
I can't do without what you won't
Give away
Baby, if you want me to stay

Chorus
You've got to burn my heart with your fire
Take the emotions higher
Lift me up with desire
Babe
And maybe then I'll spend the night

We are going nowhere fast, girl
I can't think of anything to say
If you want to know me
Then you've got to reach inside
And I can only hope you'll know the way

(Chorus)

We may never have another chance, girl
One time for all time true love may
Come your way
If we can't make it in the night
Somewhere under the moonlight
We will drift apart our separate ways

(Chorus)

Suddenly the night has gotten warmer
Baby, I don't know *soon* it could be day
I feel like I'm holding thunder

> Girl, the spell you've put me under
> Now that you have finally found your way
>
> (*Chorus*)

COLDER THAN A WINTER LEAF

I'm cold baby
Colder than a winter leaf
I said I'm cold baby
Colder than a winter leaf

My heart's freezing
It's in a winter storm
But my heart's strong
It won't be torn

I'm just cold baby
Colder than a winter leaf
You make me cold baby
Colder than a winter leaf

Now I may feel the sun again
It's warmth upon my skin
But no matter how hot I get
I'll always know I've been

Cold baby
Colder than a winter leaf
You make me cold baby
Colder than a winter leaf

I'm so cold baby
I'm colder than a winter
And I'm colder than a leaf in wintertime

IN THE COLOUR OF HER EYES

She came to me a wild surprise
And as I listened to her lies
I found out that paradise
Was in the colour of her eyes
In the colour of her eyes

I didn't know which way to turn
I've heard a heart in love will burn
I know the meaning of *to yearn*
It's in the colour of her eyes
In the colour of her eyes

Chorus
In the colour of her eyes
I see warmth on winter nights
I see arms to hold me tight
I see lips that fit just right
And I see dreams come true for me

Don't say she's too young for me
I'm in prison
Only she can set me free
And I know what freedom means
Because I've seen it in my dreams
And in the colour of her eyes
All in the colour of her eyes

In the colour of her eyes
Beauty, love and tenderness
Soft caress and gentle kiss
In the colour of her eyes
All in the colour of her eyes

EVERLASTING

I search for the everlasting love
I'll stretch the everlasting universe
To find it
I'll shape my thoughts drastically
To create it, where it isn't
But how to make my thoughts be
Everlasting

Why can't eyes be stars
And never changing
When looks of rapture
Turn from passion to indifference
You lay upon your side
Your back towards me
I touch you gently
You only snore

When the moment of climatic ecstasy
Touches we
I tremble with seemingly
Eternal joy
But the moment soon subsides

Everything is playing out
In an instant
Quick as a breath
In the twinkle of an eye
So desperately we try to hold off
To make each moment last
A little longer
How to make the moment
Everlasting

I strive for all the wrong things
I should learn to let the
Moment pass
To accept the changing shape
Of everything
For life is lived in time
And time was meant to change

There is an everlasting moment
It comes beyond the end of life
When there is nothing to change
How ironically
Dread afraid
I can barely
Whisper its name

FAR AWAY

Chorus
Far, far, far
Far away
Far, far, far
Far away

I think I'll stay
I'll unpack my bags
This is far enough
Away from you

I don't want no reminders
Of those bitter days
It's time for me to turn
To something new

(Chorus)

I think I'll learn the local lingo
Hang out down at the local bar
Dance with women
Underneath the stars

This is paradise
This can be paradise

(Chorus)

Give me some time and I'll forget you
Forget your face, forget your name
Time will come between
The memories and pain
And I'll never be hurt by you again

(Chorus)

I'm far away from you
And the hurt you put me through
Baby, I'm so far away from you

I'm
(*Chorus*)

GET INTO THE GAME

Get into the game
Get into the game
Don't waste your life
Being part of the crowd
Get into the game

Let them scream your name
Let them love or hate you
Let them cheer or boo
But whatever you do
Get into the game

Because it's not the same
Watching from the stands
Every play that's made
Time goes slipping through
Your empty hands

And you will lose
Cause only players win
So get in there and play
Before the end of the day
Get into the game

Hey Gretzky
Don't be a hog
Pass the puck

GOODBYE SALLY JANE

Goodbye Sally Jane
You're just a movie queen
Who never made it to the silver screen
A Norma Jean
Who's still unknown

Goodbye Sally Jane
You princess dressed in tattered rages
No bellhop ever took your bags
Or asked you for your autograph
And now you're gone
And I'm the only one who knows

Goodbye Sally
Goodbye Sally
Goodbye Sally

Goodbye Sally Jane
No paper ever screamed your name
In front page headlines
But I sure know you're gone
I sure know you're gone

HER DEEP DESIRE

I loved her
She was nice
But she was cold as ice
And there was no way
That I could light a fire

Though I held her close and kissed her
I can tell you mister
She never really felt any desire

She was all unto herself
She was always somewhere else
And I couldn't break
The silence
With thunder

And though I reached out with my hand
She wouldn't grab a hold
And I had to stand
And watch her
Slipping under

I loved her
She was nice
But like a star in the sky
So far away
I couldn't feel her fire

And though I held her tight and kissed her
To my regret minister
I never ever felt her deep desire

And though I held her tight and kissed her
It's to my regret minister
That I never ever felt her deep desires

HEY, HONEY, HEY

Hey, honey, hey
Hey, honey, hey
Won't you please give me
At least another day

I cannot stand
This sad goodbye
First my soul shakes
Then my heart breaks
And I slowly die

So much I want you
So much I need you
But deep inside
All I do
Is love you
You are a vision
You are a myth
You are a touch
You are a feel
You are a kiss

Hey, honey, hey
We lived through sorrow
But in the pain
We had each other
And tomorrow
Now with you gone
Tomorrow has fled
And I'd lie alone
But for the sorrow
With me in this bed

Hey, honey, hey
Won't you please listen

Without me
There will be something
You will be missing

Just like a song
Without any tune
Cold as a flower
That grows in the snow
And never sees June

HOMEWARD BOUND TO YOU

I've been running
Around the world
But I cannot seem to find
A place to stay

I've been doing different jobs
But I cannot seem to find
A life to live

I've been searching
Through my thoughts
But I cannot seem to find
An answer

The one thing I have found
Is my heart
Telling me to be
Homeward bound to you

I've been chasing after dreams
Just to find out
They're not real
Is that the way to carry on?

I've been looking
For a sun
That won't set
When nighttime comes
To always keep me warm

Now I'm running out of roads
And my heart's the biggest load
I have to carry

Weighing me down
Telling me to turn around
To be homeward bound to you
It's weighing me down
Telling me to turn around
To be homeward bound to you

I Dreamt I Was Dead

I dreamt I was dead
Cold breezes blowing through my head
Dark was the night as I bled
And the funeral went slow

The whole city cried
The kid he has died
Sang the ladies in red
But it went to their heads

Don't sing me no sad songs
Don't lay down them lily whites
It hasn't been long
Since I saw the light
So don't go bury me low

The people they gathered
The Church bells, they rang
And everyone sang
And danced in the rain

I saw tears on faces
That I didn't know
As the funeral went slow

Don't sing me no sad songs
Don't lay down them lily whites
I'm gonna be alright
I'm gonna be alright

I dreamt I was dead
And people I didn't know
Looked at my head as I bled
And the funeral went slow

I'm a Lifelong Friend

Beginnings
Beginning of my life
Seen
Near the end of my time

Loves
Loves of my life
Waking new
In a heart grown old

And faces
Faces of that love
Yours is the one
The one alone
That's looking out
Out from all the days of my life

Saying goodbye
There have been so many
It's another goodbye
Taking me away from you

But when you see me once again
You'll see a friend
I'm a lifelong friend of yours
I'm a lifelong friend
I'm a lifelong friend of yours
I'm a lifelong friend

I'm a lifelong friend
I'm a lifelong friend
I'm a lifelong friend
I'm a lifelong friend of yours

I Give to You, You Give to Me (A Duet)

September 25, 1984

FEMALE: What is love? Is it a feeling?
MALE: Yes, it's a feeling, one that can be acted on
One that can be demonstrated
And it can be expressed in a love song

Chorus (sung by male)
I give to you, you give to me
I give to you, you give to me
Love is a gift
At least partially
I give to you, you give to me

FEMALE: Do you know? Is love forever?
MALE: Well, I really couldn't say
I haven't felt it for that long
FEMALE: Is love sweet?
MALE: Well, it tastes that way to me
But I don't know how it tastes to old King Kong

(Chorus) (sung by male)

FEMALE: Is love a hunger?
MALE: In that hunger is desire
FEMALE: Is love warm?
MALE: Sometimes love can be a fire
FEMALE: Where can love take you?
MALE: Baby, it can take you higher
FEMALE: Is love something everybody needs?
MALE: Yes, love is something everybody needs

(Chorus) (sung by male)

FEMALE: How does love end?
MALE: It gets cold and wet

Time passes by
After a while, we all forget
That's how it ends
We just forget
FEMALE: I give to you, you give to me
MALE (spoken): Don't ever stop giving
FEMALE: I give to you, you give to me
MALE (spoken): Let's make it a special occasion to give
FEMALE: I give to you, you give to me
MALE: I give to you, you give to me
MALE and FEMALE: I give to you, you give to me
I give to you, you give to me

I Wouldn't Trade Your Love In
(for Paradise)

Chorus
I wouldn't trade your love in
For paradise
I wouldn't trade your love in
For paradise
Now paradise
May be nice
But it's not what I desire
All I want is your heart of fire

I wouldn't trade my life with you
For eternity
I wouldn't trade my life with you
For eternity
Let God keep His angels
Let Him keep His pearly gates
I just want to live with you
Somewhere in the States

I wouldn't trade you in for a
Better Earth
I wouldn't trade you in for a
Better Earth
Let the wars keep raging on
Let men kill for all they're worth
They're gonna do it anyway
Until the end of time
I can live with their stupidity
So long as you are mine

(Chorus)

I CHOOSE YOU

Your simple mind
Feels no pain
Don't know enough
To come out of the rain
You're always running in the storm
So very different from the norm

Chorus
But I choose you
I won't lose you
Try to run
Or stand and fight
I choose you
I won't lose you
I'll be a light
In your darkest night
You can't hide from me
You can't hide from me
You can't hide from me

Your simple mind
Screams and shouts
You ask me
What's this all about
You won't acknowledge how you feel
You don't believe that this is real

You take a knife
To stab my heart
I grab the blade
To cut away the pain
And suddenly you're running in the rain

(Chorus)

Your simple mind
Won't comprehend
The messages
That your heart sends
You fight it off and take a ride
Until you're feeling safe inside

(*Chorus*)

Do what you will to deny
Do anything not to reveal
Try your best to conceal
That I touch you like burning steel

Do not look into my eyes
Do not let me hold you tight
Run away when I come by
Try to love another guy

(*Chorus*)

IT'S A LOVELY DAY

It's a lovely day
It's a lovely day
The sun is shining brightly
Although Winter's on its way
Laughing little children
I watch them as they play
Finding such enjoyment
In this lovely, lovely day

All the people smiling
Everywhere you go
Let your worries fade away
Life is grand you know

Come and watch the leaves
Falling from the trees
Changing all their colours
As they float down on a breeze

It's a lovely day
It's a lovely day
The sun is shining brightly
Although Winter's on its way
Laughing little children
I watch them as they play
Finding such enjoyment
In this lovely, lovely day

IF IT ENDS TONIGHT, IT ENDS TOO SOON

I know this started as a lark
A game played by two lonely people
In the dark
I hadn't counted on a spark of love to flame
But it happened all the same
So you now see
If it's tonight, it ends too soon for me

We haven't even exchanged names
Just wine and laughter
Then walked in a summer rain
To a place where lovers go
It all ends with the sunrise
And no one has to know

Well, it could have gone that way
I had no intentions other than to play the game
But something happened all the same
And I'll admit that I'm to blame
But don't you see
If it ends tonight, it ends too soon for me

Well, I can't let it go that way
It's become much more than a game
Something's happened
I'll admit that I'm to blame
But don't you see
If it ends tonight, it ends too soon for me

I can tell by your smile
That you've been playing games
With me now all this while
But I'm happy as a lark
And I'm glad we're in the dark
Now that the spark of love has come to flame
Don't you think it's time I knew your name

IF YOU TRY TO BELIEVE IN MAGIC

October 25, 1984

If you try to believe in magic
But you fail
Don't you listen to them
When they say it's just as well
That there's nothing left in the world
Nothing left in the world
Nothing left to believe
Nothing left to believe
All of your wildest dreams
Are just dreams
Foolish schemes
False it seems
And magic's only make-believe

If you try to believe in life
As you die
If you try to fly, fly high
As you fall
If you look for truth
But all you hear is lies
And you feel that there is
Nothing left at all
Nothing left in the world
Nothing left in the world
Nothing left to believe
Nothing left to believe
All of your wildest dreams
Are just dreams
Foolish schemes
False it seems
And magic's only make-believe

Till someday you see
There's a sun in the sky
Till someday you hear
Music in the air
Until one day you feel
There is love in the world
And you can believe
In all your wildest dreams
They're not false it seems
Not just crazy schemes
And magic's more than make-believe

And I believe in magic too
Because I believe in you
I believe in you

IF YOU HAVEN'T GOT NOTHING

If you haven't got nothing
But a lonely heart
And a heavy load
And a long, long road
Well if you haven't got nothing
You still have got something
You must have something
Just to carry on
Just to carry on

If you haven't got nothing
But the darkest night
And there are no stars
To provide some light
If you haven't got nothing
Well you must be wrong
You've got to have something
If you're not yet gone

Not everybody's hoping
For a better day
For the sun to shine
And to light the way
Everybody's praying
For a kingdom come
But you've got to start believing
In the rising sun

When all the thoughts you're thinking
Don't lead to an end
So you say there are no answers
Well let me tell you friend
Open up your heart
Look into your soul

Search and you will find
Where miracles unfold

Now you may be shedding tears
Into an empty well
But they won't last forever
There is no such hell
Every grief and sorrow
Will be wiped away
All you've got to do is believe
And it don't hurt to pray

So if you haven't got nothing
But the rags you wear
If you haven't got nothing
But a lot of cares
If you're lost without a hope
If you're overcome by fear
Let me tell you of a place
Far away somewhere
A place you can believe in
You've got a friend up there

Kiss Me, Baby, Kiss Me

November 3, 1984

Kiss me, baby, kiss me
Don't resist me
I implore you
Baby, I adore you

Kiss me, baby, kiss me
Do not fight it
The feeling's right
Let's make love tonight

Chorus
There are stars shining in the sky
I see beauty everywhere
There is magic in the air
Baby, don't you feel how much I care

Kiss me, baby, kiss me
Don't resist me
Put your arms around me
Baby, hold me tight

Kiss me, baby, kiss me
Do not fight it
The feeling's right

(*Chorus*)

Kiss me, baby, kiss me
Now or never
This special night
Cannot last forever

Kiss me, baby, kiss me
Hold me tight
The feeling's right
Let's make love tonight

LOVE IS ALIVE IN THE NIGHT

Nighttime falls
And I
Am all alone
Somewhere
In the dark
And I
Can't get home
Suddenly
You're there
From nowhere
And heart's on fire
With the light
Of the stars
In the sky

Love is alive in the night
Her voice called to me
On the wind
That blew up
Desperately
From the frigid sea
And her eyes
Followed out of the dark
While her hand
Reaches out for my heart

Chorus
Love is alive
Love is alive
Love is alive
Love is alive
Love is alive in the night
Love is alive in the night

You and I
Have one
Night to share
You and I
Have one
Debt to bear
For all lonely souls
In the night
Can we prove
That love is alive

(*Chorus*)

Love is alive
As I
Hold you tight
In my arms
In the cold
Of the night
But we are on fire
As the flames burn on *passionately*
And the magic of love sets us free

Long Distance Love

Long distance love is something
I don't believe in
Baby, when you leave
You say goodbye to me

Long distance love is something
I can't conceive of
When you go
You throw it all away

I don't want to make you cry
But I also don't want to lie
This is only how it's gonna be

I'll look for another lover
We won't mean much to each other
We'll still be friends
That's all I can say

We'll remember less and less
More and more we'll both forget
As our lives are changing
And the years slip away

Long distance love
Can't be made to last
Before long, the feelings are
All in the past

That's not the way I want it to be
That's how it's gonna be
Baby, when you leave
You say goodbye to me

THE LAST GOODBYE

Who knew the last goodbye
Would be forever
Who knew that I would never
Be seeing you again
I wish I had said
I love you, Heather
Now I can only say I love you
To the rain

I walk around and wonder
Where you are
I come home
But you're not there
I wish upon the very brightest star
I cry a hundred million tears

Who knew the last goodbye
Would be forever
Time heals all wounds
But it can't take away my pain
I wish I had said
I love you, Heather
I do say I love you
But it's only to the rain

Now my days are cold
And nights are colder
I must not look at old photographs
I wish she was here
So I could hold her
Who knew that one goodbye
Would be the last
Since you've been gone
My clothes have gotten dirty

Who knew the last goodbye
Would be forever
If I could just turn time back
To yesterday again
I'd hold you and say
I love you, Heather
Now I can only say I love you
To the rain

Lady, Come with Me and Dance

I am a young man
In a young town
And lady
Just to touch you
I would lay my money down

I am a young man
In a young place
And I'd let a thousand years slip by
Just spending time
Gazing at your face

I am a young man
But the years go by so fast
So I'd better take you now
Lady, come with me and dance

Chorus
Lady, come with me
Lady, come with me and dance
Lady, come with me
Lady, come with me and dance

I am a young man
In a young town
You aren't the first love I've ever had
But lady
You're the one I'm loving now

Chorus

LADY, YOUR LOVE WAS NEVER FREE

Lady, your love was never free
I had to bring such precious gifts
Before you would even
Take a… look at me
Now, baby, I don't know
But I think I've lost my soul

Love was just a fantasy
A deep emotion
Two people felt for each other
But you showed me another
A kind of love I never knew
Up until I first met you

I just never did get around
To thinking that love was something
To be bought or sold

I always felt that
Women with that attitude
Were cold inside

Baby, I don't know
Why I died
To get your gold

I think I stole and lied
And cheated
And maybe even murdered
In a sense
For you
I would have taken food
Out of the mouth of a hungry child
That's how much you drove me wild

Now, lady, I don't know
But I think I've lost
My soul

Lady, your love was never free
But if I had only known
That I would have to pay forever
For things I would never do
But I did them all for you
Somehow I did them all for you

LAST IN LINE

We're a ship
Without a storm
A cold
Without a warm
Light inside the darkness
Let it be

We're a laugh
Without a tear
A hope
Without a fear
We are coming home

We're up to the witch
We may never, never, never come home
But the magic that we'll feel
Is worth a lifetime

We're a bone
Upon the cross
We're the throw
Before the toss
You can release yourself
But the only way is down

We don't come alone
We are fire
We are stone
We're the hand that writes
And quickly moves away

Chorus
We'll know for the first time
If we're evil or we're right
We're the last in line

Yea
We're the last in line

Two eyes from the east
It's the angel or the beast
And the answer lies between
The good and bad
We search for the truth
We could die along the route
But the thrill of the search
Is worth the pain

(*Chorus*)

We're up to the witch
We may never, never, never come home
But the magic that we'll feel
Is worth a lifetime

We're a bone upon a cross
We're the throw before the toss
You can release yourself
But the only way to go is down

LOVE IS WHAT YOU'VE GOT TO DO

Brother
In this life
I have found
One thing is true

It's not a mystery
But so few seem to see
That love is what you've got to do

Chorus
Love is what you've got to do
Love is what you've got to do
I know my message
Is not something new
But love is what you've got to do

Jesus
Said it long ago
And I think he was right

We've never followed
Him
But someday
We just might

We'll learn to love
Our fellow man
In a Christian way

It wouldn't surprise me
To see
A small child lead the way

(*Chorus*)

Now my song is over
Go forget it if you will
Go back to your valley
Or climb on your hill
But I hope you'll take
My message home with you
Love is what you've got to do

Love is what you've got to do
Love is what you've got to do
I know you've heard before
The words I say to you
But love is what you've got to do
Love is what you've got to do

MARRIED LIFE

If I could buy you a car
I would take you for a ride
We could drive up in the mountains
And try to touch the sky

We would leave behind the city
And the ugliness down there
We would leave behind the ghetto
And its streets of despair

If I could buy you happiness
I'd wrap it with a bow
I'd give it to you with a kiss
I love you don't you know

You make my morning breakfast
You bring my cup of tea
I thank you for all you do
But I wish you did love me

Chorus
I didn't know that married life
Could be so sad
I didn't know that love could end
So badly
I didn't know that poverty
Was such a chain
I didn't know you'd
Never smile again

We live our days in sorrow
We live our nights in pain
Knowing that tomorrow
Brings another spell of rain

All our dreams and wishes
None of them came true
I cannot make you happy
Although I do love you

I can buy you freedom
It doesn't cost a lot
Even if it means
I must give up all I've got

Let's say goodbye tomorrow
Tonight, let's just forget
Put aside our sorrow
I'll make you smile once yet

Remember when we first met
In summertime so long ago?
I held you in my arms
You said, "Never let me go!"

(Chorus)

MARY TOLD ME

Mary told me
You've got to love boy
You've got to flight
And you must be strong

Don't learn to lie boy
Or alibi boy
But understand
You can't know right from wrong

Chorus
Oh, Mary was the first girl
Who I ever loved
I sold my heart
And soul to her
She cut them up
And threw them to the dogs
So I would learn what I
Should never do

Mary told me
You've got to take, boy
You've got to make your breaks
Or you'll be broke

Don't learn to hate, boy
Don't stop and wait, boy
At least not before
Your final smoke

(Chorus)

Mary told me
So I threw her down
And I made love to her

She smiled up at me
You got it right, boy
Mary taught me things
She never told
Mary taught me things
She never told

MY HEART CAN BREAK

Take care of me
I'm not the strong man
That you see
And when you walk away from me
I can burst like a balloon

Hold on to me
I promise to hold on to you
Be careful what you do, not to lie
I can hurt so easily inside
Even if you never see me cry

Chorus
My heart can break
My heart can break
It isn't made of stone
And when it's trapped and all alone
My heart can break

Be kind to me
Tell me that you love me now and then
Could you also try to be my friend
Baby, I need someone to talk to

Find room for me
Find someplace that we two can share
Find a way to show me that you care
Baby, when I need you, please be there

(Chorus)

NOTHING IS SOMETHING

Nothing is something
Which doesn't exist
It isn't, it wasn't
It never will be
I cannot describe it
For I've never seen it
But I've been told
That nothing is free

In darkness we ponder
And fear overcomes us
Imagining what
Nothing would be
We try to dismiss it
When that won't work
While some wish it away
For reason alone
Cannot set us free

In my mind, I wonder
That something is infinite
While nothing has infinite possibilities
But when they are realized
Then nothing is something
And something is nothing
When it's for free
Like that which was hidden
Then suddenly green

My last word on nothing
Is that it's unknown
Does it exist?
Well, I couldn't say
For nothing is a mystery
Greater than life

And sometimes I think
I'm glad it's this way

It's true that being afraid
Of death is being afraid
Of nothing because that is
Truly what we fear death is

I think you have to feel
With your body

NOTHING FEELS SO FINE

Chorus
Nothing feels so fine
Nothing feels so fine
Nothing feels so good
Nothing feels so good

I've been on my own
For such a long, long time
Woke up each morning
Feeling really bad

You've been here with me
For just a little while
But in that time
I've never once felt sad

(Chorus)

Always thought I could live
Happy on my own
But it feels so cold
Waking up alone

Nothing feels so fine
As you my love
Nothing feels so good

Nothing feels so fine
As you my love
Nothing feels so good

NEVER SAY GOODBYE TO ME

Girl, don't you lie to me
And don't you cry to me
To get your way
And prove that you can use me as you choose
And, girl, don't you say goodbye to me

We are a funny pair
But I don't care
I need you here
There are things that I can't
Do alone, you see
So, girl, don't you say goodbye to me

When I'm walking home at night
And see the light
I know you're there
I feel alive
And am glad to be
So, girl, don't you say goodbye to me

I know I can be a fool
How easy you can lie to me
And use me as you choose
But if you stay
It's all okay with me
Just don't say goodbye
Never say goodbye
Don't ever say goodbye to me

NO PAYMENT DUE

No payment due
No payment due
What I did for you
I done for free
You know me
I love you

If you should go
No need to cry
No need to
Leave a farewell note
Or give me one last kiss
Goodbye

I'll understand
Your reasons why
You are free
And like a bird
You need to fly

No sad regrets
No sad regrets
The memories are sweet
I will not forget
My love for you
My love for you

And when you go
No need to cry
No need to leave a farewell note
Or give me one last kiss goodbye

I'll understand
Your reasons why
You are free

And like a bird
You need to fly
You are free
And like a bird
You need to fly

One Thing Is True: I Need You

One thing is true
I need you
One thing is true
I need you

I don't need the sun to shine
Or the sky of blue
I don't need the rain to fall
To bring spring flowers to bloom

But one thing is true

I don't need a burning campfire
To keep me safe and warm at night
I don't need someone to tell me
What is wrong or what is right
I don't need no adulation
From the man down on the street
I don't even need to wear
A pair of shoes upon my feet

But one thing is true
I need you

Chorus
I need you to hold me
I need you to love me
I need you to want me
The way I want you
I need you to hold me
I need you to want me
I need you to love me
The way I love you

I don't need to compromise
With every fool who comes my way
I don't need no expectations
There will be a better day (or false hopes for)
The earth can shake, the sky can thunder
If they're wanting to do
But one thing is true
I need you
One thing is true
I need you

I don't need a winter coat
To keep me warm against the storm
I don't even need to wear
A pair of shoes upon my feet
I don't need three meals a day
But if I'm not to lose my way
One thing is true
I need you
One thing is true
I need you

(Chorus)

One thing is true
I need you

After all my searching to discover
I'm sure of only one thing being
True
One thing is true
I need you

I don't need the birds
To sing a sweetly tune
I don't need a lot
Of friends

> To cheer me up when
> I am blue

.

PRINCESS

Come away little princess to the mountains
Come away little princess to the sea
They can't teach you nothing
In that school for journalists
Come on little princess
And run away with me

Forget your foreign languages
Forget your French perfumes
Forget that rich guy and his Mercedes Benz
He would only drive you to your doom

Come away little princess to my magic abode
Although it seems to be
Just a shack beneath the sun
Come inside and I will teach you
What everybody wants to know
And I will guarantee
You will find the learning fun

Come away princess and run
Come away little princess and run
Come away little princess and run with me
Beneath the endless sky
And the red hot burning sun

I Thought I Loved You

I thought I loved you
But I didn't
Still I married you
And lived with you for forty years
Till you were old and grey

Now I'm growing tired
Of your face
And it's time for me to leave
And go away

I'm going to leave you
With your memories
I'm going to leave you to grow old
And die alone

I'd going to take a train
To somewhere I have never been
And I'm never going to write
And I'm never going to phone

I thought I loved you
Maybe I did
Oh maybe I did
But now it's time for me to leave
And die alone
And die alone

I'VE GONE STRAIGHT OFF THE WALL FOR YOU

Girl, I've gone straight off the wall for you
I've turned myself into a fool
That's what I've done do

Climbing on your ceiling
Scratching at your door
Nobody can figure out
What I do it for

You are kind of pretty
That is sure enough
But girls prettier than you
Couldn't make me fall in love
I'd take them
Or I'd leave them
But it's not that way with you
I've turned myself into a fool
That's what I've done do

I believe it's crazy
The way I feel inside
But I want you so much
That I've given up my pride
(That I've swallowed all my pride)

I've got down on my knees
To take hold of your hand
I'll give up all my freedom girl
Just to be your man

I've gone straight off the wall for you
I've turned myself into a fool
That's what I've done do

I'm climbing on your ceiling
Scratching at your door
No one will believe it
But I'm kneeling on your floor

I See the Light

I

See the light
And I see it shining
I see the night sky
And the stars are twinkling
I see your smile
And I start to think
I'm in love with you

I

See the universe
Changing, unfolding
I see the human mind
Growing with power
And I see your smile
Always in fashion
When I touch your skin
I erupt in passion

Time
Ever flowing and falling
Deep from out of your eyes
I hear love calling
Love ever remaining
Though all things are changing
Our love carries on

Our
Love is in session
Felt from deep in the heart
Transcending all reason
Love wipes clean every sorrow
From all the past woes
Reaching far into tomorrow

I
Look into your eyes
Your heart is smiling
Always in fashion
When I touch your skin
A new love begins
We two erupt into passion
We two erupt into passion

I WILL BE FREE

I will be free
No matter what they
Do to me
No matter how they
Tie me down
Or cage me in
You'll see
I shall be free

And I shall soar
No matter if they chip my wings
No matter if it
Rains on me
If the winds blow
Ceaselessly
Always I shall soar
For now and evermore

And I shall sing
They will never
Silence me
Let them take away
The bands and the parades
Still I shall sing

And I will love you
As I was always meant to do
I'll let your fires
Reach me
And you alone
Shall teach me
Of all that love can do

And I will love you
I will love you
I will love you

I Feel, I Feel Devastated

Chorus
I feel, I feel devastated
I feel, I fell
Like a piece of shit
I feel, I feel devastated
I feel, I feel devastated

I fell in love with you
But you didn't love me too
I gave it all I had
Now there's nothing I can do

There's nothing left to try
And nothing left to say
And nothing I can take
To stop me feeling this way

(*Chorus*)

When it came to love
I thought I was quite the guy
I could break a heart in two
And make a girl cry

But when I opened up my soul
And I gave to you my heart
You ridiculed my soul
And my heart you tore apart

Now
(*Chorus*)

Perhaps it's just because I feel so devastated
But I have come to think that love is overrated
Yes, I do believe that love is overrated

I'M GLAD TO BE GOING HOME

Well, I'm glad I'll be going home
Well, I'm glad I'll be going home
Well, I'm glad I'll be going home
Well, I'm happy for a change

I was born with a broken heart
And I've tried
Almost from the start
To mend and to make it new
I have failed
But then so might you

Now it's near time to say goodbye
Now it's near time for me to die
And I'm glad to be going home
Well I'm happy for a change

I have laughed
And I've loved a bit
I have fought
And I've hurt a lot
I have made do with what I've got
And buddy so must you

Then the spring
Quickly turned to fall
So I raced
But I lost it all
While the sun
Fell out of the sky
Now it's near time
For me to die

I know I'll be welcome there
My heart will not have a care
No need for you to shed a tear
I'll be happy for a change

I WILL STILL LOVE YOU

You can hide away
But I'll still love you
You can run, run, run
But I will pursue
You can do
What you want to do
But I'll still love you
I will still love you
I will still love you

And you'll know someday
That I am the one
And you'll feel someday
That I am the sun
And you will see
Summer never fades
If you share my love
Till your dying day

You can lie to me
But I will not change
You can break my heart
But I'll rearrange
All the pieces
Back in two
Because I'll still love you
I will still love you
I will still love you

I will still love you
For I once was told
That a love that's true
Can never die

And I believe it to be true
So for all my life
I will still love you
For all my life
I will love you

IF BY CHANCE

If by chance I see you
In a year or two
What will I say to you?
Where will we wander to?

Out along the sandy shores
We've roamed before
To laugh a little more
I'll pledge my soul again to you

If, by chance, I hold on to my dying dreams
Through life's swiftly changing scenes
Will I burn bright in your heart
As the hero of your days
Or will your image of me go dim
Then slowly fade away

But if I betray beliefs we hold in twain
If my soul turns black, my mind goes suddenly insane
Will you turn your face away to hide the shame?
Or will you shed a tear then place your hand in mine again?

IT'S RAINING IN BOSTON

Now it's raining in Boston
And you're somewhere in the garden
And your hair is falling down
And you dance and dance around
How I wish that I was there with you

As I look outside my window
The clouds go slowly by below
Am I losing you behind
Just a memory in your mind
Can I turn around and find you waiting there

The sun shines brightly in Mexico
But I don't know why I've come so far
There is nothing for me here
I'm all alone and very scared
While you're so far away from me

Now it's winter in Boston
The snow falls silent in the garden
It's all so lonely and serene
How could I have ever been
So long away
Is she dancing down in Mexico
Today

ONLY THE RIGHT WORDS

I've got to believe girl
I've got to believe girl
That we could have had
Something special
But you went away
Before I got to say

Chorus
The right words
The right words
Only the right words
Stood in our way

I've got to believe girl
I've got to believe girl
Now with you gone
I've got to hold on
Anyway I can

Pictures and postcards
Long distance calling
How's the weather
How have you been

(Chorus)

I've got to believe girl
I've got to believe girl
That there's gonna be
Another chance for me to say

(Chorus)

Only the right words
Only the right words
Only the right words
Only the right words
Only the right words
Are all that I'm gonna say

OVER AND OVER IT GOES

Over and over and over and over
It goes
Changing our minds
As we change in our thoughts
As we change in the things that we know

Chorus
Changing our lovers and
Changing our beds
Changing our looks as we
Changing in our heads
Over and over and over and over it goes
Over it goes

Once we were smiling
And now we are crying
We should have laughed
All of the while
Each day was different
We were so in love
Before love went out of style
"Nothing is permanent,"
I said as you painted your toes
Over and over and over and over
And over it goes
Over it goes

What lessons has life to teach
Nothing it seems
I have learned more
In some of my dreams
Tears fall, I wave goodbye
When did I learn to cry?
Over and over it goes

(Chorus)

Life ends without a bang
Butler says, "Sir, have you rung?"
The monster lies dead in his bed
Not a dream in his heart
Not a thought left in his head
Over and over and over and over
It goes

OLD KATE

Got bored
On a summer's day
Old Kate said
To go away
Said I don't need love no move
I don't need love

Cold tears in the pouring rein
Just got off the midnight train
Old Kate said to go away
Said I don't need love no more

Old man in the summer's warm
Young girls watch him walk alone
And they cry
Cause he's lost his love

Old man well you feel brand new
Live the day until it's through
Still believe
That your dreams
. Will all come true

Old men on a summer's day
Meant to end your world this way
Walk alone
Till your dreams
Come true

RACE, RACE, BABY FLY

Hello, hello sweety pie
How you doing?
Don't you lie
The sun is flying through the sky
Its rays will find you out

Don't you doubt
That life is real
Even for those made to feel
Afraid of growing up
And getting out

Chorus
Race, race, baby fly
Or come and lie down by my side
This is not the Victorian age
And sex has become all the rage

Don't you realize all you've lost
Waiting bears a heavy cost
Time is always slipping by
Before long, you're bound to die
You can't escape the fate of all
Even if you try

You are wasting years and youth
Is it because I'm uncouth?
Or is the truth that you're afraid?
If you are, I don't know why

(Chorus)

We all make lots of mistakes
But that is just what living takes

To try to do, to do, to try
To laugh and love, to hurt and cry

Until there is no sun
No places, nor no anyone
No sad time to forget
No bad deed to regret
Till love and life are through
And all things have been done

(Chorus)

SADIE

Sadie was a dreamer
With her hair in her eyes
And her head in the clouds
And she reached for the sky

Chorus
And by and by
I always wished
That I
Could bring her down
And show her
Paradise
Was on the ground
With me
But Sadie truly loved to fly

I would see her on the street
Wearing a pretty dress
She always seemed to look her best
She turned and smiled into the sun
I'm sure that she was lost within a dream

(Chorus)

Now it's been years since she left town
There have been rumours
Stories passed around
That she met some man
Who brought her down
Who broke her heart
And she died tragically

Me? I've cried and cried
And tried so hard not to believe
Because Sadie always meant something to me

(Chorus)

SHE SAID NO

And the answer came to me
In a letter that she wrote
It arrived on my 27th birthday
She sent her photograph along
It was to haunt my final nights
Because I couldn't turn my gaze
From her tortured eyes

Chorus
She said no
She said no
She said I like you
But I do not love you
She said no
She said no
She said,
"I would marry you
But I never could be true"

She was honest I suppose
And that must count for something
In a world of lies
And scarce concealed hypocrisy

So I burned the letter
But I kept her picture
And I think I kept a tiny piece
Of the dream

She said yes
Kiss me love
She said yes
I'll be yours forever
She said
Hold me for all eternity

She said yes
Kiss me love
She said yes
I'll be yours forever
She said, "You know I'll always be there
With you in your dreams"

Now I know I'm going to die
There's no reason left to lie
I must face the truth of my life
Before the chance is gone

(Chorus)

Now I look into the mirror
And I see my tortured eyes
I touch her photograph
And I want to say goodbye
But I don't quite know to who

SMILE YOU'RE ALIVE

Smile you're alive
All's well with the world today
The sun is in the sky
And there is much going your way

I know I'm a stranger
But I am not a danger to you
I only want to say
There's no reason to be sad today

Walk on your way
To the mountains or the streams
Smile as you go
And try to share some of your dreams

Other people need you
You are not alone
There is much that is true
And much that can be known

The world is not so cold
And summertime comes every year
As you are growing old
Try to live without fear

Love yourself and love your neighbour
Do your best to understand
Give help when help is needed
Just do the best you can

Smile you're alive
A gift only God could give
The stars are shining bright
A billion more reasons to live

I know I'm a stranger
But I am not a danger
I only stopped to say
There's no reason to be sad today
There are no reasons to be sad today

SOMETHING WILD

Hey baby
You drive me crazy
And I do believe
There's something wild
Inside of you

A sunshine
That feels fine
True delusions
For me to look up into

A darkness
Surrounding
To evaluate
What life is all about
Leaves me living half in dreams
And half in doubt

This fog that
Covers all the land
The cries of thousands
Struggling to survive
Reach out
Touch my hand
Let me know
We are alive

Hey baby
You drive me crazy
But I do believe
There's something wild
Inside of me

SHE'S A ROCK 'N' ROLL CREATION
August 20, 1984

She's a rock and roll creation
Burning hot with pure desire
She'll leave you standing
With your heart
Held in your hands
And though she stares at you with passion
That's just a small part of her action
To her, you're only one of many fans

She's a show queen
Dancing in blue jeans
Turning you on
With the wave of her hand

Rising like thunder
Moving like lightning
Filled up with emotion
Running into the stands

She's a rock and roll creation
Burning hot with pure desire
She leaves me standing with my heart
Held in my hands

And though she stares at me with passion
I'm wanting much more of her action
Baby, tell me I'm your one and only man

She's my show queen
Dancing in blue jeans
Turning me on
With the touch of her hand

We're rising like thunder
Moving like lightning
Filled up with emotion
We're gonna break up the bank

Rising like thunder
Moving like lightning
Filled with emotion
We're gonna break up the band

SUZY DOESN'T LIVE HERE ANYMORE

Dirty socks stuffed in my bureau
Smelly clothes flung on the floor
Got a beer beside my bed
A case of empties by the door
Mail comes flying through that slot
I wonder who it's for
Probably Suzy
Don't them lovers know
She don't live here anymore

Got my football hero sweater
It's all stained with bacon grease
I don't know how it got that way
I ain't eaten in a week
Got a picture in my pocket
Done worn out from too much wear
Keep me looking at that Suzy
Just to know she once was here

I ain't got nobody
To call me on the phone
They all ask for Suzy
Ask me, when she coming home?
Hey, lover, don't you know?
She don't live here anymore

Got her picture in my pocket
Done worn from too much wear
I just keep looking at that Suzy
Hey, lover, you want to look?
You want to look
Just to know she once was here

TAKE MY NAME

I don't have much
Only one troubled life
But I could be happy
If you were my wife

Wouldn't need fortune
And wouldn't need fame
I could be happy
If you'd take my name

Chorus
Take my name
Take my name
Don't think of money
And don't think of fame
Put this ring on your finger
And don't be ashamed
Darling please
Take my name

Trouble is
I know you love someone else
And while you're off with him
I'm all by myself

Dreaming of what a sweet life it would be
Darling, if only
You would marry me

(Chorus)

(Spoken by Preacher)
Now do you take this woman
For the rest of your life
To be her husband

As she'll be your wife
To have and to hold
Till death do you part
To love one another
With all of thy heart

If there is a girl you want
For all your life
Play her this song
And she might be your wife
But if she says no
Could you please kindly see
Would she consider marrying me?

(Chorus)

TAKE YOUR WOMAN

Take your woman
Take her down
The sun's setting
And it's time to lay around
Take her gently to your side
Don't let your baby cry

Travelled five miles through the storm
Just to reach my baby's home
Though she'd be waiting all alone
I saw her light
Saw her loving in the night
She thought I'd stay somewhere warm

(*Spoken*) Now that man struggled blindly in the storm
He stopped a mile down past his baby's farm
She found him in the morning
Lying frozen in the snow

So, guys, when you go home

Take your woman, take her down
The sun's setting
And it's time to lay around
Love your baby when you're home
There will be nights
She'll spend waiting all alone

THE HURTIN'S OVER (THE PAIN IS GONE)

The hurtin's over
The hurtin's over
The pain is gone
The pain is gone
It took a long time baby
But I've managed to hang on
I've put the pieces back together
I can start my life anew
It's been hard on me
But I finally see
I can make it without you
I can make it without you

The memories
No longer make me cry
I no longer wake up hoping
To find you lying by my side
And the tears
Cried into my pillow have all dried

The feelings changing
And change is due
Time has stood still for too long
I couldn't just stop loving you
I had to realize life goes on
After love comes to an end
But baby don't ask me
To be your friend

The hurtin's over
The hurtin's over
The pain is gone
The pain is gone

My world is sunny once again
I have made it through the rain
And the tears
Cried into my pillow
Have all dried

THERE ARE TIMES TO SAY GOODBYE

There are times, times, times
We must say goodbye
We must say goodbye

And it's hard for lovers
Not to cry

But turn away
Face the bright tomorrow
Don't let our love
End in sorrow

And I'll know that
You once were mine
And I'll look back
On those happy times
And I'll rejoice in memory
Because I once loved you
And you loved me

Now it's time, time, time
We must say goodbye
We must say goodbye
You must go your way
And I'll go mine
And should we meet in distant years
We'll smile for never were there tears

And I'll rejoice in memory
Because I once loved you
And you loved me

THERE'S HEARTBREAK

I saw a man working
On a job that led nowhere
For almost no pay
His life passed away

For things he needed
Clothes for the children
Food on the table

Chorus
There is heartbreak
When each day
Is endlessly the same
No different in no way
From the day before

There is heartbreak
Can you take it?
Can you serve to survive?
Can you make it
Through the day alive?

I saw a girl walking
The streets in the night
Stopping so often
Under a lamp light

She was young
She was lovely
What was her reason?
Why did she choose
To do this to survive?

(*Chorus*)

I saw an old man
Feeding gulls in the park
His eyes were smiling
His life was a lark

The sun was shining down
Out of the sky
There was heartbreak
But the old man was alive

(Chorus)

Me? I'm a dreamer
My vision is vast
But whenever I look
Far into the past

I see nothing has changed
After all of my pondering
Isn't it strange
That I am still wondering?

(Chorus)

There's No Going Back

Well, I saw you
The other day
I didn't know
What to say
It's been too long
And everything has changed

It hurt me to
Just pass on by
I thought I saw
Tears in your eyes
I almost stopped
I almost called your name
But

Chorus
There's no going back
There's no going back
Time heals wounds by changing things so
Drastically
That there's no going back
There's just no going back

I kept walking
Down the road
My heart bore
The heavy load
The memory
Of how things use to be

Nights together
We were young
Love and joy
Two happy ones

Before you caught
Me with another girl

(Chorus)

You were hurt
But so was I
I was at fault
Still I cried
But worst of all
I never tried to make it up to you

Turning around
For one last look
I see you've gone
Have I been wrong?
Should I have stopped?
Should I have called your name?

(Chorus)

There's a Place in My Heart

There's a place in my heart
I keep warm for you
Somewhere for you to come to
When you're cold and blue

When you feel alone
With the rain coming down
And you've got no home
Look around, look around

Chorus
There's a place in my heart
I keep warm for you
A place
I keep always warm for you

When the snow's too deep
And the wind's too cold
When what you owned
You've already sold

When you want to die
But you only cry
Come around
To the light in my eyes
Come around
I've a warm place for you

(Chorus)

There's a place in my heart
I keep warm for you
A place
I keep always warm for you
A place I keep always warm for you

There's a place in my heart
I keep warm for you
A place I keep always warm for you
A place
I keep always warm for you

TIME IS SLIPPING AWAY

Chorus
Time is slipping away
Down the hollow chambers of my heart
Realities of life are dulled by the pain
Riding youthful childhood memories are blocking my way
Time is slipping away
Each passing moment will never be regained
Time is slipping away

There's an old beat up sofa on an
Empty sun porch
A boy lying so content
He had nothing but a pillow to lay
Down his head
"Peace of Mind" was all that it meant

(Chorus)

There may come a time when life will
Cloud up your mind
With echoes of pain overdue
There may be a way to break up those
Binds
Find your pipers and pay them their
Dues

(Chorus)

As long as the pipers of life are unpaid
And the pain that is due clouds your
Head
You'll never know what life you
Might have made
If your clouds of pain were dead

(Chorus)

To Kill and Die

Chorus
We will kill
And they will die
We will die
And they will kill
And all of us
Will do our fill
To kill and die
And die and kill

Come on armies
March and fight
Kill by day
Die by night
Sound and fury
Fill the sky
As the bombs
Go flying by

Do it—cause they tell you to
Do it—cause you think you should
Do it—for those whom you love
Do it—for what's right and good

Nobody can say you're wrong
This is just a stupid song
But I think you're dumber still
To kill and die and die and kill

(Chorus)

WHAT DO YOU MEAN TO ME?

Sometimes
You're living in smiles
Sometimes
You're living in tears
Just who
Is it you are?
And what do you mean to me?

You're lost
Under your skin
Touched by the sun
Touched by the rain
I know
Life is more than just to breathe
But what do you mean to me?
What is it that you mean to me?

I'm
Loving your face
Is it okay
To spend time like this
When each end of the day
Steals the sun away
But what do you mean to me?
What is it that you mean to me?

WELL I WANT TO KNOW

Well I want to know
Where you're going to go
When you go leave me
Love I think you'll see
That the world is cold

And I know you'll find
That the nights are long
And the days are hard
And it's not so nice
Being on your own
Being all alone

Think of yesterday
When you had me there
To hold you tight
Through the lonely nights
And overcome your fears

How you've got no one
Who you can whisper to
Who will share your dreams
And help you do the things
That you want to do

Well I want to know
Well I want to know
Well I want to know
Where you're going to go
When you go leave me

And I think you'll find
And I know you'll see
That it's not so nice

Being on your own
Being without me

No, you won't enjoy
Your silly little boy
Being without me
Being without me

WHY, WHY, WHY, WHY DON'T YOU LOVE ME

Chorus
Won't you tell me
Why, why, why, why
Don't you love me?

Won't you tell me
Why, why, why, why
Don't you care?

When the sun comes shinning
Through my window
Won't you tell me
Why, why, why
You're never there?

Are there reasons
That I'm not aware of?
Is there something
That you haven't said?
I know that I'm the only one in love
But it's hard to get it through my head

(Chorus)

If you say it all
In simple English
I will try hard
To believe it's true
But if I should call you
When I'm lonely
You will know
It's because
I love you

(Chorus)

WHERE HAS LOVE GONE

First spark of love
As joy
Fills my heart
I see your eyes
Shine in the dark night
Now I wonder
Where has love gone

First touch of flesh
And flame
Begins the game
We spin and twirl
Above the world
We're free
But now I see
And wonder
Where has love gone

Our hearts unite
In flight
We join our names
Our love is such
As gods have touched
But now I wonder
Where has love gone

The sky grows dark
And clouds thunder
I feel the rain
And watch you
Slipping under
The treacherous sea
What can it be
That grips us
And where has love gone

I see you
Turn and wave
As you pass beyond
My horizon
I know the sun is setting
There is no forgetting
But still I wonder
Where has love gone

Where has love gone to?
Where has love gone?

WITHOUT A KISS
August 29, 1984

I feel so awful
I don't know why that is
Perhaps it's just because
You left me last night
Without a kiss
A kiss
A kiss
Without a kiss

I cannot comprehend
The way that you behave
I treat you like a queen
You just use me like a slave

And everything I do
No matter what it is
Finds no pleasure with you
So you leave without a kiss
A kiss
A kiss
Without a kiss

I don't want this to last
I've got to break the chain
Find myself some shelter
Get in out of the freezing rain

But when I see you smile
It all begins anew
My heart fills with desire
And I'm mad in love with you
With you
With you
In love with you

Time goes on
Are you mine or his?
Where did you go last night
And why did you leave without a kiss
A kiss
A kiss
Without a kiss
A kiss
A kiss
Without a kiss

YOUNG GIRL OLD MAN

You're a young girl
And I'm an old man
So many years
Past the end of my prime

You're a young girl
Growing up fast
Almost a woman
You're looking oh so fine

I have a big house
Just near the ocean
We can listen
To the windswept waves

You're a young girl
And I'm an old man
Take me back, back, back, back, back
To my younger days

Young girl, Young days
Young girl, Young days

Young girl
Give me one more chance
To fall in love in a dance
Like in my younger days

A PERFECT CIRCLE

As I looked into the sky
With my all-revealing eye
I couldn't help but wonder why

So I drew a perfect circle
In the sand
Then made a line
Straight through the middle
Dissecting the perfect whole
Into perfect halves

I split the halves into quarters
The quarters into eighths
The eighths into sixteenths

Then for want of something else to do
I tampered with perfection
And smeared two sixteenths
Out of existence

It is just a feeling
For there is no science in it
And a thought
Without a feeling to it
I had to do it

Tears fell
And drowned two more sixteenths
Of the perfect circle
The wind came up and blew
The rest away

I looked into the sky
With my all-revealing eye
And watched the sun fall
On a less-than-perfect day

I'll Be Seeing You Again

Ain't no reason to say goodbye
I'll be seeing you again
Ain't no reason for us to cry
I'll be seeing you again

I got no intentions
Of letting time slip by
I'll be seeing you again
Before the sun passes
Too many times across the sky
I'll be seeing you my friend

I love you don't you know?
And that's a feeling that will last forever
Although I have to leave
I promise soon we'll be together
Together again
I'll be seeing you again
I'll be seeing you again

You can kiss me and turn away
But I'll be seeing you again
When you miss me
Know that someday
I'll be seeing you again

And if you find the one you love
Please don't forget me
Good memories are not enough
But if you let me, if you let me
I'll be seeing you again
I'll be seeing you again

So keep on smiling, I'll be at your side
On your coldest, darkest day

When you're all alone and think I've lied
You'll see me walking your way

I won't forget to come around just when you need me
You can believe me, you can believe me
You can believe me
You can believe me

I'll be seeing you again
I'll be seeing you again

WHY I KEEP LOVING YOU

One more day
That's all that is waiting
One more day
To watch the sun from my cage

One more night
Filled with fear and with hating
One more night
Before the world passes away

Is it real?
Are there stars in the heavens?
Is it real?
Was it me who did this?

I can't recall
Just the scent of her perfume
I can't recall
Just the touch of her lips

One more day
In the morning, they hang me
One more day
Oh if I had a gun

One more night
Oh I wish that I was free
One more night
If the chance comes, I'll run

WHY DO THE BEST THINGS IN LIFE NEVER LAST?

Why do the best things in life never last?
Why do all good things so quickly pass?
That's what I ask
When I think of you
And the love we had
That's lost
That's gone away

Always the stars
Shine in the sky
The sun's always there
The moon when it falls will soon rise again

But why do the best things in life have to end
Why do they break
Rather than bend
Why couldn't our love have lasted for eternity

Why must the happiest heart
Turn to tears
Why does it all fall apart?
Through the years
All that is left is a memory of you
And the love we had
That's lost
That's gone away

Why do the best things in life never last?
Why did the love we had so quickly pass?
Why couldn't our love have lasted an eternity?
Why couldn't our love have lasted for eternity?

YEARS FROM NOW

Many years from now
Many years from now
When you're older
When you're older
When your world has gotten colder

You will think of me
Amra, you will think of me
While you stand alone
With a cold rain falling down
As you're walking home
You will think of me
And feel as lonely as the night

Amra, you know this isn't it
None of this has to be
You don't have to take that plane
And fly away from me
No, you don't have to fly away
From me

Many years from now
I will think of you
When I hear Pink Floyd playing
Or I see someone
Who looks like you
Escaping in the crowd

YOU ARE GOING AWAY

October 25, 1984

It's just not right
That this should be
The way I have to say goodbye
It's just not right
Am I a man
That all I ever do is cry

But you are going away
For how many days
You cannot say
And I am so afraid
That days stretch into years
Days stretch into years

It's just not sweet
The taste is bitter
I'm so cold
As summer turns to winter

And though time passes ever slow
My eternity is ending
While all the world I used to know
Is buried under snow

It's just not right
That I
Should have to say goodbye to you
It's not the thing
That I would ever choose to do

But I'm a slave
With fate as my cruel master
And all it ever gave

Was not what I was after
Until I saw you

Now you are going away
For how many days
Who can say
But I am so afraid
That the days stretch into years
Days stretch into years

The world revolves
Trees grow old
And mountains fall
I don't care at all
What happens in a billion years
Just

If you return
I hope
That I'll be here to see you smile
If you return
I hope
That I'll have lasted through the while
Between

Fate, don't let my eternity end
Before I will see you once again

You are going away
For how many days
Who can say?
I am so afraid
That the days will stretch into years
Days stretch into years

Appendix One:
THINGS I'D LIKE TO BE
BY EDNA ANITA THOMAS

I would like to be a butterfly
So I could fly all day
From buttercups to daisies
To pass the time away

I would also like to be
A little bird that sings
I would want to be a blue jay
With beautiful blue wings

I'd like to be a firefly
They meet their friends at night
It's nice to watch them fly around
And see their nice bright lights

I would like to be a moonbeam
When they light up the sky
If you watch closely
You'll feel happy
And often wonder why

But most of all I'd like to be
A quiet little park
With lots of popular trees around
Where lovers like to park

Where butterflies can fly around
And birds can sing all day
Where fireflies come out at night
Cause it's their time to play

And moonbeams come out at night
To meet these lovers in the park
And make it bright with moonlight
As they hold hands in the dark

Where they'll put their initials
On the iron bridge
For all the world to see
Little knowing that those initials
Will be there for many years to come

If I could, you know those are
Some of the things I'd like to be

Appendix Two:
DANNY'S DREAM

I cannot run, yet I will fly. I have no strength, but with what strength I have, I will fight on until death. I will cry, but not a tear will fall. I will smile as I wave goodbye. Although it breaks my heart that I am weary, but I will not rest!

The beginning is no place to begin. I would have you know me better by telling you my perhaps never to be realized dream.

I wonder how many weary people there are who only wish their burdens would end. I have lived with a burden, a heavy burden. I too wished that it would end. But it hasn't ended; it hasn't even become lighter.

I finally realized that I must grow stronger. That is my dream: to grow stronger so that my burdens will not bury me, but I will carry it with me to the top of the mountain.

There have been times I felt very strong, able to run with my burden on my back undisturbed by its presence. There have been times I have been crushed under its tremendous weight, unable to rise and face the day.

I have often felt like a little boy dragging a suitcase as he walked with his father, the man taking long, quick strides, causing the boy to fall farther and farther behind... the boy exerting all his strength and energy in a fierce and desperate attempt to keep up until the father finally laughs as he lifts the boy and his suitcase onto his shoulders.

I love you, son, the man thinks. *You are not my burden. I am strong and I will carry you to the top of the mountain.*

When I was a boy, my father carried me to the top of the mountain. It was a warm spring day and he took me on a bicycle trip through the valley. The river ran calm as it winded through the valley. We stopped and splashed our faces with the cool, clear water.

We drank the sweetest-tasting water from a farmer well on the top of a hill, then we got on our bicycles and raced down the other side until we hit the bottom at full speed and let ourselves coast a bit up the next hill. Then my father's legs began to pump hard and he floated to the top. My legs ached and I struggled to push farther up the hill as it became steeper, higher, and more impossible to climb.

It wasn't long before my father came running down to meet me. Then he pushed me and my bike up the mountain.

"Do you want to rest, Dan?" he asked when we got to the top.

My brother carried me on his shoulders all the way from the Canadian National Exhibition home along the waterfront. It must have been six or seven miles on a hot summer day. He never got tired, or maybe I just never noticed.

My mother has carried me all my life. She has carried me up many mountains. When I look at her, I see that she has grown tired. Her burden has never gotten lighter. She can no longer carry it effortlessly, with a spring in her step as she did when she was younger. But she still carries it.

My father, brother, and dear mother helped me to reach the top of many mountains. They never rested and I never wanted to rest. When they saw I was tired, they asked, "Do you want to rest, Dan?" I never wanted to; I had to. I was forced to! My burden took away my strength and energy when I wanted it most: when I was climbing with them up rugged cliffs to the top of the mountain.

Then I became their burden. They lifted me onto their shoulders and climbed, surefooted as mountain goats, to the summit. Together we watched the clouds float by, just out of reach, the sun's piercing rays streaking down to the green valley below.

I was their burden and they never tired. I have no burden but myself, and I tire. I was born without strength, without energy, having to struggle to walk; that is my burden. They were born strong, able to run with the wind. They have lifted burdens onto their backs, burdens that have slowed then down, stole away their strength, and made them weary. Tired? Of course they're tired. But they never stopped to rest!

What's their secret? What gives them the strength to lift another effortlessly onto their shoulders? What enables them to endure, to continue carrying another up the mountain to the summit long after they've grown weary and lost their strength? Is it love?

I want to be strong, strong enough to carry someone I love up the mountain to the top. That is my dream!

Appendix Three:
Eulogy to Daniel B. Thomas

Public speaking isn't something I'm very comfortable with, so I trust you will forgive me if I read from a prepared text.

Many years ago, shortly after I first met Dan, I undertook to read through the Oxford Shorter English Dictionary. As you may have guessed, when faced with such formidable opposition I was hardly able to make a dent in it. Danny's life was also a formidable book. Although I knew Dan for twelve years, I suspect I really only read through but a few chapters of his life's story before the book was closed and taken away from us.

During those years, however, I was fortunate enough to co-author a few paragraphs of his story, and as such I would like to speak briefly on his life.

To have met Dan was to know him, and to have known him was to have loved him. I could stop here and feel satisfied that I had done him justice. That, however, only scratches the surface of what was the essence of Danny Thomas. Perhaps the greatest part of that essence was his zest for life. That may be a matter of semantics, which at this point is unimportant. What is important is that there was an intangible quality about Dan that caused him to live with such an intensity, an intensity which at times few men could ever dare hope to match.

This zest for life was reflected in the way Dan was always going places and doing things. Prior to his stroke, Dan and I used to attend college football games on Saturday afternoons. At the games, Dan would get caught up in the atmosphere, the excitement amongst the spectators, the activity on the field. There was a vitality there that one could feel pressing against one's skin. It was this vitality that a vibrant Daniel Thomas lusted and lived for.

Dan loved to be with the people, to be involved, to be part of their lives. It was this love of life itself, combined with his spirit for adventure, that drove Dan to go places and do things the rest of us consider wistfully and then only for a moment before our inhibitions entrap us.

Once Danny and I discussed how Sir Winston Churchill lived on in the spirit of the English people through the legacy he had left them. Dan too, given time, could have enchanted a nation. But it really doesn't matter. Those of us who were close to Dan were affected and changed by that association. Danny has left us a legacy of memories that is certain to last a lifetime.

As I look around me today, I see Dan's inner circle of friends. I don't think it is necessary to mention your names, you know who you are. That circle is noticeably broken by some who wished they could be here but were unable to attend for various reasons. I am certain, however, that their thoughts are with us. To those who were able to attend, I wish to thank you. You are the people who meant a lot to Dan, and because of that your presence means a lot to me.

I would also say a word about Mrs. Thomas and the rest of Danny's family. I have never seen a family as full of love as the Thomases. I have no doubt that at times it was only this love that kept the flame flickering within Dan.

Through my conversations with Dan, I know this love was reciprocated. He loved you all very dearly, especially you, Patti. As your older brother, he was always worried about your well being and tried to protect you from the realities of life whenever he could.

I know that everyone here is full of sorrow over the loss of Dan. While the sorrow will never fully dissipate, I believe after almost a week of reflection that gratitude would be a more appropriate emotion for us to leave with here today. Every day Dan lived, he enriched someone's life. I am grateful that Danny was a part of my life for so very long. For those who didn't know Dan for that long, you should be grateful that you were able to call him a friend.

I would like to finish by reading a passage from a poem, the title of which will be obvious:

> To you from falling hands we throw
> The torch be yours to hold it high
> If ye break faith with us who die
> We shall not sleep though poppies grow

The torch that was once Daniel Thomas has passed to all of us. The obligation is now on us to see that the flame never dies.

—Randolph Kinghorne

ABOUT THE AUTHOR

Daniel Broderick Thomas (November 6, 1958—October 5, 1985) was born in Halifax, Nova Scotia at a time when Halifax was still predominantly a Navy town, albeit with two universities established in the 1800s—Saint Mary's University and Dalhousie University, both developed in the urban core.

Halifax, being a coastal city, was and still is busy with incoming and outgoing shipments. Daniel's father, Johnathon Thomas, worked as part of the Merchant Marine for many years, dating back to the Second World War. His mother, Edna Thomas, worked as a nurse in Halifax.

After a tumultuous upbringing in Halifax in the 1950s and 1960s, Daniel's mother relocated her seven children to Toronto where he later pursued a Bachelor of Arts, majoring in philosophy and minoring in English at the University of Toronto, graduating in June 1983.

An operation he required as a corrective measure for his congenital heart defect in October 1985 was ultimately unsuccessful due to post-op complications.